T5-DHI-692

AMANDA'S NIGHTMARE . . .

She tossed about on the cot, her sleeping mind still aflame with violent noises and a kaleidoscope of bursting colors.

Then she realized what had awakened her . . . Heavy breathing sounded in the tent like a bellows, and rough hands clawed at the waistband of her trousers, trying to pull them down and off.

Her eyes popped open, a scream of outrage ripping at her throat, and in the reddish light she recognized the leering face looming over her. He had her legs forced apart and was kneeling between them. His trousers were open . . .

"Knock off the screaming, you bitch," he grunted. "Let a real man fuck you for once."

She shuddered in revulsion. "You're not a man, you're an animal!"

She managed to twist to one side drawing her legs up. Then she drove one knee into his crotch, against his engorged manhood.

He yowled like a wounded dog. Doubling up, clutching at his groin, he rolled off the cot, landing with a thud on the ground.

Amanda sat up, grabbed her shirt and was startled to see Dudley push aside the tent flap and charge inside, yelling, "Amanda, Amanda, let's get out of here . . ."

"WHEAT FIRE!"

Also by Clayton Matthews from Pinnacle Books:

The Power Seekers

WRITE FOR OUR FREE CATALOG

If there is a Pinnacle Book you want—and you cannot find it locally—it is available from us simply by sending the title and price plus 50¢ per order and 10¢ per copy to cover mailing and handling costs to:

Pinnacle Book Services
P.O. Box 690
New York, N.Y. 10019

Please allow 4 weeks for delivery. New York State and California residents add applicable sales tax.

_____Check here if you want to receive our catalog regularly.

THE HARVESTERS

CLAYTON MATTHEWS

PINNACLE BOOKS • LOS ANGELES

This one is for Patty.

This is a work of fiction. All the characters and events portrayed in this book are fictional, and any resemblance to real people or incidents is purely coincidental.

THE HARVESTERS

Copyright © 1979 by Pyewacket Corporation
Lyrics to "Honky-Tonk Woman" © 1979 by
Patricia Matthews

All rights reserved, including the right to reproduce this book or portions thereof in any form.

An original Pinnacle Books edition, published for the first time anywhere.

First printing, June 1979

ISBN: 0-523-40448-4

Cover illustration by John Solie

Printed in the United States of America

PINNACLE BOOKS, INC.
2029 Century Park East
Los Angeles, California 90067

Prologue

The man in the wheelchair waved a hand at the broad expanse of glass. "You want to know about wheat, look out there. It's all around you."

The man with the portable cassette recorder nodded. "Yes, I know, sir. Wheat was all I could see for miles driving in."

He fell silent, staring out through the glass. The two men were alone in the glassed-in veranda of the sanatarium. It was late afternoon, and the rays of the westering sun slanted across the wheat fields, turning them to gold. A strong wind from the south blew across the endless plain of wheat, setting it to billowing with the rhythmic motion of the sea.

In the distance four combines moved in military lock step, pluming four yellow clouds of wheat straw and chaff. The red combines, like iron locusts, moved at about three miles an hour, each shaving a swath twenty feet wide through the grain.

The only building breaking the table-top expanse of wheat was a pearl-white structure some miles distant, a building that appeared to

1

consist of a number of interconnected structures. One building at the west end was rectangular; the others, an even dozen in number, were cylindrical in shape.

The man with the recorder said, "I drove in from the other direction. What are those white buildings?"

"Prairie cathedrals."

"Prairie *cathedrals*?"

"Grain elevators."

The man in the wheelchair brooded on the acres of wheat. His left side sagged, the arm hanging uselessly. He laughed, a barking sound. "You know, when I had this stroke and they told me I had to be put in a place like this, I said only if they could find me one surrounded by wheat. Better still, one smack dab in the middle of a wheat field. And by God, that's just what they did!" He slapped his knee with the one good hand. "Look out any window in this hellhole and you'll see wheat!"

His voice died abruptly, and he stared again out the window. The man with the recorder waited, with the acquired patience of any good journalist.

"The staff of life, that's what they call it," the man in the wheelchair said with what seemed to be customary abruptness. "Did you know that that crew out there with the combines will have harvested close to a half-million bushels of wheat by the time they reach the Canadian border in mid-September?"

"No, sir, I didn't know that. But that's why I came to you, to find out these things."

2

The wheelchair occupant's head swung around with agonizing slowness. It was difficult to guess his age. Late sixties, certainly. Yet he could easily be eighty. "Just why do you need to find out these things, young feller?"

"I'm a free-lance writer, as I told you. I write and try to sell articles that might have current appeal to the reading public. There is a lot of public interest in grain right now, wheat in particular. This year's near crop failure, the high price wheat is bringing . . ."

"And the business with Russia some time back, right? Who'd have ever thought the day would come when the Russians would be involved in such a big wheat deal with the United States? We certainly never would have figured it to happen back when I started in the wheat business. Yup, I guess you're right, young feller. Folks are goddamned interested in wheat these days. The price, for instance. Back in 1931, wheat sold for thirty-four cents a bushel! What is it today? Ten times that, and more!" He laughed without humor, but the hard planes of his face had softened. "But the thirty-four cents was as hard to come by as five bucks is today. Probably even harder for many folks. Oh, times were tough, the Great Depression and all, no doubt of that. Yet, in many ways, it was a kick in the ass, young feller, a real kick in the ass . . ."

1

Dudley Graham saw his first wheat-threshing machine one hot July afternoon just outside of Newton, Kansas. He was riding a gondola aboard a freight train, which was barely creeping along due to repair work on the roadbed. The railroad paralleled the highway, and stopped up ahead was a caravan, which consisted of several cars, trucks, pickups, and two strange-looking machines that caused him to rub his eyes in disbelief.

Dudley, an avid reader of the pulp magazines, especially science fiction, thought instantly of weird machines from a distant planet that had landed on earth bent on conquest. A Californian by birth, Dudley had been riding freights for close to two years now, ever since the Depression had sent unemployment sweeping across the country like a tidal wave; but this was his first time in this section of the country. In a part of his mind he knew he was seeing wheat-threshing machines, yet he preferred the more fanciful notion.

On sudden impulse, he reached down for his suitcase and tossed it off the gondola, then clambered over the side himself. The long train was moving so slowly, it posed no problem. By the time he was off, the train had drawn abreast of the stalled caravan. Dudley picked up his suitcase and walked the short distance to the highway, where about twenty people were crowded around a tractor that was hitched up to one of the ungainly machines.

He stood unnoticed for a few minutes on the fringe of the group of men, staring in fascination at the machine the tractor had apparently been towing. The long, partially flexible snout that protruded behind the machine reminded Dudley of pictures he'd seen of elephants with their trunks bent back. The entire contraption rested on four fragile iron wheels, even smaller than wagon wheels. The word CASE was stamped on the side of the machine in large letters.

Still staring, he took out his sack of Bull Durham and rolled and lit a cigarette. Finally he nudged the man standing to one side and slightly in front of him. When the man—a tall, scrawny, fortyish individual, with corn-colored hair, washed-out blue eyes, skin burned a leathery red by the sun, and a long, turkey-gobbler neck—glanced around, Dudley jerked his head, "What the devil is that object?"

The man took his time about answering, those washed-out eyes studying Dudley's travel-stained clothes and cinder-blackened face and hands with mounting contempt. "Ain't you ever seen a threshing machine?" His Adam's apple bobbed like a cork on his long neck as he spoke. He was wearing faded overalls, so long unwashed the legs were stiff as stovepipes.

"Can't say that I have. So that's what it is. Well, I'll be damned!"

"Are you on the bum?"

"You might say that."

"Just dropped off that freight, did you? If I was you, bo, I'd git while you can. Miss Amanda don't take kindly to bindle stiffs."

"And just who is Miss Amanda?"

"Amanda Cayne owns this shebang and she bosses the threshing crew."

"Tractor's broke down, I take it."

"That's why we're stalled here. Guy who takes care of our machinery just up and took off the other day."

Dudley looked at the men gathered around the high-wheeled Farmall tractor. "They don't seem to be having much luck fixing it."

"Aw, those guys don't know shit from Shinola about fixing busted machinery." The man spat brown tobacco juice into the dust. His eyes gleamed, then his thin lips cracked in a smile and he muttered, "Here comes Miss Amanda! Now you're in for it!"

Dudley glanced in the direction of the man's gaze and saw a tall woman, her black hair worn in a bobbed cut, coming toward them. She was wearing a man's shirt open at the throat and whipcord breeches tucked into riding boots. That alone was enough to make her stand out, but she was also smoking a tailor-made cigarette and her long legs moved in a mannish

7

stride. Yet the narrow face was attractive enough, if now smudged with grease, and the thrust of the full breasts against the tight shirt was undeniably feminine.

She stopped before them, booted legs set wide apart, her glance settling on Dudley. Her eyes were the green of limes he had seen once in a California citrus orchard. In a rich, full voice she said, "And who are you?"

"He's a bo, Miss Amanda. He just hopped off that passing freight."

Amanda gestured imperiously. "I didn't ask you, Bud. Is what he says true, stranger?"

"My name, if that's of any interest to you, is Dudley Graham. And yeah, I just dropped off that freight. That's not much of a crime nowadays, is it?"

"That all depends."

"If you were the law, you might vag me. Since you're not . . ." Dudley shrugged. "I'm not bumming you for anything, if that's what you're thinking."

She was silent for a little while, studying him closely. Dudley grew uncomfortable under her scrutiny, well aware of what she was seeing. A week had passed since he'd had a bath—he knew he had a ripe aroma—and he hadn't shaved for a couple of days. Road dirt and cinder ashes were caked into the stubble of beard, and his clothes—khaki shirt and trousers—were stiff with dirt and grease, automobile grease. The last money he'd earned had been for a ring job on a Model-A Ford a week before down in Oklahoma, and his clothes hadn't been washed since. In addition, he had skinned down since hitting the road, losing some fifteen pounds, so the clothes were now a loose fit.

For the first time in a year he was suddenly, and somewhat ashamedly, aware of his appearance. He remembered how his mother used to tease him for taking a bath every day and insisting on clean clothes from the skin out!

Yet his unease sprang from a little more than that. There was an arrogance about this woman, a disdain for common folk, that stirred his temper. She seemed to be peering into his very soul and arriving at the conclusion that he lacked one.

Finally she spoke. "I wasn't worried about your asking for a handout. I don't feed bums. We could use another hand or two, but from the looks of you, I don't know . . ."

"To put your mind at ease, I don't know anything about threshing wheat. This is the first time in my life I've even see a threshing machine."

"You don't have to know much. But you do have to be willing to work your tail off. You're so skinny that you'd blow over in a high wind, and from the looks of you, you don't know the meaning of an honest day's work."

Dudley grinned, slouching a little. "I don't recall saying I was looking for a job."

Her gesture was contemptuous, yet curiously elegant for such rural surroundings. "I understand that your kind would rather hop freights than look for work."

"My kind, is it?" He dropped his cigarette

into the dust and ground it out with a vicious twist of his toe. He felt like telling her to go straight to hell, but his belly rumbled, reminding him that he hadn't eaten since the previous night. Keeping a tight rein on his temper, he glanced up. "I might be able to fix your tractor, in exchange for a hot meal."

Her gaze grew intent. "You can repair tractors?"

"Tractors, trucks, Henry Ford's finest." He shrugged. "There isn't all that much difference." In truth, he'd never worked on a tractor in his life, but he hadn't the least doubt about his ability to get it running again.

Amanda Cayne said, "I can't lose anything by letting you try. It'll certainly be worth a hot meal to me if you can fix it." Her full lips shaped a slight sneer as her glance flicked toward the stalled tractor. "God knows you can't do any worse than this collection of smart mechanics." She raised her voice, just loud enough for it to sting with the whip of authority. "You men there, stand back! I have a man here says he can fix it." To Dudley, she said, dropping her voice, "You have a half-hour, freight rider. If you don't fix it by then, drag your tail!"

Already rolling up his sleeves, Dudley started toward the stalled tractor with his usual loping strides. The man Amanda Cayne had called Bud trotted alongside him. At the tractor, Dudley touched the motor block.

"Still hot. Hasn't been down long, has it?"

" 'Bout a half-hour, is all."

"What exactly happened, do you know?"

10

"The driver said it spluttered a few times, then just died."

"I suppose somebody checked the fuel tank?"

"Oh, Miss Amanda always insists we gas up everything whenever we hit the road. She'd have our asses if'n we didn't." The Adam's apple bobbed up and down in silent laughter. "We only came five miles since the place where we finished threshing yesterday."

Dudley's long fingers were moving here and there about the huge motor—touching, twisting, testing, then moving on. To the unknowing he seemed to be idling away time to little purpose, but anyone with a fair knowledge of machinery would have discerned a virtuoso touch to those hands.

Dudley said, "How come a woman is running this outfit? The whole thing hers?"

"Belongs to her daddy, Amos Cayne. Old Amos has been in the wheat-threshing business since the early twenties. This year, not long after the season started, he had a pretty bad stroke." Bud laughed, baring tobacco-stained teeth. "So Miss Amanda had to take over, else the Caynes would have been out of business."

"How do the men take to working for a woman?"

"They don't." Again Bud laughed soundlessly.

He's a great laugher, this guy, Dudley thought sourly.

"By the way, my name is Bud Dalmas."

11

"Glad to know you, Bud."

Bud continued, "The men're all grumbling, threatening to quit. But they're between a rock and the hard place. The season's already well along, where would they go? The other crews are already filled. But she ain't getting much work out of them. A couple of months into the season, and she's over a week behind schedule."

Dudley said suddenly, "Find me a roll of friction tape, will you, Bud?"

From an open toolbox nearby, Bud got a roll of black friction tape and gave it to him.

"Now see if you can scrounge up a can of gasoline."

"A can of *gasoline*?"

"That's what I said."

While Bud was gone, Dudley carefully wrapped the fuel line with friction tape. When Bud returned with a five-gallon can of gasoline, Dudley instructed him to fill a coffee can first, then pour the rest into the fuel tank.

"Now how about giving a turn or two on the crank."

Obediently Bud went around to the front of the motor. Dudley advanced the spark, then primed the motor with the contents of the coffee can.

"Crank away, Bud."

With a grunt Bud spun the crank. The motor caught and died.

"Again."

When Bud spun the crank this time, the motor caught with a stuttering roar. Bud came

12

around from the front, beaming proudly, as if the accomplishment had been his.

Dudley glanced around to see Amanda Cayne striding toward them. Skidding to a stop, she looked at her wrist watch. "It only took you ten minutes."

Dudley throttled back the motor. "The trouble wasn't hard to find. The gas tank was dry."

"But that can't be." She glared at him as though he'd insulted her. "That tank was filled this morning."

"That may well be, but it was bone dry," Dudley said calmly. "Of course, the fact that the gas line was punctured may have had something to do with it."

"Punctured? Then why didn't these men catch it?" She glanced around at the circle of faces, some sullen and closed against her, others openly grinning at her discomfiture. "But, of course! Maybe they didn't *want* to find it! Maybe they even did it!"

Dudley, cleaning his hands on some waste Bud had given him, shrugged. "That's your problem, lady. I'd suggest you get that gas line soldered first chance you get. The friction tape won't hold for very long. Now, when do I get my hot meal?"

"You'll have to come along with us until we stop for supper." She stood with one arm across her breasts, the other elbow propped on her arm and a thumb flicking against her teeth, a mannerism Dudley would soon become familiar with. "How would you like a job full

13

time, keeping my machinery going? Two dollars a day, three hot meals."

Dudley stopped wiping his hands, staring at her thoughtfully. He grinned suddenly. "Why not? I've got nothing better to do."

2

The following morning, arriving at the next farm on their schedule, Amanda put Dudley to work driving a bundle wagon.

"What the hell!" he said in disgust. "You hired me to keep your machinery running, not to drive a goddamned wagon!"

"Everybody has to pull his weight around here. If there's some mechanical problem . . . okay, you work on that. But I can't pay you just to sit around on your tail the rest of the time."

"You have to have an oiler around the threshers."

"I have one."

"But I've never driven a team of horses in my life."

"Nothing to it. These mules are trained for it. There *is* a difference between a mule and a horse, Dudley." Her smile was edged with malice. "You just head them toward the threshers when you get a full load. You can drive a car?"

Dudley stared. "What does that have to do with the price of apples?"

"When you want a team to go right, pull on

the right rein. Left, the same thing. Just like turning a car. Okay?"

Dudley glowered at her, once again tempted to tell her to go to hell.

"But now if you don't want to drive a wagon, I can put you to feeding the shocks into the separator. At the end of the day you'll have wheat chaff in your ears, nose, eyes, and other more indelicate parts. You'll get some of that on the wagon, but it won't be so fierce."

The reason he didn't tell her to go to hell would have struck most people as strange. It even struck him as strange.

Amanda Cayne intrigued him. At twenty-five, his experience with women had been limited. He'd certainly seen very few at close range. Even in this Depression time, women didn't have much interest in an unwashed hobo. The little sex Dudley had experienced recently had been with whores, when he had the money, or the occasional grunting, animal-like coupling with a female hobo, as gamey as he, in the corner of some boxcar. And the encounters with girls before he hit the road had been strictly adolescent.

Yet Dudley liked women: he liked their company, their endless contradictions. He often thought of himself as a people watcher. And he'd had little opportunity of late to observe the female sex. But sex, as such, had little to do with Amanda's fascination for him. As constantly horny as he was, Dudley doubted that he would lay with her even if a miracle should occur and she were to consent. She was attractive enough physically when she made the effort, but Dudley, at least in those first few days, was always reminded of a bristling porcupine. Couple with her and a man could wind up with a quill embedded in his balls.

His staying around had certainly not come about because he was that desperate for a job. He didn't back away from hard work, not if it involved repairing machinery; but sheer, mindless, backbreaking physical labor held little appeal for him. And wheat threshing was backbreaking, dirty labor. It was hot as the fires of hell under the blistering Kansas sun. Usually they couldn't start until after nine in the morning, when the night's dew had dried off the wheat.

Long before noon, Amanda's warning had come true. Wheat straw and chaff were inside Dudley's nose and ears, and under his clothes, digging into his flesh like needle-nosed lice. Every time he took a drink of water, he spat out a mouthful of the stuff.

Dudley saw a certain irony in the situation. They had camped by a river the previous night and Dudley had taken out his other pair of khakis, which were reasonably clean, and sneaked down to the river. There he had taken a bath and shaved in cold water, then put on the clean clothes. He had been proud of himself.

And all for what? he reflected with some bitterness.

No one had noticed, at least no one had commented, and long before noon, he had sweated through his clothes. He felt dirty and far itchier than he had *before* the bath.

It was his chore to drive down between the rows of shocked wheat, stopping every few yards. He had to get down and pitchfork the shocks onto the wagon, which had low, slatted sideboards to keep the shocks in. Then he clambered aboard the wagon and repeated the procedure until he had loaded the wagon, which he drove to the threshing machines, getting in line with the other bundle wagons. When it came his turn, he pitched the shocks to the men feeding the separator. Not even there could he escape the wheat chaff. If anything, it was worse. The two threshers, set up side by side, threw a high, steady stream of wheat straw out of the blowers onto a steadily growing straw stack, and the faint breeze carried the stuff everywhere.

However, the activity was fascinating to watch whenever he had a moment to spare. It took him awhile to get the function of each man sorted out.

The man who seemed to be the most indispensable, and in a sense the kingpin of the operation, was the separator tender. The tender on the thresher Dudley was delegated to was named Jack Rollins, who also seemed to be in charge of the crew when Amanda wasn't around. Like the captain of a ship, he stood up on the high, vibrant steel deck of the thresher, supervising the transfer of the shocks from the bundle wagons onto the slow moving, chain-slatted feeder.

Dudley had had an opportunity to observe the whole process shortly after the threshing had begun, watching the wheat bundles chewed up by the whirling, oscillating knives cutting the binder twine. Then the grain spread out into an even layer as it disappeared inside the machine to be separated, grain from straw and chaff, between stationary concave and whirling cylinder teeth. Then it flowed out into the vibrating straw racks, where the grain kernels were sifted onto a series of oscillating sieves. Here the fan housing blew away the chaff that remained, and the clean grain flowed in a never-ending stream into the spiraling augers to be carried to the high Dakota elevators and poured down spouts to the baggers and the sack-sewers.

The sack-sewers alongside the threshers were busy as beavers, sharp needles flashing in the sun. They tied half-hitches with new linen twine over the ears of the grain sacks, working almost too fast for the eye to follow. The sacks full, they sewed them up tight, neatly spaced stitches across the tops of the jigged sacks. Then they lugged the sacks to the five-high sack pile, later to be picked up by the trucks hauling the grain into town. The sacks, Dudley learned, weighed about 135 pounds, and around two thousand sacks in a twelve-hour day could be expected from a good crew. The sack-sewers wore gunny sacks laced around their overall legs to keep them from wearing out by the constant rubbing of the grain sacks on their knees.

Occasionally the separator tender would adjust the blower at the control wheels, moving it left to right, telescoping it, raising or lowering it, adjusting the flow of straw to make a well-formed, rain-resistant straw stack.

On the ground the oiler moved around the threshers, attending to oil holes on the pulley shafting with a squirt gun, and servicing the grease cups on the rapidly revolving journals. Or staggered about, Dudley thought dourly. Apparently he was drunk as a skunk. Now, why the hell couldn't *he* be doing that job instead of breaking his back pitching shocks?

The cookhouse wagon stood on the edge of the field, in a grove of trees near where Amanda Cayne had pitched her tent. Smoke plumed from the stovepipes as the cooks inside prepared the noon meal for over thirty hungry harvest hands.

Dudley saw the water wagon coming across the field, a team of six mules pulling hard, leather lines and bridles glittering in the sun.

His own wagon empty once more, Dudley resignedly clucked to the recalcitrant mules and got them headed toward the nearest row of wheat shocks.

Less than an hour into the morning, his thigh muscles were aching, and he knew that he was going to be stiff and sore the next day.

And midway through his last load before the noon hour, something happened that almost made him walk away and never come back.

Plunging the pitchfork into a shock of wheat and starting to lift it, he heard a rattling sound and froze. A rattler was coiled underneath the shock, diamond head weaving. Since childhood Dudley had had an irrational fear of snakes, poisonous or otherwise.

As the snake's head drew back to strike, or so it seemed to Dudley, his inertia snapped. With a strangled yell he threw himself backward. He stumbled and fell, flesh cringing away from the expected prick of fangs.

A shadow darted past him, and Dudley sat up in time to see Bud Dalmas charge the snake with upraised pitchfork. Sunlight glinted off the three tines as the fork came down. With a triumphant yell, Bud held the pitchfork high, the writhing reptile impaled on the middle tine. Then he buried the pitchfork into the ground. With the toe of his heavy work shoe Bud calmly peeled the snake off the tine and ground the head to a pulp. He spat an accurate stream of tobacco juice at it and grinned around at Dudley.

"Booger spook you, did he, Dudley?" He shook with his silent laughter. "Hardly ever see a rattler curled up under a wheat shock. They like it where it's hot and dry, but I reckon he went to sleep there yesterday in the heat and hadn't stirred yet."

Dudley climbed shakily to his feet. To his shame he noticed the wet trickle down his leg. He had pissed himself.

Bud didn't seem to notice. In a drawling voice he went on, "Reminds me of something happened last year. I was working with a threshing crew up in South Dakota. This crew was threshing with these new-fangled com-

21

bines. We got a skunk caught and ran him through the combine. Chewed the booger up good, but not before he had let loose his stream." His sly glance dropped to Dudley's crotch, and Dudley knew that he had seen the spreading stain after all. "Sometimes a pole cat does that, hides in the wheat and gets chewed up in the combines. The wheat stinks so bad, the grain elevators won't accept it. That time we started a small smudge fire and let the combine pull the smoke through. That cut the smell some, leastways it changed it around a little." The faded blue eyes took on a strange, set expression. "Have to be goddamned careful of starting any kind of fire around wheat. Wheat ranchers, and harvesters as well, are scared shitless of wheat fire."

Bud worked his jaws and spat a brown stream, Adam's apple bobbing. "You okay now, Dudley?"

"I'm okay. Thanks," Dudley said somewhat ungraciously.

"Don't mention it. We all got to learn some time. Tell me something, will you, Dudley? Why are you sticking around here? This ain't your kind of life. Miss Amanda'll work your ass down till there ain't nothing left of it."

Dudley snapped, "It's none of your business, Bud! You're a nosy bastard, you know that?"

"That I am." Bud laughed, not offended in the least. "Didn't mean any harm. Just trying to be friendly."

Dudley turned his back and advanced on the wheat shock, avoiding the dead snake. When he turned around with a pitchfork load of wheat,

Bud was climbing into his own bundle wagon.

This time when Dudley reached the threshers with the loaded wagon, everything had shut down for the noon meal. Despite his bone weariness, Dudley was ravenous. This was a fact of his life that he had learned to live with. For two years now he had been constantly hungry. Even when he was flush and could eat all he wanted for a week—or a month, for that matter, which was the longest period of time he had ever eaten regularly—he might glut himself until he could hardly walk and still not dull the edge of that hunger.

The food was served from the cook wagon. It was not fancy, but it was good and filling: thick ham sandwiches made with freshly baked bread, crocks of cold milk, pots of coffee, and apple pies right out of the oven.

As Dudley stood in line with a tin plate and cup, waiting his turn, Bud said from behind him, "This is a part of your pay, Dudley, so you'd better eat all you can hold. No limit on the grub."

Dudley felt a jab of irritation. Bud seemed to be attaching himself for some reason, trying his best to be ingratiating, to be a buddy. More like an albatross, Dudley thought. It wasn't so much that he disliked the man, but there was a quality of eagerness about Bud, as though he didn't have any close friends among the crew and Dudley was his last chance. And Dudley was somewhat of a loner. He had never been able to make friends easily. Yet he didn't know what to do about it, short of being downright insulting. Also, he had a hunch that Bud didn't insult easily.

Plate piled high with sandwiches, Dudley found a bit of shade in the lee of a bundle wagon. Bud joined him shortly.

After a few bites, chewing noisily, Bud said, "Guess you noticed that Her Ladyship don't eat with the hands?"

Dudley glanced around. "I hadn't thought much about it, but I don't see her."

Bud grinned. "Bet your ass." He jerked his head toward her tent in the grove of trees at the edge of the field. "She's eating in her tent. Working men's food ain't good enough for the likes of her."

It occurred to Dudley that she was probably wise not eating here, the only female among men as randy as goats. But he didn't say that, he just grunted and went on eating. Bud stopped talking, too. At least he seemed to have enough sense to know when someone didn't want to talk. Or more likely, Dudley thought, he can only do one thing at a time and stuffing his face is first on the list right now.

They finished eating in silence, Dudley going back for two wedges of pie. Then he rolled and lit a cigarette. Bud bit off a chaw of tobacco and sat chewing as contentedly as a cow chomping its cud. After Dudley had smoked the cigarette down, he put it out in the dirt and stretched out with his hat over his eyes.

He was awakened from a light doze by Bud nudging him with an elbow. The other man muttered, "Here she comes. We're supposed to have an hour. As usual, she's fudging ten minutes."

Dudley sat up. He saw Amanda striding toward them. She stopped by one of the threshers, hands on hips, her glance flicking over the scattered crew.

"All right, you men!" She clapped her hands together. "Time to get back to work. I'm not paying you just to sit around on your tails!"

There was much grumbling, some murmurs of rebellion, but one by one the men got to their feet and began returning to their assigned jobs. Bud made a move to get up, getting as far as his knees, where he stopped and stared at Dudley, who sat without moving, arms wrapped around his drawn-up knees. Laughing without a sound, Bud sank back onto his haunches.

In a moment Amanda's gaze found them. She advanced with long strides. "That goes for you too, Bud . . . Dudley. Get off your tails and back to work." When she received no immediate response, her voice harshened. "Either that or draw your time." Without waiting for an answer, she turned her back on them.

Dudley got to his feet, clapping his hat on his head.

Bud stood up with him. He spat a long stream. He said admiringly, "Ain't she a darb?"

"I'll say this much . . . she's not the most tactful person I've ever worked for, even in these days of no jobs."

"Wasn't for the Depression and just that, no jobs, she'd have lost this crew long ago."

And yet, curiously enough, as he trudged back to his bundle wagon and rousted the dozing mules into sluggish activity, Dudley didn't find himself resenting Amanda for her whip-cracking tactics.

Instead he found her somewhat amusing. He had never worked for a woman before, except for the occasional odd job, and Amanda Cayne was about as comfortable bossing men as a whore in church. But the next few weeks promised some interesting moments—if he could stick them out.

The afternoon brought some respite. After two hours on and off the bundle wagon, just when he was certain that his legs would not make one more climb into the wagon, Amanda came striding toward him.

"You're needed at the threshers, Dudley. One of the grain trucks won't go."

Dudley tried to stand erect. His back felt as if it had a pitchfork embedded in it. "How come you're responsible for the trucks? They don't belong to you."

She shrugged. "That doesn't matter. True, I don't have to fix it. But it would take the rest of the afternoon to get a man out from town, and that'll only slow us down. We're behind enough as it is."

The trucks, four of them—an ancient Model T, a Chevy, and two Internationals—were used to haul the threshed wheat into town to the elevators. The Chevy was the one down. The motor ran all right, but the clutch was so old and worn that it wouldn't move the vehicle out of its tracks. After a half-hour's work, Dudley said to the driver, "It'll move now, but you'd better garage it in town, get a new clutch band put on. It's liable to go out again any minute, for good the next time."

Wiping his hands on some waste, he watched the loaded truck pull out for town.

Then he walked over to the water barrel for a dipper of water. He drank the contents, dipped it full again and, removing his hat, splashed the water over his head.

His glance settled idly on the nearest tractor. It looked like the one that had had the punctured gas line. When the threshing machines were set up in a new field, the tractors used to tow them were then used to operate the separators, a long pulley belt spanning the tractors and the threshers.

Dudley thought he could detect the stink of hot gasoline. He strolled over to the tractor. It was indeed the one he had worked on, and the friction tape had worked loose, a steady stream of gasoline, like a boy urinating, squirting onto the hot motor block.

There was no one attending the tractor. With a quick movement he disengaged the pulley drive, then shut off the motor.

He heard an outraged bellow from Amanda. "What the devil do you think you're doing!" she said.

"You didn't have that gas line soldered. The tape had worked loose and gasoline was spilling out. You're lucky the tractor didn't catch fire. I warned you."

She scowled at the tractor. "Why didn't you fix it better yesterday?"

"I wasn't working for you then, remember?"

She fixed him with an icy glare. "Well, fix it now!"

He smiled slowly, being deliberately insolent. "I'll strike a bargain with you. This machinery is falling apart, all held together with baling wire. It needs constant attention. Take me off that blasted bundle wagon and I'll fix it, then watch over the others. It'll save you many breakdowns in the long run. In between times I can work as an oiler. The one you've got is falling down drunk, anyway. Put *him* on the bundle wagon, sweat some of the booze out of him."

Her face flushed, and she started to raise a hand as if to slap him. Dudley stood his ground. Then her hand changed its direction, fingers delving into the pocket of the man's shirt for a pack of cigarettes. She took her time about lighting one, studying him coolly.

Dudley, beginning to know Amanda slightly better now, had to admire her self-control. He knew her temper was as touchy as a cap pistol, and that her inclination at the moment must have been to tell him to get his tail in gear and clear out.

"Why should I make any kind of a bargain with you, freight rider?"

"Up to you."

She crossed one arm over her breasts, the other propped on it. "A bargain with a hobo, a bum?"

"A hobo who can keep your machinery going.

That's what I hired out to do, not drive a team of stubborn-ass mules. So either I do what I was hired to do, or I take a walk."

"Okay, Buster Brown. It's a bargain . . . providing you keep everything in working order. If you don't, *I'll* give you your walking papers. Now, get to it and fix that gas line. You'll find a toolbox, along with a soldering iron, in the back of my pickup."

Amanda turned on her heel and walked away, leaving Dudley feeling that she had somehow won the skirmish, when in fact she hadn't at all.

He got the toolbox out of the red pickup and went over to the tractor. Bud, just coming up with his bundle wagon, jumped down and came over to him, grinning. "What was Miss Amanda chewing you out about, Dudley?"

Dudley grunted, kneeling over the toolbox. "Tell me something, Bud . . . what's wrong with this chickenshit outfit? I know it's the Depression and all that, but you said her father had been in the wheat-threshing business since the early twenties. It strikes me that most of his machines date back to around then, and he hasn't bothered to even keep them patched up. Why is that? Can't he afford new machinery, or at least keep up what he has?"

"Depends on what you mean by afford." Bud spat a brown stream and shook with laughter. "He could have afforded it, I reckon. Old Amos, the way I get it, made good money, even in these years of hard times. But he likes women and booze and living high on the hog.

He spent it as fast as it came in, putting off buying new machines until tomorrow. And now . . ."

"And now it *is* tomorrow and it's a little late."

"Yup. That's about it." Bud grinned cheerfully. "Way I understand it, the Cayne bank account when Miss Amanda took over was just about kaput. Everything mortgaged to the hilt. She can only make the payroll from Saturday night to Saturday night. She gets paid by the bushel, so much for each bushel threshed. Comes a time when some wheat farmer don't ante up on time, she likely won't meet the payroll."

Dudley stood up with the soldering iron. He glanced at Bud curiously. "Seems to me you're looking forward to this happening."

Bud's grin disappeared. He dug into the dirt with his toe, eyes cast down. "Ain't that exactly. Much as I don't cater to her, I'd hate to see these men thrown out of work. But threshing with these machines is behind the times. Combines, that's the coming thing. Time the wheat farmers learn that, they'll be better off. You can harvest faster with combines. Cheaper, too."

"If that's true, why don't they all use combines then?"

"Aw, they're old-fashioned. Their daddies used threshers, and what was good enough for their daddies is good enough for them."

"Must be more to it than that," Dudley said

absently, staring dubiously at the soldering iron.

"Well . . . combines, you see, mow and thresh the wheat in one operation. You don't mow it first and shock it up to dry for several days like with threshing machines. There's some that claim combines spoil harvest-wet wheat. Ain't true but many still believe that. The millers started it, claiming that much of the combined wheat was too wet to mill. Lots of farmers believe that too . . ."

"Shit!" Dudley said explosively. "The damn soldering iron's broken! Doesn't *anything* work around here?"

Bud for once had nothing to say. He just stood there, shaking with his silent laughter.

Since it had been a rhetorical question anyway, Dudley hadn't anticipated any response. He concentrated all his attention on repairing the soldering iron, which took him until close to sundown. Consequently, it was nearly dark when he had the gas line on the tractor fixed, and the other thresher had shut down for the day. As he stood wiping his hands, Dudley saw the crew gathering around the cook wagon for supper.

And he saw a car trailing dust along the edge of the field. It was a new, glistening black 1933 Ford V-8. This was the first year that Henry Ford had ventured away from the Model A. Dudley felt a pulse of longing. He had yet to see one of the new V-8's at close range. He would give a day's wages for just one peek under that hood.

Then he laughed shortly. A day's wages at the rate he was being paid here didn't amount to all that much.

The Ford skidded to a stop a short distance from Amanda's tent, and a big man crawled out of the low-slung car. He was too far away for Dudley to see what he looked like. The man started toward the tent.

Bud approached just then with a plate of food. Dudley asked him, "Who's the gink with the V-8?"

"That's Seymour Hooker."

"And who is Seymour Hooker?"

"He runs a crew of combines. He's harvesting over on the next farm this week. He's Miss Amanda's chief competition."

"So what the hell is he doing here?"

"Come to take her out, I'd guess. He's been courting her since she took over this crew. Oh, not to marry!" Bud laughed silently. "Hooker ain't the marrying kind. But he likes his women, and I know he'd purely admire to get into her drawers!"

3

Seymour Hooker thought of himself as a child of the century. Born five minutes into the new year—and the new century—on January 1, 1900, great things were predicted for him.

It hadn't worked out quite that way. His parents, while not dirt poor, had owned a scrub-oak ranch in West Texas and were never more than a month ahead of the mortgage payments on the ranch. Seymour had left home at the first opportunity, being just old enough to volunteer into the Army in 1918. He had served in France with distinction, was wounded in the Battle of Belleau Wood, and spent the rest of the war in a hospital outside Paris. At the close of the war he had a medal and a leg that turned gimpy on him in cold or wet weather.

Both his parents were dead when he returned to Texas. He sold the ranch. After dividing the money with his only surviving relative, a sister, he had a few hundred dollars left. The oil boom was going strong in Texas, and investing in wildcat leases was the thing, so Seymour invested with several partners in a lease. A few months later the drillers came up with a dry hole, and Seymour was flat.

He went to work for the wildcat driller. Seymour had been fascinated by the term "wildcatter" from the first time he had heard the word. It had a flavor to it, a flavor of adventure, of free wheeling, the ultimate in free enterprise. It was a man's game, a man's profession. And there was also the possibility that a wildcatter could, if lucky, make a strike and become a millionaire overnight.

But eventually Seymour realized that would never happen, not for him, in the oil business. After a half-dozen years of some of the hardest labor he could imagine, he wasn't any closer to being wealthy. True, he was earning top wages. He could do any job around an oil rig, including boss a crew. But by nature he was a big spender, an enthusiastic womanizer, a two-fisted drinker. These traits, together with a love for fine cars, devoured all the wages he earned. If he worked long enough and saved his money, he might in the end accumulate enough capital to buy a drilling rig of his own and put together a crew, but Seymour was honest enough with himself to admit that wasn't likely to ever happen. Saving money just didn't appeal to him.

Soon, another factor was added. The long hours of hard labor around oil rigs, combined with working in all kinds of severe weather, especially rain and cold, began to affect the old leg wound. He knew he had to find some other employment.

What he found was J.C. Fallon. He came across a "Help Wanted" ad in the *Dallas Morning News* for a man to boss a threshing crew. Seymour wasn't even sure he knew what a threshing crew was, but he answered the ad anyway.

J.C. Fallon—an operator, entrepreneur, conniver—was into as many pies as he had fingers for. No one knew what the J.C. stood for. To his many enemies, it stood for Jesus Christ, naturally in the profane usage. J.C. had neither chick nor child, and he lived in a palatial mansion in the Highland Park area of North Dallas, alone except for a household of Negro servants. He was desiccated, as dried up and crumbly as an autumn leaf.

When Seymour was ushered into his presence, he thought the man had to be nine years older than God. Later, he learned that J.C. was in his mid-sixties. Yet it didn't take him long to discover that J.C. Fallon had a mind as sharp as a recently stropped razor.

Beady black eyes raked him from head to toe.

Seymour liked good clothes and could be a sharp dresser, but since the ad had asked for a crew boss, he came in working clothes—sweat- and oil-stained khakis, a crumpled Stetson and muddy boots. Of course, no tie.

In a bull roar J.C. said, "What kind of a get-up is that?"

Unsettled, Seymour said defensively, "I'm on my way to work, couldn't spare the time to change."

"Ain't that. Shitfire and save matches, I like

to see a man in working duds." J.C. batted the air with a bony hand. He wrinkled a nose as curved as an eagle's beak. "But oil, I smell the stink of oil on you."

"I'm not surprised," Seymour said, recovering his aplomb, his temper beginning to stir. "That's what I do for a living."

"Working for some wildcatter, I'd reckon."

Seymour drew himself up to his full six-feet-two. "I'm a tool dresser and a goddamned good one!"

"Damned country's gone oil mad," J.C. grumbled. "Every jackleg in the state of Texas who can rub two dimes together is going around poking holes in the damn ground!" He leaned forward. "No future in it, boy. It's all a gamble, pie in the sky."

"If you hit it, you can hit it big."

"How many do? Most of the time you go around with your ass hanging out. How long you been fooling around in it?"

"Six years."

The ancient face cracked gleefully. "And you ain't got those two dimes, have you? But at least you're showing some sense, answering my ad." He rubbed his hands together with a sound like crackling paper. "Wheat, that's the thing. They talk about black gold. Well, wheat's red gold." He fumbled in his coat pocket and produced a cigar as thick as a man's thumb. He bit off the end, spat it on the expensive carpet, and looked at Seymour expectantly.

With a sigh Seymour struck a match for the cigar, wondering if he was going to be offered one. The offer wasn't forthcoming, and in time Seymour learned that J.C. Fallon had a reputation for stinginess. "So tight," one story had it, "that his asshole is stitched shut for fear his shit might accidentally fertilize his neighbor's garden." Yet Seymour was to learn that J.C. Fallon paid top wages if a man working for him produced.

Wreathed in cigar smoke, J.C. grumbled in that lion's roar, "Goddamned doctors tell me that the stogies will kill me. According to them, anything that gives a man pleasure will kill him." He lowered his voice a decibel. "Did you know, boy, that wheat was the first grain domesticated by man? It was first cultivated in the Nile Valley under the Pharaohs. It was introduced into this country by the English colonists in Virginia in the seventeenth century . . ."

For a half-hour Seymour was subjected to a lecture on wheat in all its aspects, his first insight into the depth to which J.C. Fallon immersed himself into anything that interested him financially.

". . . thing you have to remember is that oil may make a man a millionaire overnight, but oil ain't permanent. What is more important to a man: what goes into his automobile or what goes into his belly? Sure, the automobile is growing in popularity, but some fine day it's going to all come to a screeching halt. Shitfire, either they run out of oil, or they start making so blamed many automobiles a man can't move. But wheat? Man will always have to fill his

37

belly with bread." He squinted at Seymour through thick cigar smoke. "That's why I'm into wheat. I've got several threshers, run three threshing crews. I own a couple of flour mills, a passel of grain elevators. Now I'm investing in a harvest-machine factory. I've put a big pile of money into a factory that's getting ready to turn out these new-fangled combines. That's the coming thing, boy. Combines. Soon put all these old threshing machines out of business. Oh, there're only a few combines working so far, and it'll take some little time before they get all the kinks out. But it's the coming thing."

"How about wheat land?"

"Nope, don't own any."

"Seems to me, if you're into wheat, you'd want to be in at the source, grow and sell it."

"And that's where you'd be wrong." J.C. waved a bony finger. "Most of the farmers in this country are land poor. They're stupid as pigshit, disorganized, and if a man handles it right, he can buy cheap from them and sell high at the other end. That's where the money is in most things, boy. The middle man, he's the one makes the dough. And another thing . . . farmers have crop failures. Have one crop failure, there goes a whole year's investment. Harvesting and milling, you just get your product from some other part of the country. And come the panic, most farmers will go under."

Seymour stared. "What panic?"

"The one that's coming. Mark my words well, boy, it's coming. A real bad one, probably the likes of which this country has never seen. All these people gambling money on oil wells, the stock market, and what all. Pure-dee foolishness. The bubble's going to bust. Wait and see."

Seymour started to tell Fallon that he was crazy as a coot, they were in the middle of an unprecedented boom. Then he checked himself. You don't tell a prospective employer that he's crazy. And that brought up the next question. Did he *want* to work for this man? Well, he knew for a fact that J.C. Fallon was one of the ten richest men in the whole state of Texas. And someone had once said to him, "The only difference between a crazy rich man and a crazy poor man, Hooker, is money. You don't have to be crazy to make a million, but it helps."

Seymour didn't know about the wisdom of this aphorism, he'd never been this close to a millionaire before. So how could he know?

He came to with a start, realizing that J.C. was speaking. "I'm sorry, Mr. Fallon . . . what did you say?"

"I said . . ." J.C. turned the volume up. "Do you want the job?"

"Well, yes . . ." Seymour hesitated, then took the plunge. "But I'll be honest with you. I don't know the first thing about wheat threshing."

"Didn't think you did." J.C. nodded smugly. "And I would have been sorely disappointed had you lied to me. Shitfire, there ain't all that much to learn about threshing wheat. I'll have one of my other crew bosses fill you in on all you need to know. The important thing is can you ramrod a crew of men. They're mostly a sorry lot, rumdums and bums. You'll have to ride their asses to get a full day's work out of them."

"I've bossed oil-rig crews. And they're usually a pretty rough bunch of peckerwoods."

"Fine and dandy. Then you're on my payroll as of today. This is May, the season starts in a couple of weeks. That'll give you all the time necessary to learn the things you need to know."

His being hired so suddenly and casually stunned Seymour a little. He could only say lamely, "Thank you, Mr. Fallon."

J.C. let him get almost to the door before saying, "Hooker? Do you want to know why I really hired you?"

Seymour turned back. "Well, now that you ask, I reckon I am curious."

"You're not the only one who came for the job, you know. Been a half-dozen others. But they all came duded up in a white shirt and suit and tie. You're the only one came in working duds. Maybe you did that on purpose, but at least it shows you ain't afraid of hard work and sweat and a little dirt. All of which you'll get plenty of, working for me!"

That interview had taken place eight years before. Seymour was still with J.C. Fallon, and reasonably content with his lot.

One thing he had learned early on—J.C. was crazy like a fox. His prediction of the 1929 stock market crash and the country's plunge into a long depression had been only one example. The years had seen J.C. grow in wealth and power. He hadn't lost a penny in the market crash, and everything he was involved in financially was still making money.

He sat in that house down in Dallas, like a spider spinning a web, only the threads of his web each led directly into the heart of some economic enterprise. He didn't seem a day older and that bull roar was undiminished. He now owned a controlling interest in the farm equipment factory that had pioneered the new combines, although his name never appeared in connection with it in public, and he was scheming hard to convert every wheat grower and custom threshing crew to the use of combines, *his* combines.

In a manner of speaking, Seymour was his chief salesman, although his function had nothing to do with selling as such. J.C. schemed and Seymour carried out the plotted moves. Seymour now bossed the largest crew of combine harvesters in the wheat belt, and J.C. gave him carte blanche to bring about the wholesale conversion from portable threshers to combines. He was to accomplish this by any means he saw fit, by nefarious methods if nothing else worked.

And Seymour loved it. In effect, he was his own boss. It was a rough-and-ready life, giving him the opportunity to use his own initiative, and the freedom to wench and booze and wheel and deal. He drank with his men, whored with them, and there wasn't a man in his crew that he couldn't whip in a fist fight. Seymour often thought he had been born into the wrong time. He should have been a gun-handy trail boss rawhiding a crew of cowboys and a herd of longhorns up the old Chisholm Trail. Or maybe a swashbuckling buccaneer, with a crew of bloodthirsty, unscrupulous pirates at his command. Since neither of these pursuits were open to him, he was satisfied with what he had.

It paid well. And Seymour knew, without consulting J.C., that he had earned his choice of jobs with J.C.'s far-flung enterprises. But he wasn't at all interested. Most of the jobs available to him would be behind a desk, and he knew he would wither away and die confined to an office.

Over the years that he had worked for J.C. Fallon, Seymour had succeeded, by various means, in driving a large number of threshing crews out of business, by using intimidations, threats, bullying tactics and, when all else failed, outright sabotage. He had been most effective in heckling the wheat ranchers, convincing them to convert from the portable threshers to combine harvesting, thus killing two choice birds at the same time by eliminating competition and increasing J.C.'s sale of combines.

Seymour saw nothing at all wrong in the tactics he employed. To him, it represented private enterprise at its finest; in a manner of speaking, the survival of the fittest. The other thresher men were free to do the same thing to him, if they had the guts and the resources to do it. Few did.

There had been little repercussions from the

law. The authorities in the small towns throughout the wheat belt were just as happy not to interfere in warfare between harvesting crews, so long as it didn't directly involve the towns they presided over, and the local citizenry, rural or otherwise, were not harmed. The few times there had been legal problems, a simple phone call to J.C. had fixed it.

There was one thresherman, however, that Seymour had not as yet been able to intimidate. Amos Cayne was just as tough, just as shrewd, as Seymour, and all of Seymour's efforts at coercion had failed. Old Amos had been around a long time, he knew the threshing business from the word go, and he had built up a tremendous reservoir of good will and a strong loyalty from the wheat growers. Even Seymour's efforts to lure away members of the Cayne crew by threats or offers of higher wages had largely failed. Old Amos's men were loyal to him.

His failure to drive Amos out of business was a burr under Seymour's hide, and an irritant to J.C. as well. Therefore, it had been welcome news when J.C.'s call came in early summer. "I just got the word, boy. Amos Cayne has suffered a bad stroke and can't finish out the season. His daughter, a slip of a girl of twenty-five, is taking over for him. You think you can handle her any better than you've been able to handle her old man?"

It had been on the tip of his tongue to retort that J.C. himself was older by several years than Amos Cayne, yet it would take one tough son-of-a-bitch to handle *him*! He didn't say it, of course. There were some things he could say to J.C. in talking back, but that wasn't one of them.

Instead he had said, "I can handle her. I would have forced Amos out of business before this season was over. I had him on the ropes. The thing is . . . she *is* a woman. You want me to handle her just like I would anyone else?"

"Shitfire and save matches! Yes!" J.C. roared. "She's playing a man's game, ain't she? If a woman was playing tailback for the Mustangs—God forbid *that* should ever happen!— you'd tackle her if she was carrying the pigskin, wouldn't you, boy?"

Seymour hadn't figured on one thing— Amanda herself.

He had known Amos Cayne for years and had a sneaking admiration for the tough old fart, but his daughter was something else again. Seymour had seen her for years, hanging around Amos, looking more like a boy than a girl. But he hadn't been prepared for the sheer physical impact of Amanda as a woman instead of as old Amos's daughter. Seymour had seen women more beautiful, sexier, more feminine, but she had corners as unexpected and as hard as a hidden rock in a wheat field that could rip the guts out of a combine.

Yet from his first glimpse of Amanda bossing her crew, high-stepping among them like a high-born lady in a cow barn trying to avoid the steaming chips, he was hooked.

44

She was attractive, she appealed to his competitive spirit—he had the whimsical notion that she wore iron drawers—and he figured that if he could service her, get her off guard and mooning over him, she would be that much easier to drive out of business. Well, he had yet to service her, she sure as hell wasn't mooning over him, and he hadn't been able to force her out of business. He'd had a couple of grumpy calls from J.C. about *that*.

At least she was still going out with him occasionally—like tonight—so all wasn't lost yet.

He drove Amanda into town for supper and talked her into going to a honky-tonk for a drink before returning to camp. Although Prohibition had come to an end nationwide earlier that year, Kansas was still dry. Somebody once said it would find a way to remain dry even if a second Flood hit, a flood of booze instead of water. But the lure of the threshing crews passing through with money to spend was too strong. A long, low building just beyond the city limits, at the moment called Annie's Place, housed a honky-tonk, which served 3.2 beer, under-the-counter hard stuff, and very little food. Kansas *had* approved for sale the weak 3.2 beer, and many similar places were springing up across the state in advance of the threshing crews.

The honky-tonk had a monstrous juke box, playing only "shit-stomping" music, and a cleared area for dancing. Many of the girls who worked these places, Seymour knew, operated in a camp follower fashion. They followed the wheat harvest, moving from town to town as the harvest advanced.

Seymour had learned that Amanda drank very little, yet she had very advanced ideas about the status of womankind. If a man could drink, in public or private, why couldn't a woman?

So, at his suggestion, she agreed to stop at Annie's Place on the way out of town.

As they pulled onto the lot, gravel splattering like shot against the undercarriage of the V-8, Amanda said, "I'll bet Annie is a man. They usually are. Why do you suppose they always put a woman's name on a place like this?"

"Because men coming to a honky-tonk are looking for more than just a drink." He took a deep breath and dared to add, "They're horny and hoping to get in Annie's drawers, even if they have to pay for it."

"Men!" Amanda snorted indelicately. "Their lives are ruled by that thing between their legs!"

"Many women's lives are, too, you know. I've known a few."

"More than a few, I'm sure it's safe to say. I've heard about your reputation with women."

He grinned lopsidedly. "It's all an exaggeration, sugar. Don't believe a word of it."

He hopped out of the car and hurried around to open her door. Among the best features of the 1933 Ford, in Seymour's view, were the front doors. The cars were built low to the ground and the doors opened toward the front.

46

No matter how careful a woman was getting out, she couldn't help showing a lot of leg.

Amanda did it with dignity and style, but she gave him a show, and she had fine legs, very fine legs indeed. These rare dates were the only times he saw her in a dress.

Keeping a poker face, Seymour offered her his arm and they walked inside, the raucous music hitting them like a thunderclap. The place was brown with cigarette smoke, and smelled of spilled beer and whiskey and urine. It was about half-full, eighty per cent male. As they made their way to an empty table against one wall, Seymour waved greetings to several men, all members of his crew.

Holding a chair for Amanda, he said, "I don't see any of your men here."

"I'd better not see any here," she snapped. "They'd be out of a job tomorrow! This isn't Saturday night."

"Sugar, sugar," he said, sitting down. "You ride those old boys too hard. A working man needs some relaxation."

"They can relax on Saturday night, so they'll have all day Sunday to sleep off a hangover. If they came during a week night like this, I wouldn't get a day's work out of them tomorrow."

"*I* manage," he said dryly.

"You manage! What kind of work is that, sitting on their tails on a combine all day?"

"If it's all that easy, why don't you switch to combines? Before those old threshers of yours wear out?" He searched his pockets for a cigar

47

and lit it. "You and your daddy are behind the times, Amanda."

"Daddy would never hear of it, how many times do I have to tell you that?"

"Daddy ain't in the driver's seat now, sugar. You are. You can do what you damn well please. I can get you a good deal . . ."

"With J.C. Fallon, I know. I'll never go into hock to that vulture."

He sighed. "Amanda, you're in hock up to your eyeballs now."

"It would kill Daddy if I ever switched over to combines . . ."

"Hello, stud," said a husky voice behind Seymour. "How are you all?"

Seymour glanced around, beginning to grin. "Annie! I didn't know you were here yet. You look good enough to eat!"

"Don't be vulgar, stud," said the woman behind him.

Laughing, Seymour stood up. "Amanda Cayne, meet Annie Mae Delong." He grinned down at Amanda. "You see, there is an Annie, after all."

Amanda said coolly, "How do you do, Miss Delong."

"Not Miss, honey." Annie gestured carelessly. "I ain't been a Miss since I passed sixteen. I've had three husbands since."

The two women studied each other warily, and Seymour could sense the sparks of antagonism that sprang up between them immediately.

Annie Mae Delong was a big, voluptuous

woman in her late thirties, with a peaches-and-cream complexion, a hive of blonde hair running counter to the current fashion, and bright blue eyes. Heavy breasts spilled out of a low-cut blouse. Seymour had known her for some years and she had been a honky-tonk woman for more years than that, yet she still had a blowsy, fey charm, and very little of the hard gloss usually acquired in honky-tonks.

Then Annie turned to face him, dismissing Amanda with a flick of her fingers. Seymour had to suppress a grin as Amanda's lips thinned, a tide of dark color sweeping her face.

Annie said, "What would you all like to drink?"

"I'll have a snort of whiskey and water. Orange gin is Amanda's drink. Correct, Amanda?"

She nodded stiffly, her mouth a tight line.

Annie said, "Whiskey and water, one orange gin coming up."

As Seymour sat down, Amanda said tartly, "What's the shit-eating grin all about?"

He glanced over at her, realizing the depth of her displeasure. Despite her daily proximity to field hands, Amanda rarely resorted to gutter language.

He said, "Annie's an old friend. I'm just happy to see her, is all."

"I'll just bet you are, *stud*! How many times have you been to bed with her?"

Seymour's temper flared. "That's going a little far, Amanda. It's a question a lady would never ask, and besides it's none of your god-damned business!"

The drinks came, Seymour paid, and they sat in sulky silence, Seymour downing his drink in a single gulp, Amanda sipping hers and making a face at the taste.

The juke box abruptly fell silent, and all the lights went out, except one over the small stage at the end of the room opposite the bar. Seymour looked that way in time to see a man pushing a small, white upright piano onto the stage from a side door. Annie Mae Delong followed him in carrying a swivel stool in one hand, a tall glass in the other. An expectant hush fell over the crowd, the dancers all drifting back to their tables.

Annie sat down, took a swallow of her drink, struck a couple of chords on the keyboard and, without any announcement whatsoever, began to sing a current juke box favorite. The lyrics told of a man who had just lost his sweetheart and nothing mattered to him now. The song had been credited with inspiring a number of recent suicides.

Annie's voice was untrained, and she occasionally went flat, but her voice had a strangely compelling quality and somehow, even with such a melancholy ballad, she managed to give it a roguish, rollicking lilt.

The crowd applauded lustily as she ended the song. With only a nod of her head, a flashing grin to her audience, she swung into another one—"Honky-Tonk Woman."

It was a song Seymour hadn't heard before, and he listened to the lyrics intently.

I know what they've been talking,
I know just what they say.
They talk about the way I used to be.
But they don't seem to realize
I'm not like that today,
That girl is gone, and she's no longer me.
I was a honky-tonk woman,
No better than I should be.
I layed around, and played around,
My life was wild and free.
I was a honky-tonk woman,
Yes, I led me a real wild life.
But that was before you asked me to be
your wife.

Suddenly Amanda leaned across the table and spoke in an intense whisper, "Seymour, I want to leave now."

He looked around at her. "Aw, c'mon, sugar, I haven't heard this one. Besides, it's rude to walk out on a singer."

"Rude or not, I'm leaving. With or without you." She got to her feet and started out.

With a sigh Seymour got up and followed her out. She was already in the car when he reached it.

He got in. Before starting the motor, staring straight ahead through the windshield, he said, "Sometimes, Amanda, you can be a real bitch."

"Why? Because I don't approve of your honky-tonk sluts? Because I won't drop my pants for you like they do?" She paused. "Or because I, a woman, can hold my own with you in a man's business?"

"Jesus Christ, Holy Jumping Jesus Christ!" he said in disgust, hitting the steering wheel a blow with his fist. He started the car. "I don't know why I bother with you."

"I don't recall asking you to."

Yet he knew he would keep bothering, no matter how difficult she was. And, driving back to the Cayne camp, a startling thought came to him. Could she be jealous, jealous of Annie? Was that why she had acted the bitch? He started to accuse her of it, then changed his mind. That would probably roil her even more.

They rode the rest of the way in silence.

But the thought of her possibly being jealous so buoyed him that, after stopping the Ford alongside her tent, he turned to her, and said, "We seem to have got off on the wrong foot tonight, sugar. Let's not go to bed mad at each other."

She shrugged. "Who said I was mad? It's not that important."

Further encouraged, he slid across the seat, put an arm around her shoulders and started to pull her into his arms. Amanda gave a lithe twist, right hand coming up and around. The heel of her hand struck him under the chin, jolting his head back.

"Why don't you go back to your honky-tonk woman, Seymour? She's probably expecting you."

With a flash of leg she was out of the car. She ducked into the tent.

Seymour sat for a moment, seething. Then he laughed aloud at himself, gave the wheel a twist and gunned the Ford around. As he headed back toward the highway, he saw a fire over by the threshers and Amanda's crew gathered around it. He slowed the car immediately, not wanting them to guess that he had struck out with Amanda again.

Once on the highway, he took note of the weather for the first time all evening. It had been a hot night, and now there was a sullen, brooding quality to it. It was very still, no breeze whatsoever. In the southeast ominous clouds, a bilious green, were piling up.

Tornado weather.

Seymour trod hard on the gas. He'd better get back and see that all his equipment was battened down in case a twister struck.

4

Dudley had found the threshing-crew encampment much like a hobo jungle. Even though it was a hot night, they all gathered around a bonfire and swapped lies. He supposed the need to collect around a fire went back to primitive times, when the discovery of fire was considered a great force to hold back the unknown dangers of encroaching night.

There was another resemblance to hobo gatherings: he had yet to learn the full names of most of the crew. He was Dudley to them—none had evinced any interest in his last name—and they were Red, Swede, Bud, Slim, and so on, to him.

Although his first day at wheat threshing had left him feeling beat, he sat half-dozing around the fire with the others, listening idly to the lies. There was a blackened coffeepot on the coals, but he didn't partake. He also heard the clink of a bottle in the firelight and knew that liquor was being passed around. He wasn't offered any.

The man they called Swede—tall, bony, around fifty, with a red face, a blond cowlick, and a wad of snuff bulging his lower lip—was talking. "The best man with a bundle wagon I ever seen was a feller called Handy Andy. He was called Handy Andy because he could do just about anything asked of a man working around a threshing crew. But he was best on a bundle wagon, a holy terror." Swede spat into the fire. "Fact is, he was so durned good at it, he soon did nothing else. It was something to watch him load a rack. He would heave whole shocks onto the wagon at once and end up with a stack so high a man couldn't see over it, and the mules would grunt and fart hauling the wagon to the separator. He fed the thresher all by hisself."

Swede grinned at the circle of skeptical faces. "It's all a fact, fellers, I swear to the Almighty. First time I ever saw Handy Andy was back in 'bout '22 when I went to work for Harvey Wiggins. Harve had only the one thresher then, and just a three-man crew, me, Handy Andy and Harve himself. Harve and me, we handled the separator while Handy Andy hauled the bundles. It took only two, three minutes for old Andy to unload the wagon, and the separator would still be sputtering and spitting out straw by the time he was back with another load. We kept ten, fifteen wagons busy that year just hauling the threshed wheat into town to the elevators. That first year, with just the one machine and a three-man crew, we harvested out half the counties in Kansas and up into the Dakotas. The next year Harve decided it'd be worth his while to buy a second thresher. I ran one separator and Harve t'other. Now mebbe you fellers won't believe this, but old Handy Andy fed *both* machines. We operated both rigs side by side and Andy would park his bundle wagon between them, pitching bundles into first one feeder, then t'other. He had to work a little faster, but he managed her, yessir! That year he wore out I don't know how many teams of mules. We kept over fifty wagons busy just hauling wheat into town and we threshed durn near all of Kansas by ourselves!"

Grinning, Bud Dalmas said, "Swede, you are without a doubt the goldarndest liar I ever listened to!"

"So what happened to this Handy Andy?" asked a voice from across the fire. "How come he ain't still around?"

"Well now, that's a queer thing. Old Andy had this one terrible failing, you see. They raise a heap of corn through here, well as wheat, so they've a lot of silos. You fellers must have noticed. During the three years Handy Andy worked with us, there was a lot of ensilage spoil in the silos. It was late into the second year before we found out the reason for this. Handy Andy didn't show up for work one morning. He often stayed away all night somewheres, but he always showed up for work.

"Well, me and Harve finally went looking for him. We found him about two miles away sleeping snuggled up like a babe against the bottom of a silo. He had a straw in his mouth, a straw that ran into a hole in the bottom of the silo. We tried to get him away. It weren't easy. I took the straw out of his mouth, it was stained brown from something, and sniffed it. It smelled to hell and gone of corn juice!

"When we finally got Handy Andy awake, we got the truth out of him. He had been sneaking off at night, boring holes in the silos and getting soused on corn juice!

"That's what had been happening to the silos, you see. We got him to promise to stop it, and we swore we wouldn't give him away to the farmers. Actually, we wouldn't've anyways." Swede grinned. "Had the farmers found out what old Andy had been doing, they'd've run him out of the county on a rail. 'Course, Handy Andy didn't stop what he was doing. He kept sneaking off at night to find a silo from which to sip corn juice. But me and Harve, we couldn't complain. Handy Andy kept doing the work of a dozen men, keeping all them wagons busy hauling away threshed wheat. And he showed up for work, most times."

Swede paused to take a fresh dip of snuff.

The voice across the fire said, "You still ain't told us why that feller Handy Andy ain't still around!"

"Well, sir, that's an even queerer thing." Swede paused for effect, looking around at the circle of faces with a grave countenance. "The third year, '25 I recollect it was, was a bad year for the farmers all through here. There was a real bad drought. The wheat was poor, hardly worth threshing, but we worked it anyways. Poor Andy almost wore hisself out loading the bundle wagons, the shocks were so far apart. Not only that, but he had to walk several miles every night to try and find a silo that wasn't empty. He got down to a shadow of hisself. Then we hit a county that had been struck real bad by the drought. The corn crop had failed, as well as the wheat.

"One morning Andy failed to show up at all. Harve and me waited until near noon, then went looking. We finally found him on a run-down farm near twenty miles away. He was lying next to a tumble-down old silo. When he saw us coming, he staggered to his feet, gave us a look made me think of a dog with the rabies, doubled himself up into a ball and went rolling across the prairie away from us. Just like a tumbleweed! He rolled right on out of sight toward the Dakotas.

"We asked the farmer there what was in his silo. He said he hadn't raised a single ear of corn all year, so he'd filled his silo with tumbleweeds!"

Swede nodded solemnly. "And that was the last anybody ever heard or saw of Handy Andy. I did hear tell that he was seen somewheres up in Canada, still rolling along like a tumbleweed."

There were hoots of laughter, a few snorts of derision, but no one said anything for a few moments.

The first to speak was the man across the fire who had been needling Swede. "That ain't the way I heard it atall. In the first place, this feller was called Flagpole Slim because he was

59

thin as a fence post and wore a red bandanna around his head to keep the sweat out'n his eyes while he worked. But he could load and unload bundles like no other man alive and he did slip off at night to sip at a silo with a straw. That part's correct enough. But the last silo he tapped was filled with locoweed, not tumbleweed. The last time Flagpole Slim was seen, he was spinning around on his tippytoes like one of them fairy ballet dancers, going faster and faster until he finally just took off, rising and dipping across the country like a tiny tornado. Fact is, last summer he was seen a'dancing across a wheat field over in Nebraska and was mistook for a twister. And that's what really happened, fellers, don't believe old Swede's lies."

"Aww, hell," Swede grumbled, "that was a different feller entire from old Handy Andy."

Beside Dudley, Bud got to his feet and stretched. He spat a brown stream into the dying fire. He drawled, "That's enough lies for this old boy for one night. Miss Amanda'll be rousting us out early enough come morning."

Dudley got up and wandered out of the firelight to urinate. His attention was caught by bouncing car lights at the edge of the field. The car stopped, illuminating Amanda's tent. Almost immediately the sound of a car door slamming carried across the field. The car made a sharp U-turn and drove away, faster than it had come. Dudley felt a stab of satisfaction, a feeling that annoyed him.

Then Bud ranged alongside him, opening his trousers. "Speaking of tornados, look at that, will you? That sure looks like twister weather to me."

Dudley, buttoning up his fly, followed the direction of Bud's gaze to the southeast. "Have you ever been in one, Bud?"

"Naw, but I've seen them at a distance. Small ones. This one looks like a big'un. And I've seen what they can do. They can tear up everthing in sight. I saw once where a twister had driven a straw smack dab through a telephone pole!"

"My God, you're right! I think we've got one coming!" It was Jack Rollins, a lean, intense individual of about thirty-five. "We'd better tie down anything we can!" He whirled, running back toward the fire, shouting at the men.

"Won't do much good," Bud said. "If it hits, Katie bar the door. Shit, a twister can pile up a tractor like a toy . . ."

Dudley hurried after Jack Rollins. The next quarter-hour was hectic, with men shouting at one another and scurrying frantically about. Ropes and stakes were brought out. The stakes were driven into the ground and the ropes used to tie the threshers tightly to the stakes. Rollins was everywhere, shouting orders.

Through it all Bud moved unhurriedly, doing very little that Dudley could see.

Rollins yelled, "Leave the tractors be. They're heavy enough to be safe . . . I hope."

The threshing machines were staked out now, and Rollins directed the men to tie down the bundle wagons.

Suddenly a man yelled, "Here she comes!"

Dudley halted what he was doing and looked toward the southeast.

At the bottom of a black-green cloud, like some obscene growth, sprouted a black, inverted funnel. Dudley stared in fascination. The funnel seemed to be moving very slowly, dipping and weaving with the sinuous, deadly grace of a snake. There was a faint coating of brown around the funnel, like a protective shell around the functioning inner core, and Dudley figured it must be dust that had been picked up from the ground. The twister had an awesome beauty. Having heard many tales of tornados, Dudley had some idea of the terrible, sometimes capricious, violence contained in that spinning cone. A roar could be heard now, like the rumbling approach of a fast-moving freight. It was about two miles distant and appeared to be headed straight for them.

Beside him Bud said, "Even if the twister misses us, there's usually hail follows. Wheat farmers are as scared of hail as they are of fire. Best thing to do if it hits, Dudley, is to lie flat on the ground, hands over your head."

Suddenly, Dudley was struck by a realization that spun him around. "Amanda! She doesn't know, nobody's warned her!"

He started toward her tent a hundred yards distant, running flat out across the field. He knew it was risky. There was a kind of eerie, greenish light now, but it wasn't enough to show up any obstacle. Hit a rock and he could easily break a leg. He sped on.

Bud's voice pursued him. "Don't be an asshole, Dudley! You don't have time to reach her!"

Dudley didn't slacken his speed. By the time he had reached the edge of the field, his lungs were laboring mightily, his breath whistling. He fell once, felt his trousers rip and a stinging sensation in his knee. He scrambled to his feet, risking a glance to the southeast. The twister was closer, looming up like a black pillar vaulting into the heavens, still moving with that beautiful grace. It seemed dead on target for the threshers.

Dudley didn't stand on ceremony. He burst into the tent and plowed to a stop. Voice raw in his throat, he said, "Amanda! Twister, there's a tornado headed this way!"

There was light enough for him to see her sitting upright, blinking in confusion and outrage. "What the devil are you doing in my tent?"

He took a step, grasped her arm and hauled her from the bed. She was wearing only a thin nightgown. "There's a tornado headed directly for us, goddamnit!"

Her eyes flared wide. "The threshers!"

"They're all latched down, as well as we could. Now come on, you've got to get out of this tent!"

As though suddenly realizing the inadequacy of her garment, Amanda pulled away from him. "Get out of here while I put on some clothes."

"For God's sake, woman, you don't have time for that!"

"You think I'm going out there like this?"

"Oh, shit!" With a gesture of disgust he wheeled about and stomped from the tent.

To his astonishment the tornado didn't seem any closer. It appeared to be hovering just beyond the edge of the field. With fingers that shook slightly he rolled a cigarette, shielding his hands around the match to light it. A few drops of rain were falling. For the first time he noticed that a weird quiet prevailed. The freight train roar had stopped.

He heard a rustle beside him. He looked around as Amanda emerged from her tent. She had thrown a slicker around her shoulders, but a glance down told Dudley that she had taken time to also put on her boots.

A rumbling sound began in the distance, the freight-train roar building. The funnel was moving again, coming straight for them.

"Get down!"

He threw an arm around Amanda's shoulders and tumbled them to the ground, his body half-shielding hers. She struggled for just a moment, then was still. The wind came, pelting them with debris.

Dudley looked up just in time to see the funnel heading straight for the threshers. The roaring sound was building to an ear-splitting crescendo. The funnel had almost reached the threshing machines when, unexpectedly, inexplicably, the bottom of the funnel swooped up, like a high jumper clearing a hurdle, swooped up and over the threshers and sped on, leaving the separators untouched, dipping to the ground again near the opposite side of the wheat field. It appeared to gain momentum once more as it raced away, the roar diminishing as it was swallowed up by the night.

It was quiet again, with very little wind and just a splatter of raindrops, fat as marshmallows and about as soft.

Dudley said, "We can get up now. It's all over."

He helped Amanda up.

"Everything looks all right, nothing seems to be damaged," she said. "If I were at all religious, I suppose I'd fall down on my knees and give thanks. It doesn't look like we'll even get any hail, which usually follows on the tail of one of these things."

Dudley looked over at her. There was still just enough of that weird light to show him she was strangely exhilarated by the whole incident, her color high, green eyes sparkling. In that moment she was very beautiful, the abrasive edges of her personality softened, or blurred momentarily, by the night, the excitement.

And, as she looked back at him, her mouth made soft and vulnerable by a musing smile, he realized that he was still holding her hand.

Realization seemed to strike her at the same instant, and she pulled her hand away, not angrily but briskly. She said, equally brisk, "I'd better go check, see if everything is all right."

She started across the field in that long-legged stride, Dudley hurrying to catch up.

As they neared the threshers, the shadowy

figures of the men could be seen moving about, their voices rising and falling in agitation. The fire was out, the rain had stopped and, incredibly, the moon was out, bathing the field in a benign glow.

Suddenly Amanda began to hurry, and in a moment Dudley saw the reason. They hadn't escaped unscathed, after all. One of the tractors setting off to one side had been overturned. Then men were gathered around, attempting to flip it back onto its wheels.

As they came up, Jack Rollins stepped in front of them, barring Amanda's way. "Better not, Miss Cayne. Swede is . . . well, he's trapped under the tractor. We're trying to . . ."

A muted cry came from Amanda. "Is he all right?"

Rollins cleared his throat. "I don't think so. He's not moving. The motor block ended up on his chest. He must have ducked under the tractor before the twister hit and it flipped over on him."

Amanda shouldered him aside and strode on. Rollins made a move to stop her, then desisted. Now the men gave a shout as the ungainly tractor reared up, landing on its wheels with an earthshaking thump.

The men saw Amanda and stepped back. All their faces were silently accusing. A few mutters of resentment sounded. Amanda ignored them, arms crossed over her breasts.

Rollins kneeled by the prone figure, which was almost buried in the soft ground. In a moment, still kneeling, he turned his stricken face around and dolefully shook his head. "He's gone."

"Dear God," Amanda whispered. "What have I done?"

Her face worked, and for a moment Dudley thought she would weep. Then her shoulders went back, and she half-turned away to light a cigarette. She took two steps toward her tent.

She halted and, without turning her head, said in her normal, her ordering voice, "Call into town, Jack. They'll let you use the phone at the farmhouse. Have them come out and . . . do what has to be done. Then get the men bedded down. It'll be morning soon. It won't take long for the shocks to dry, what little rain we had."

5

The earliest memory Amanda Cayne had retained of her father—she couldn't have been more than four or five—was of a big man with a shock of coal-black hair tossing her high into the air and saying in a great, rolling voice, "You got some sugar for your old daddy?"

Squealing, half in fright, half in delight, she had kissed him, feeling the raspy stubble of beard on his cheek and smelling the sour-sweet odor of his breath, a smell she later came to identify with whiskey.

He had loomed over her like a towering tree, blue eyes merry and bright, and she should have been really terrified when he tossed her nearly to the ceiling. But she knew even then that he would never, never let her fall. Despite his size and voice like thunder, there was a gentleness about him that she was to see manifested in many ways down through the years.

Even when he fought—and how he loved to fight!—it was rarely ever in anger. A rough-and-tumble fight was a game to him, and he never battled with his enemies, only his friends. In fact, Amos Cayne had few enemies. Who could hate a man who laughed as he fought, who was the first to pick his victim up off the floor after he'd won, who was so generous he would forego putting food on his own table to help a friend in need, who could gentle a stubborn mule with those huge hands? The few times she had seen him confronted by an enemy, Amos would turn his back in icy disdain, refusing to dirty his hands. If forced to fight, he would search out any means to end it quickly, using anything handy to coldcock his opponent. In those early days in Texas, just past the turn of the century when it wasn't unusual to see a man walking the streets with a Colt strapped to his waist, Amos refused to tote a gun, fearful he might use it in an emergency.

Amanda's mother was a frail little woman who walked in the shadow of her husband; she had been a school teacher before marrying Amos Cayne. She worshipped him; he could do no wrong. She never criticized him when he came home roaring drunk, never uttered a word of censure when the money he made was gone within a month or two of the end of the threshing season. By the time Amanda was twelve she had long since been aware that her father was seeing other women. Her mother voiced no complaint about that, either.

One day, well into Amanda's fourteenth year, she had made a poor attempt at explaining her attitude. "Men, they're different, honey. They have certain . . . physical needs that must be met. I love your daddy very much, but I never cared much for that sort of thing. And these past few years, I've had so many . . . uh, female complaints, that I just haven't been able to. Your daddy understands, and doesn't try to burden me with a physical relationship. So I can't complain if he finds his womanly comfort elsewhere. You'll understand, Amanda, when you're older."

Amanda came to understand, right enough. She understood more than her mother ever had, or would have admitted to. Amos Cayne had a lusty appetite for women. He would have ranged outside his own bedroom, even if his wife had been willing and able. But since her mother didn't seem to mind, Amanda decided, why should she? She knew by then—somewhere around seventeen—that there were men like that, and she was slowly discovering that they were usually far more interesting than the faithful sort. If a girl knew how to protect her own heart from being broken. And since she had this forewarning that most girls her age didn't have, Amanda believed she could hold her own with men, any man.

And, generally speaking, she had held her own. In that, she had followed one of the few pearls of worldly wisdom from her father's lips: "People may disappoint me, honey, but they hardly ever surprise me!" Therefore, since Amanda's standards for male conduct weren't high, her disappointments had been few. Certainly none had been heartbreaking.

The man who had disappointed her the most, actually, was her own father. But this fact did not diminish her love for the man. Even with

71

both eyes open, well aware of his multitude of faults, she adored him.

The worst disappointments, naturally, were financial. During the lush times of the twenties, Amos Cayne would earn a great deal of money, from late May until early November, being much in demand by the wheat ranchers. He kept very little of it, however. Most years the money was all gone by Christmas or thereabouts.

The Cayne home was in a small town not too far from Wichita Falls, Texas, on a thirty-acre ranch, where Amos kept the threshing equipment during the winter months and raised mules. Or tried to raise mules. Raising mules profitably was a year-round occupation, and Amos would rather drink and whore during the long, cold winter months than work at raising mules. He worked his ass off during the threshing season, didn't he?

By the time Amanda was big enough, caring for the mules became largely her chore, which she attended to on weekends and after school. What few mules they raised were herded along with the threshing crew during the season and sold to the wheat growers along the way. The animals were mostly a scrawny lot, not the healthily sleek and rambunctious creatures they were supposed to be, and it didn't take Amanda very long to figure out that the farmers bought the mules as a favor to Amos Cayne.

Shortly past Amanda's sixteenth birthday, her mother died. Since Amanda was an only child and there were no close relatives, she began going with the Cayne crew during the summer months, up until school started in the fall. Then she stayed with a neighbor down the road until Amos returned for the winter.

She was of little help with the threshing, never allowed to do more than a few small chores. That first summer Amos had growled, "Best thing you can do for us, girl, is just stay the hell out of the way!"

Even so, Amanda had had a great time during those summers. Mostly it was the traveling, and the circus-train or gypsy-camp atmosphere, the seeing of new places, the meeting of new people. Later, when she was forced to take charge of the crew, Amanda discovered that she had picked up more knowledge of threshing operations during those summers than she realized.

Most of all during those harvesting summers, she had been impressed by the respect shown to Amos Cayne as a thresherman. Combines were little more than a rumor in those days, and Amos's competition came from other threshermen with the same sort of operations. It was no competition really. He always had his pick of the farms to harvest, and others had to be content with second best. And although Amos tried to hide his private life from Amanda, she was also impressed by his widespread reputation as a carouser.

She soon came to understand that her father exercised great restraint while she was around, but there were weekends when he would be gone all of Saturday night and most of Sunday. The first time this took place, Amanda was frightened that something dire had happened to him, but in time she came to expect him to show up Sunday afternoons with a sheepish look, red-eyed and smelling to high heaven of cheap liquor.

Amanda had continued to spend her summers with the crew, even during her college years. She was astonished that her father had managed to squirrel away enough money for college tuition for her, but she wasn't all that eager to go. But since he *had* saved the money, she went. She majored in Liberal Arts at Amos's insistence.

"I think I should take something that will be of use to me afterward, Daddy, so I can get a job. Maybe some secretarial course."

Amos had waved this suggestion away with a grand gesture. "A proper lady doesn't have to work. Certainly no daughter of mine will ever have to. I'm raking it in, girl. You won't ever have to worry." This was two summers before the '29 Crash. "Besides, some day you'll be getting married."

A sensible streak in Amanda, or perhaps some sort of hunch, had impelled her to sneak in two years of shorthand and typing. But even after the Depression had begun, Amos was still making fair money, still much in demand by the wheat growers.

Yet he had complained only mildly when Amanda began looking for work after graduating from college in 1930. She had been fortunate, landing a job in the courthouse at Wichita Falls. It slowly dawned on her that Amos wasn't doing nearly so well as he pretended. His equipment was getting old, and he didn't have enough money to buy new. Yet he cut down very little on his big-spending habits, and he had to scrounge every spring to get together enough cash to start the season, even shamefacedly accepting a small loan from Amanda once.

However, it hadn't been until the stroke cut Amos down and Amanda took charge of the crew that she learned the full extent of his indebtedness. Both the farm and the threshing equipment were mortgaged for far more then their market value, and there wasn't even enough money in the bank account to meet the payroll.

Amanda had been at work in the courthouse on that Monday morning when the call came from Oklahoma. It was Jack Rollins. "Miss Cayne, I've got bad news. Your daddy is bad sick. He's in the hospital . . ."

"Was he out drinking all weekend?" The words came out curt and harsh, without any forethought.

"Miss Cayne, your daddy's had a stroke," Rollins said reproachfully. "It's bad, real bad."

"I'm sorry, Jack." She scrubbed a hand down over her face, giving her head a hard shake. "I'll get the first bus out. I should be there some time tonight."

Amos was sleeping under heavy sedation when Amanda had finally arrived at the hospital in the small town in northern Oklahoma. Fifteen minutes with the doctor, whose horse-face looked as if it had never known a smile in sixty-some years, convinced Amanda that her father would thresh no more this season, if ever again.

"He will probably live, Miss Cayne, if he survives the next twenty-four hours . . . and *if* he stops drinking, smoking, eating too much, and all the other things that nearly killed him last night. And that includes working so hard. I assume one of your questions will be the one that your father's foreman, Jack What's-his-name, has been pestering me with. The answer is no, he will *not* be able to go back to work anytime soon."

"From what little I know of strokes . . ." Amanda hesitated, then blurted out the question. "Is he paralyzed?"

"At the moment his whole right side is paralyzed, yes, and his speech is impaired. In time, with the proper therapy, that should be remedied. It is far too early to tell at this stage."

Jack Rollins was pacing the hospital corridor when Amanda came out from the conference with the doctor. "What did he say, Miss Cayne?"

"If you mean will Daddy be able to go back to work this season, the answer is no."

Rollins's narrow shoulders sagged. "What are we going to do?"

Amanda lit a cigarette. "We're going to finish out the season."

"I'm not sure I can handle it on my own. I might get through a couple of weeks, but a whole season? I'm not cut out for that kind of a job."

"Then we'll have to put somebody in charge who can do it, won't we?"

"But who? This late in the season, the good threshermen are already hired. Hell, I doubt we could even hire a lousy one."

Amanda crossed one arm over her breasts, tapping her teeth with a thumbnail. "I've already thought of somebody."

"Who?"

"Me. I'm going to take over, Jack. The Cayne crew will finish out the season." She felt both satisfaction and pique at the consternation she saw in his face.

"But you can't . . . a *woman*?" At the sharp look she gave him, Rollins subsided, muttering, "Your daddy won't like it."

"It seems to me he doesn't have much choice. I'm not going to tell him right away, not until he's much better. So don't you go blabbing it to him."

"Oh, I won't," he said fervently. "I wouldn't have the guts."

"Don't worry, Jack. Together we'll manage okay," she said with far more confidence than she felt. "After all, I did travel with the crew summers during several seasons. Daddy has already lined up the farms to thresh. Now all we have to do is meet the commitments."

That was the theme she had struck over the next few weeks. She never for an instant showed a lack of self-confidence. Even when she hadn't the faintest idea what she was doing, she never let it show. She made whatever decision was required at a given moment and stuck with it unwaveringly, never once admitting that she was wrong, and she often was.

But there were a number of factors she hadn't reckoned with. First and foremost was the strong animosity of the crew toward a woman boss. Recognizing this, and also knowing that the only reason they remained with her was because it was too late in the season to get another job, she was harsher with them than was her wont, growing more dictatorial daily. The more resentment they showed toward her, the harsher she became, knowing full well that she was doing it all wrong, yet not knowing how else to handle it.

And she was appalled to learn the true facts of the Cayne financial situation. There was rarely enough money in the bank account to pay the crew on Saturday nights. A number of times she had to press the wheat growers for payment, so she could wire the money to the bank in Wichita Falls to cover the paychecks. That was also a matter for resentment from the men. Threshing crews were accustomed to being paid in cash every Saturday night. They grumbled at having to accept checks, grumbles she ignored.

The equipment—the threshing machines, the tractors, anything that had moving parts—was falling apart. Daily the problems with the machinery mounted.

Many times she felt like giving up. It would have been no disgrace, heaven knows. Everybody *expected* her to give up. Even a man, a man without Amos's drive and determination, probably would have given up.

But Amanda had that stubborn streak. Even more than her stubbornness, the thing that firmed up her determination to continue was the confrontation she had had with her father about a month after his stroke.

When she had finally gotten in to see him the morning following her long bus ride to the hospital, Amanda had been shocked at the gray, shrunken, unmoving man in the bed. That enormous vitality and drive was all gone, leaving an almost lifeless hulk. He hadn't been able to move his right arm or leg, his speech was so badly slurred she could scarcely understand him, and he dribbled out of the side of his mouth.

The doctor had allowed her only a few minutes that time. Amos's interest in the threshing operation had been nil. He had merely mumbled that he supposed they would have to close down, and she replied, brightly, that no, she had found someone to boss the crew.

She had visited him three times during that month. On the third visit she found him much improved. He could speak more clearly and there was some movement in his right arm, although none in his leg. And he had shown a revived interest in the threshing crew. Amanda had avoided most of his questions, assuring him that everything was going well.

To his question about who was running the crew, she had responded, "It's nobody you know, Daddy. Don't worry about it." Still, she knew she wouldn't be able to evade the truth much longer.

She had seen the doctor briefly on her last visit, and he had told her she could take Amos home soon. "We've done about all we can for him here. For a man who has been as active as your father, too long a confinement in a hospital can have an adverse effect. As long as he has someone to take care of him at home and is taken in for proper treatment at regular intervals, he'll be better off. They have much better facilities at Wichita Falls than we do here."

Knowing this would come about eventually, Amanda had already arranged for a couple, a man and wife eager to do it for little more than room and board, to stay with Amos during the remainder of the threshing season. But she knew she would have to tell Amos the truth. Naturally he would demand an explanation of why she wasn't living at home. At her next visit Amanda explained this to the doctor.

"Tell him," he said with a shrug. "Tell him the truth. He's a tough old character and I don't think another stroke right now is too likely. He may, as you say, rant a little about you, a woman, taking his place, but it'll pass. And wouldn't he fret more knowing your crew is out of business completely?"

Amanda was sure that the doctor was wrong in one respect—Amos's opposition wouldn't pass that easily.

What she wasn't prepared for was the violence of his opposition. "You must be crazy, girl! That's no goldanged job for a woman! Those men have no respect for a lady. They figure any woman who'd mix with men in the fields is no better than a honky-tonk woman!"

"Just like you, Daddy?"

"Those men are little better than scum, a bunch of hard-drinking, whoring bums!"

"Nobody's tried to rape me yet." She paused, then added deliberately, "In fact, nobody's even tried to get into my pants."

"Amanda! I never learned you to talk like that!" His drawn face registered shock. He leveled a shaking finger. "You see, you see what's happening? Already you're talking dirty "

"That's not exactly what I'd call dirty." She remembered the ordeal he'd just gone through and felt a stir of compassion. But her temper was rising now, and she drove on. "I've heard far worse than that in the girl's outhouse at school, before I ever took over the crew. I haven't led all that sheltered a life. Not with the example you set for me, Daddy."

It had been a cruel taunt to throw at him at this particular time, and she knew it. Amos's face turned ashen, and he jerked his face away from her.

Contrite, she went to him and cupped his trembling hand in hers. "I'm sorry, Daddy. I shouldn't have said that. It was rotten of me."

His face worked, and for a moment she thought he was going to weep.

Then he said humbly, "No, girl, you're right. I ain't set what might be called a good example." He sat up a little, squaring his shoulders.

He flung her hands away with a gesture almost angry. "But it ain't only that. I reckon you can handle yourself well enough in that respect. I ain't so much afraid they'll get out of line in that way. They all know they'd have me to deal with if they did! But I'm talking about their respecting you as boss. They just won't work good with a woman over them."

"We're going along all right so far," she said tartly.

"That's because nothing's come up yet. How long's it been . . . less'n a month? Wait until something bad happens, a breakdown maybe. Maybe the crew'll be laid up for a few days. They'll probably all take off like jackrabbits, afraid they won't be paid."

"And whose fault is that, Daddy? Is it my fault that there's no money in the bank?"

"It's hard times, girl," he mumbled, glance sliding away again. "And don't forget all that money I had to lay out to put you through school. Just about then the Depression hit, and I never did make it all back."

"Daddy, don't evade the issue! All those years you've spent money like water, drinking, chasing women, honky-tonking . . ." At the hurt look on his face, she softened again, placing her hand over his. "I'm sorry. What you did with your private life is none of my business. And I do appreciate your sending me to college, I really do."

"Then don't let it all go to waste, Amanda," he said eagerly. "You've got all that schooling, you have a good job. Think how many girls in the country'd be happy to have a good job like yours, have your education." He stopped to stare at her. "You've quit your job, ain't you?"

"Of course. I had to."

"So what if you can't finish out the season? What if you go bust? Then what'll you do? You're running behind already, I know you are. You get too far behind and the farmers will start looking around for somebody else to do their threshing."

"Daddy, what would you have me do? Fold up the threshers? You know if you miss a season, you won't be able to get grain to harvest next year."

"I don't care, goldang it!" Amos said with some of his old vehemence. "I'd rather see the threshers setting somewheres rusting away than you running them!"

Amanda stepped back from the bed. She said distantly, "I'm already doing it, Daddy. And nothing you can say or do will stop me. The way I see it, you don't have much choice in the matter."

He raised up, anger twisting his face into an ugly grimace. "Then it'll be on your head, girl! Whatever happens will be on your head!"

"Nothing will happen, Daddy."

Striding down the hospital corridor, Amanda had been puzzled by her behavior. Never before had she scratched at her father so. Was it because the stroke had leveled him, leveled him to common clay, tumbling the king from the hill? She wasn't ashamed of the things she'd said,

83

perhaps a little abashed at her temerity. She was . . . well, yes, she was exhilarated!

But now, after the twister had hit, she wasn't so sure that nothing could happen. Now, a man was dead, and because of her. Oh, she wasn't responsible for a freak tornado. Everyone, even the members of the crew, she was confident, would consider her thinking that the silly reasoning of a female.

Yet, she knew, deep down she knew.

If she hadn't kept the threshing crew on the road, if she had followed Amos Cayne's advice and folded up her tents, the man called Swede wouldn't be dead now. It was a fact she couldn't escape. It was a fact that she would have to live with for the rest of her life.

6

"The twister tipped a tractor over, J.C.," Seymour said into the telephone. "There was a guy under it. He was killed. They were damned lucky at that. The twister could have wiped them out."

"Man wasn't yours, was he?" said the voice of J.C. Fallon, roaring away undaunted by those many miles from Dallas.

"Nope, wasn't my guy. The dead guy was named Swede."

"Then they're still in business?"

"Still in business, but not for long. They're falling behind more every day."

"Then maybe it's time you spread the word. Can you leave your crew on its own for a few days?"

"No problem, J.C. My crew could run itself if necessary. And Rooster Cockrun, my foreman, is a good man."

"Then here's what I think you should do. Go on ahead, contact all the farms the Cayne crew is due to thresh. Let them know how far behind she is. Scare the shit out of them, tell 'em she'll never make it . . ."

Seymour only half-listened to the roar of J.C.'s voice. It was what he had in mind anyway. He twisted about so he could squint through the fly-specked window of the filling station, watching the attendant gas up his V-8 at the one pump out front.

". . . up in the northeast corner of Kansas. What's the guy's name, Martin?"

"Right, J.C. Thaddeus Martin."

"Yup, that's the bird I mean. Get to him, convince him that Amanda Cayne will never make it in time to keep his grain from rotting in the field. He's got the biggest wheat acreage in Kansas. Scare *him* off, and that'll put her tits in the wringer for sure!"

"I'll talk to him, J.C., sure. But he and Amos are long-time buddies. I've felt him out every year. He won't even listen when I try to bad-mouth old Amos's operation."

"But things are different this year. Shit-fire! Amos ain't around this time, his daughter is. This Martin, he's a bachelor, ain't he?"

"Not exactly. His wife died some years back, and he's never married again."

"Probably hates women. Don't matter anyway. If he finds out a woman is ramrodding the Cayne outfit and might not make it in time to harvest his crop, he'll come to tow."

"I'll give it a try, J.C. I'll swing up through the state for a couple of days, pass the word on to several of these old boys. I'm sure I can get some of them out of the Cayne camp."

"You get to this Martin and you've got it made." J.C. hesitated, coughed delicately, then said in a subdued voice, "Tell you what, get that Martin acreage for my combines, and there'll be a bonus in it for you."

"A bonus! You sick or something, J.C.?" Seymour said in mock concern. "That's not at all like you!"

"You know what you can do, boy? You can go straight to hell!" J.C. barked. "Let me tell you this, smarting off to me like that . . . if you don't put the Cayne outfit out of business *before* they harvest the Martin place, you can look for another job come next year, 'cause you'll be through with me. Now how do you like them apples, Hooker?"

The receiver crashed down on the other end, causing Seymour to wince at the reverberations against his eardrum. He cradled the receiver, knuckling the offending ear with the other hand, grinning broadly. Then he got the operator and asked the charges on the long-distance call. Hanging up again, he saw the station attendant shambling toward the shack. Seymour went out to meet him.

"Comes to ninety cents, sir. She didn't take any oil. That's one fine automobile you've got there. First one of them models I've seen around here."

"I like it just fine." Seymour paid for the gas. "And here's what the phone charges came to. Thanks for the use of it."

The man shrugged. "No big deal. I'm surprised it's still working. You're the first one to use it in a month of Sundays. I know I sure as hell don't use it much."

Typical, Seymour thought as he drove away in the V-8. If the man had any gumption, he'd be using the telephone to drum up some business.

It seemed to him that the attendant's apathy reflected the attitude of the whole country. With the nation sunk into an economic depression that just kept dragging on and on, most people seemed content to drift, doing nothing but whining and complaining, sitting on their asses. A man with get-up-and-go could still make a buck. Look at J.C. Fallon. Look at Seymour Hooker. Both those old boys were doing all right, Depression or not.

J.C.'s threat didn't bother him too much. J.C. was always making threats like that. He figured it would keep a man on his toes. Of course, Seymour had to admit there was always the possibility that J.C. might someday carry out one of his threats, if he got riled enough. And since he, Seymour, had been battling the Caynes for some time now without success, another year's failure just might provoke J.C. enough to do it. But Seymour was confident that he would drive Amanda Cayne to the wall before the season was well along.

He unwrapped and lit a cigar. He didn't smoke much as a rule, but he liked a cigar after supper and when he was driving long distances. It helped to pass the time. He loved fast cars and he loved to drive, but long distances bored the teetotal crap out of him, as did any long stretch of enforced idleness.

Twenty miles north of the filling station, he

turned the Ford off onto a gravel road and went down it five miles before turning into a farmyard. This was one of the places on his threshing schedule. The farmer came out to greet him, offering him supper.

Seymour declined. "Can't stay that long, Bob. I have a lot of driving to do before this day's over. Just wanted to let you know that my crew is ahead of schedule. We'll be hitting your place late next week."

He drove on, Kansas land stretching for miles in every direction, stretching to the horizon. Most of it was planted in wheat, ripe and golden, rippling in the faint breeze. The only thing breaking the flat monotony of the fields was a grain elevator rearing up in the distance now and then.

A few miles farther on he came to another farmhouse. The farmer here, Don Barnes, had a whole section in wheat, and was one of the Cayne customers. Seymour had been trying unsuccessfully for two years to get the man to switch over to combines. So far, Barnes had remained loyal to Amos Cayne.

But this time Seymour had more leverage, and he didn't waste any time using it. He found Barnes—a short, stumpy man in his mid-forties—outside his barn in the back of the house, checking over his mowers before shocking his wheat in preparation for the Cayne crew's arrival.

After the amenities were out of the way and he had offered Barnes a cigar, Seymour said abruptly, "Hear about old Amos Cayne?"

Barnes, struck match halfway to the cigar, paused to stare. "Hear about Amos? What about Amos?"

"He had a bad stroke. He'll be laid up for the rest of the season, maybe for good."

"How come nobody . . . ?" Barnes broke off with a curse as the burning match scorched his fingers.

Seymour struck one of his own matches and held it to the cigar.

After the wheat rancher had the cigar going good, he said, "How come nobody told me about this?" He glowered at Seymour as though the whole thing was his fault. "What am I supposed to do about my wheat? I'm about to cut it and here I find out there's nobody to thresh it!"

"Oh, they're not out of business," Seymour said blandly. "His daughter, Amos's daughter, is running the crew."

"Oh, well, that's different," Barnes said in relief. Then, in a classic double take: "His daughter! A *woman* running the crew?"

"Yup. That's the truth of it." Seymour paused to let it sink in good, then added, "Last I heard, she's about a week behind schedule."

"Hell and damnation! And here I'm about to cut." Barnes spat into the grass beside the mower and turned to stare out over his stand of wheat. "I can't wait much longer to mow, but if my wheat stands too long in the shocks, I may lose my whole crop."

Seymour let him ruminate a few minutes before saying, "I don't much like to say I told you so, Don, but I've been trying for some time to get you to switch over to combines. You let my crew come in here and combine your wheat and you can forget about mowing and shocking and all that crap."

The man swiveled his head and stared at Seymour out of flat brown eyes. Yet Seymour detected a small flare of hope in those eyes and he strove to keep any elation out of his own face.

Barnes said slowly, "Think you can manage to fit my place into your schedule?"

"No problem, Don. Like I said, we're ahead of schedule. We can be here in about a week. If need be, I can always have a couple more new combines shipped in."

"No hike in the bushel rate?"

Seymour assumed a wounded air. "Now you think I'd take advantage of a man in your fix? The same rate as I'm charging everybody else. And I don't have to remind you that our rate is a couple of cents a bushel cheaper than what Cayne would be charging you."

"Then it's a deal. I'll send old Amos's daughter a wire telling her that since she's gonna be late, just not to bother."

The two men shook hands and spent a few minutes working out the details. Seymour restrained his jubilance until he had the Ford out of the lane and arrowing down the gravel highway. Then he let loose an exuberant shout.

This was a coup, oh this was a dandy coup! He thumped the steering wheel with the heel of his hand and laughed aloud. This called for another cigar. He dug one out and lit it, letting the V-8 wander dangerously back and forth across the road, correcting it twice just as it was about to swerve into the ditch

Now if a few more growers with big acreage would fall in line that easily . . .

At the first available telephone, at a garage in a little crossroads village, he stopped and called J.C. to tell him about Don Barnes.

J.C. grunted. "You say he has a section to thresh?"

"At least that, I'd say."

"Then why're you wasting money on long-distance telephone calls to pass on piddling news like that, Hooker? Shitfire, boy! Get this Martin into your camp, *then* you'll have something to brag on."

But Seymour was grinning hugely as he drove on. He'd long since learned to look behind J.C.'s grumpiness. He liked to be apprised of any good news, and the grumpier he sounded, the happier he usually was.

The farmers Seymour talked with the next two days were a mixed lot in their reactions. Three were agreeable to switching over to combines; the others were skeptical of Fallon and willing to gamble on whether or not the Cayne crew would show up. Two were even downright hostile, threatening to throw him bodily off their farms.

One said, "Knowing you, Seymour Hooker, you're probably lying. I wouldn't put it past you."

Seymour grinned cheerfully, winked and went on his way. Late in the afternoon of the second day he turned north toward the Nebraska state line and the farm of Thaddeus Martin. He purposefully planned to arrive late so he would be invited to stay overnight with Thaddeus. Since Martin was his prime target, Seymour wanted to relax and chew the fat with him.

Despite their being on opposite sides, in a manner of speaking, Seymour liked the big, rawboned wheat grower. In temperament Thaddeus and he were completely different, but there was much Seymour found to admire in him. Slow-moving, equally slow to anger, stubborn in his convictions, Thaddeus was something of a leader in this part of the state in spite of himself. According to the stories, he had come to this region from Ohio at eighteen, with a wagon, a team of mules, several milk cows, and his wife. He had bought a section of land. Since then he had carved out a niche for himself, becoming something of a legend among the wheat farmers, just as Amos Cayne was among threshermen.

Through the years Thaddeus had stood rock firm against hard times, droughts, and locust plagues, gradually extending his empire until he now planted several thousand acres in wheat every year. To Seymour, Thaddeus represented a dying breed, a man of pioneer spirit, a man who had done it all on his own, without help from any man. Even in these hard times he still survived and prospered, refusing to accept help from the ever-expanding farm aid program, while most of those around him eagerly embraced any aid offered by the federal government.

And Seymour knew that J.C. was right. If he could get Thaddeus Martin to switch to combines, the rest of the wheat growers in the area would fall in line like toppling dominos.

Thaddeus's wife had died in an influenza epidemic a half-dozen years ago, and he had not remarried, refusing even to make an effort in that direction insofar as Seymour was aware.

Seymour had often wondered what the man did for pussy, but that wasn't a question you asked of Thaddeus Martin.

He reached the boundaries of the Martin wheat acreage miles before he ever approached the house. Finally he turned off the gravel highway and drove a half-mile down a narrow dirt road, dust boiling up behind the car. Tall elms lined the lane like sentinels, making of it a tree-shaded tunnel.

It was Seymour's understanding that Thaddeus had lived with his wife for fifteen years in a sod shanty, which had been put up before the turn of the century, before he finally built his own house. The story had it that his wife died just one week before they were to move into the new house. Thaddeus had lived there alone since. The few times Seymour had been in the house he had only been in the kitchen, the hall and one upstairs bedroom. The glimpses he'd had into the other rooms of the house had shown him ghostly shapes of furniture covered with dust shrouds. It had occurred to him that Thaddeus probably never went into the other rooms at all, but Seymour had not dared inquire about it.

Such were his thoughts as he drove down the lane. The sky was like an inverted bowl, brassily reflecting the fierce sun. In the weeds beside the lane grasshoppers sang their drowsy heat-songs. The sun was slanting low in the west when he stopped the Ford in the grassless yard before the square, two-story house. Another odd fact that perhaps revealed more than a streak of eccentricity in Thaddeus Martin was the outside appearance of the house. It had never been painted. The legend had it that the painters had been due the day his wife died, and Thaddeus had chased them off, vowing to never have it painted during his lifetime.

Whatever the reason for its unpainted state, the house looked strange out there in the middle of wheat fields, its boards weathered a uniform gray while most of the other farmhouses were kept a pristine white by being painted every few years if the farmer could afford it.

As Seymour got out of the V-8, Thaddeus came around the corner of the veranda from the east side of the house. The veranda, unscreened, ran along two sides of the house. Thaddeus stood at the top of the steps, big frame clothed in faded overalls and a once-blue shirt, big feet in work shoes planted wide apart on the porch. He looked as solid, and as timeless, as the elms Seymour had passed through on the way in. Around forty now, Thaddeus's thick mane of brown hair was already showing streaks of gray. He towered well over six feet, weighed over two hundred pounds, with shoulders barn-door wide. His craggy face was burned a dark red from the sun and the prairie wind. Gray eyes regarded Seymour without expression.

"Thaddeus, how you?" Seymour went up the steps, bootheels clicking with the sound of bullets. At the top of the steps he accepted Thaddeus's firm handshake.

"Middling, Seymour. Middling. You're looking good." His gaze went past Seymour. "Quite a fancy-looking automobile you've got there."

Seymour turned around to follow his glance, making no attempt to keep the pride out of his voice. "She is something, ain't she?"

"Must have cost you a pretty penny. I'd guess you're doing right well for yourself this year to be able to afford an automobile like that."

"Considering the hard times, Thaddeus, not too bad." He turned to look out across the fields of wheat. "Looks like you've got a fine crop of wheat this year. Since the price's up a little, you shouldn't do too bad."

"Middling crop, fair to middling. Figure to start mowing some time next week."

Seymour itched to tell him that Amanda Cayne and her crew might be late, critically late, but he knew his man. Now was not the time.

"Supper'll be on the table soon, Seymour. Maybe you'd like to wash up at the pump out back before setting down."

Seymour made the expected protest. "You sure it's not too much trouble? I was just passing near and thought I'd drop by to chew the fat a little. Didn't realize that it was so close to supper time."

"No trouble. This time of the year I always keep a kettle of stew simmering on the stove. Never know who might drop in. All I have to do is bake a pan of biscuits. That won't take long. And your bed's all made upstairs, Seymour."

"We-ell." Seymour pretended to consider. "Reckon I can stay over. Nowhere I'm really expected until morning."

"Happy to have you stay the night," Thaddeus said. He gazed off. "Man gets lonely sometimes living all by himself. Good to have company once in a while."

The two men went around the corner of the house. Thaddeus turned into the kitchen, and Seymour went on down the steps to the well out back of the house. Stripping off his shirt, he commenced to wash, looking forward with pleasure to the Martin supper table. There were other unmarried wheat growers he spent the night with from time to time. They fell into two categories. Either they had a housekeeper to do the cooking, or they did it themselves. Almost without exception they were lousy cooks.

Thaddeus Martin, however, *was* an exception. He could cook better than most women, Seymour knew, and he did it, seemingly, with little effort. Other men were prideful of their terrible cooking. Cooking was woman's work, or for one of those la-di-da boys. A real man had no place in the kitchen. Thaddeus showed no great pride in his cooking; any praise he simply shrugged off. Yet the fact remained that he was a good cook, and he was one of the most masculine men of Seymour's acquaintance.

Some people might say, "What's so hard about a pot of stew?" but they had never eaten Thaddeus's stew. Or his biscuits, either. The stew had a blending of subtle flavors that must have come from a private garden of witches' herbs. It gave everything a flavor defying description. And his biscuits were light as a feather and tasty enough—no other way to say it—to melt in a man's mouth.

Seymour dried himself on a sack towel and put on his shirt. Shooting a glance at the house, he detoured around it with a tin cup of cold water from the well and out to the Ford. He dug the pint bottle from under the seat and poured a generous dollop of whiskey into the cup. He knew that Thaddeus would not allow booze in his house. Although far from a religious fanatic, he had many of the old Biblical notions about morality, a morality that frowned upon the use of alcohol in any form, sexual relations outside marriage, and women swearing, smoking cigarettes, or wearing pants.

Halfway through the cup of whiskey and water, Seymour stopped, struck by a sudden thought. If Thaddeus met Amanda *before* the crew arrived here, and saw for himself the things she did that he was sure to consider beyond a woman's bounds, he just might cancel his agreement with her on those grounds alone. Now the question was, how to bring this about?

Seymour knew he couldn't just come out and tell Thaddeus without a little ground-work first; he wouldn't be believed.

Belly warmed by the whiskey, he started back to the house. The sun had gone down, and dusk was closing fast. With the sun gone, some of the day's heat had dissipated.

But it was still fierce in the kitchen. The heat from the cast-iron cookstove was intense. For a man of his size, Thaddeus seemed unbothered by it as he took the pan of biscuits from the oven and put it on the table.

They sat down and pitched in. There was little conversation at the supper table. Eating was too serious a business in this, the hardest of hard times. Seymour dug into the stew and buttered biscuits with a good appetite, as did Thaddeus. The meal was finished off with a fresh-baked peach cobbler and mugs of steaming coffee.

Then they took themselves out to the front porch, Seymour sweating freely, and occupied two straightback chairs side by side. It was full dark now, the stars bright in a clear night sky. The earth was cooling, and the crickets chirped to each other in the night. Fireflies darted about, blinking on and off like traffic lights.

Seymour fired a cigar, while Thaddeus crimped tobacco out of a packet and tamped it into a short black pipe with his thumb, then lit it with a wooden match. That old pipe was Thaddeus's only vice that Seymour knew of.

Seymour hooked his bootheels on the porch railing and tilted the chair at an angle on its back legs. Thaddeus didn't move, his feet planted solidly on the porch planks.

Seymour patted his stomach and burped gently. "Fine supper, Thaddeus, mighty fine."

"One thing about a man with a farm. He won't starve to death, even in bad times."

"That's true," Seymour agreed. Then he added, forcibly keeping any slyness out of his voice, "Still, a lot of farmers have been losing their places right along, banks foreclosing right and left. A bad crop year, fall behind on the mortgage, then whap! Something happen to your wheat crop maybe. It could even happen to you, Thaddeus."

Thaddeus's only response was a soft grunt.

Seymour figured that he had planted the seed; he knew better than to cultivate it until the big man by his side had time to think on it a little. Striking off on a tangent, he drawled, "What do you think of our new president, Thaddeus? Franklin Delano Roosevelt?"

Thaddeus grunted again. "I'd guess it's a little early to tell yet. He's been mighty busy, I'll have to say that for him."

"That he has, proposing and passing bills right and left."

"Can't say as I much approve of this liquor repeal business. Thank the good Lord we folks here in Kansas had the good sense to remain against it, except for that 3.2 beer."

Seymour had brains enough to steer the conversation away from that particular subject. "Some things the new president's done ain't so bad. Maybe too early to tell yet how they'll work out. But the CCC is giving some poor kids jobs. And he's shored up the banks. Way I understand it, ain't so many banks going under now. And some farmers think this crop subsidy is a good thing . . ."

Thaddeus stirred now, a tremor of anger in his usually mild voice. "Subsidies!" He spat over the railing "Man's a mighty poor farmer if he needs government help to keep going. This reducing crop acreage is a bad thing, Seymour. We should be producing more, not less. This Cotton Control Act now, telling a man how much cotton he can plant and how much he can't, taxing him for going over his quota! Next thing you know, they'll be doing that to wheat farmers, too!"

He was silent for a bit, blowing angry clouds of smoke, as though waiting for Seymour's comment. Seymour kept quiet.

"You know what's wrong with this country?"

"I have my own ideas, Thaddeus. But I'd admire to hear yours."

"Greed, that's what it is. Too many people were greedy, trying to make all the money in the world, that's why we're in this Depression. A man should be satisfied with what he's got!"

Seymour recognized the inconsistency of this position. Thaddeus Martin had the most acreage under cultivation of any wheat grower in the state. But, since J.C. Fallon could be considered the greediest of men and Seymour himself would dearly love to have J.C.'s money, he withheld comment. In his private opinion, he thought the country would be better off if more men were greedy, out there fighting and scratching for every nickel they could lay their hands on, instead of being content with what they had, or what the government would let them have.

Thaddeus seemed primed now and he ran on for a spell, a long spell for a man who rarely used two words when one would do the job. Seymour smoked, making a response when one seemed called for.

All at once Thaddeus fell silent. He leaned over the railing to knock the dottle from his cold pipe. "Time for bed. Morning comes early and the cows don't like to wait to be milked." He stood up. "But you don't have to rush off to bed, Seymour."

"Oh, no, I'm ready to hit the feathers." Seymour also stood up. "I've had a long day myself."

Hitting the feathers wasn't far from the mark. The feather bed was still in place in the bedroom that Thaddeus showed him. The custom was to remove the feather beds in summer. It was comfortable, of course, but it was also hot as hell. One of a feather bed's functions was to keep a person warm in winter. Apparently Thaddeus, not being all that accustomed to having overnight guests, had neglected to remove it.

After a time Seymour, sweating like a laboring horse, had to move to a quilt spread on the floor. Even so, he slept very well, because he was so tired. Since he was used to sleeping on the ground during threshing season anyway, it wasn't that much of a hardship.

He heard Thaddeus moving around shortly after daybreak. He stood at the window in his shorts, stretching and yawning. Down below he saw Thaddeus on his way to the barn carrying two milk buckets. There was a pink cast to the sky in the east. It was going to be another clear, hot day.

Seymour got dressed and went downstairs. There was already a fire in the stove, a kettle of water heating and coffee perking. He went out to the car for his razor, poured a pan of hot water and shaved at the wash bench out back. He had wondered before why Thaddeus hadn't installed an indoor bathroom; he could certainly afford it. Probably didn't hold with all these modern conveniences.

By the time he was finished and went into the kitchen, Thaddeus was there, putting breakfast on the table. They ate ham steak, red-eye gravy, three eggs apiece and the usual pan of biscuits.

They sat for a while over coffee, even though it was beginning to heat up in the kitchen. Thaddeus didn't fire up his pipe and Seymour refrained from lighting a cigar. Thaddeus seldom smoked in the house.

Taking a sip of coffee, Seymour said casually, "I reckon the Cayne outfit will be threshing for you again this year?"

Thaddeus glowered at him and growled, "You know he is, Seymour. He always will, long as he's around. Our friendship goes back a good many years."

"Then I reckon you ain't heard the news. Amos ain't with the crew."

Cup halfway to his mouth, Thaddeus stopped to stare. "He's not?"

"Nope. Amos had a stroke a little over a month ago."

Thaddeus set his cup down with a crash. "Then if they're not still threshing, why ain't I been told?"

"Oh, they're still threshing. Amos's daughter, Amanda, is running the whole shebang. Did you ever meet her?"

"His daughter?" Thaddeus frowned, looking off into the distance. "I seem to recollect a girl hanging around. A slip of a girl."

Seymour grinned. "Oh, she's all growed up now, a fine figure of a woman."

"But a woman running a threshing crew?"

"Something to think about, ain't it?" Seymour nodded wisely. "Some of the growers are a little concerned. Seems she's running behind schedule, way behind."

"Hooker . . ." The other's voice was harsh now. "You ain't lying to me?"

"Thaddeus, old friend, would I do that?"

"I wouldn't put it past you, if you thought it'd get you my wheat to do."

"Thaddeus, I swear to you . . . look, if I did a thing like that, you'd catch me out eventually, right? Then were'd I be?"

Thaddeus held his gaze a moment longer, then looked again out the kitchen door, his coffee forgotten and growing cold. "So Amos came down with a stroke, did he? Can't say I'm too surprised, the way that man lived . . ." As if of its own volition, one hand dipped into his pocket and came out with the old pipe. He fondled it between his big hands, as though warming the bowl. "Where is Amos now?"

"Down home outside Wichita Falls, the way I get it."

"And his girl took over?"

"That's right."

"You say she's falling behind?"

"I swear that's the gospel truth, Thaddeus. I wouldn't lie to you about something like that. Look, let me put it to you this way." He leaned forward intently. "Why don't you let the mowing slide for a few days. What can it hurt, man? Then hop into your pickup and drive down to find out for yourself? I'll tell you where to find her. Don't be content to take my word for it, Thaddeus!"

7

Thaddeus Martin stood on the porch and watched Seymour Hooker's fancy Ford speed up the lane toward the highway, a cloud of dust boiling up to linger in the air long after the car had disappeared.

And Thaddeus was still standing there long after the car was out of sight, staring blankly in the direction Seymour had gone and considering what he had told him. Somehow he felt that, in this instance, the man was telling the truth. For some strange reason, knowing full well that he was a liar, a conniver, a man who would do just about anything to make his way in the world, Thaddeus liked Seymour Hooker. Maybe it was because the man was hungry for life and lived it to the hilt, maybe it was because Seymour was the exact opposite of Thaddeus Martin. Or maybe it was because of something Martha, who had never met Seymour, had said once, "You have to learn more tolerance, Thad. You have to cultivate a tolerance toward people different from yourself, accept them as they are."

Although not overly educated, Martha had

been a bookworm. For a time after her death, Thaddeus had cursed and raged at her reading addiction, blaming that for her fragile health. He knew this was only an excuse, of course, an excuse to remove the onus from himself for working such a delicate person down to skin-and-bones and onto her deathbed.

And that, of course, was swinging to the other extreme. Martha had been robust enough when they'd married back in Ohio—he eighteen, Martha sixteen. Certainly she had worked hard, right along with him in the fields as well as cooking and tending house, if that sod shanty they had lived in for so many years could be called a house; but that had been of her own choosing. Martha had possessed a will of iron. If she hadn't wanted to work, she would not have done so, no matter what Thaddeus had said or done. "If we are to make anything of this land, Thad, I have to do my share. I never gave you any sons to help."

Her barrenness had been Martha's one bitter disappointment in life. How many times had he assured her that it didn't matter all that much?

Martha had known better; she had been able to read him as easily as she could one of those books of hers. "A man wants sons, Thad. There would be something unnatural about him if he didn't. I could say it is my cross to bear, if I was a very religious person, but I don't know why God should punish me. I have tried to live a good life!"

She had indeed lived a good life. She had been a good woman, a fine wife to a man, and he missed her with an ache that would not go away. Martha was dead six years now, but Thaddeus still caught himself talking aloud to her, discussing daily problems as he had when she was still with him.

With a sigh Thaddeus crossed to lower himself heavily into one of the porch chairs. He took out his pipe, filled and lit it. He recognized how unusual it was for Thaddeus Martin to sit on the porch in mid-morning and smoke a pipe. There was much work to be done. Right now he didn't have the heart for it. He sat and smoked and let his thoughts range back down through the years—the good years and the bad.

He knew of the many stories about him. He never bothered to confirm or deny them. Most of them were true, if heavily embroidered, as legends will become with time.

"I never dreamed I'd end up married to a living legend," Martha had said with that puckish grin. She was then on her deathbed, but she retained her sense of humor right up to the end.

"You embarrass a man, Martha."

"But it's true, Thad! You *are* a legend. You came out here riding on a wagon behind a team of mules. You were one of the first to realize that the prairie uplands were the best for wheat. You started with a section of land, now you have over two thousand acres in wheat. You have a green thumb . . . or should I say a gold thumb?" She had grinned again. "You have thrived and prospered where others have gone under, fought and won against drought and wheat rust and wind and hail and fungus, survived two grasshopper plagues. You remember the one five years after we came out here? Remember, I was wearing that old straw hat? The grasshoppers ate it right off my head before it was all over."

Thaddeus remembered, he remembered very well. . . .

It was a drought year, as it always seemed to be when the locusts came. It was a clear, hot day.

Suddenly, around four o'clock in the afternoon, the sky darkened, the day becoming almost as black as night. Martha's chickens ran clucking to their roosts, obviously terrified. Thaddeus came hurrying in from the fields. With a whirring sound the grasshoppers came from the northwest by the thousands. They covered everything like a living shroud. Thaddeus was blanketed from head to foot before he could reach the sod shanty. They hit his face and hands with a sound like rotten fruit bursting. The ground was covered to a depth of four or more inches by the time Thaddeus reached the shanty, and they were advancing across his fields of ripening wheat.

Martha saw him coming and ran out of the shanty, batting at the caroming insects.

"You get back inside, Martha!" he yelled at her. "I just wanted to make sure you're all right. I'm going to start a fire in the fields, like a backfire against a prairie fire. Maybe I'll be able to save some of the grain."

"I'll come with you, you can't do it alone."

Her face was set, and he knew it was useless

110

to argue. He would only waste valuable time. Martha ducked back inside to clamp that straw hat on her head. They toted cans of coal oil and torches made of tow sacks wrapped around broomsticks out to the fields and started a line of fire. Fortunately the wind was in their favor and they were able to save about half of the wheat crop. To Thaddeus's dying day he would never forget the sound of grasshoppers frying and the smell, dear Lord, the smell! It was enough to make a man sick to his stomach.

But Martha worked by his side all the while. He well knew that most women would have been terrified, more likely to hide away in the storm cellar. Of course Martha was frightened, she had to be, yet she never uttered a word of complaint.

When it was over, near sundown, and the grasshoppers were gone, as quickly as they had come, she took off what remained of the straw hat and looked at it with a rueful laugh, that puckish grin alive.

"Well, Thad, it could have been worse. You lost a passel of wheat, but I only lost a straw hat."

Walking back to the sod shanty, they passed along the creek bank. Many of the trees had branches broken off, so overloaded had they been by the insects, and the water in the creek was so thick with drowned grasshoppers it flowed sluggishly.

As they rounded the henhouse, Martha suddenly skidded to a stop and began to laugh helplessly, pointing a finger. The two dozen hens she kept had come out of hiding and had clearly been gorging themselves on dead grass-hoppers. Now they were so full they could eat no more and stood around with heads hanging, pecking listlessly at the insects littering the ground.

Martha got her laughter under control. "Like some smart man once wrote, 'There's always a silver lining to every cloud.' First time in my life I ever saw chickens so full they couldn't eat!"

That was Martha, indomitable, eternally cheerful, fearful of none of God's creatures, and only defeated by death. Few women would have run away from a reasonably comfortable life in Ohio to elope at sixteen with a boy not yet twenty, to come all the way out to Kansas in a wagon, and then to stand by her man through thick and thin.

Thaddeus knew that many of his neighbors here in Kansas considered him a religious fa-natic, a fact they admired him for since all had a bedrock faith and an abiding belief in the ways of righteousness. Yet this was not quite the truth; they would have had to know of his childhood and growing up to understand. His father had been a drunkard and a woman-chasing fornicator, putting his wife into an early grave by his dissolute ways. Thaddeus's grandfather on his mother's side had owned the Ohio farm when his daughter married John Martin against his wishes. Disapproving of his son-in-law, he had left the farm to any grand-son he might have, said farm becoming the property of said grandson on reaching his eighteenth birthday.

Thaddeus stoically endured the abuse, the drunken rantings and beatings from his father, waiting until that fateful date. And on that birthday he sold the farm and everything on it, taking whatever he could get for it. He kept only a milk cow, a wagon and team. Then he prepared to marry Martha and leave Ohio forever. Also on that day he raised his fist to his father for the first time.

Weaving drunkenly, John Martin barred his way with a shotgun, demanding the money from the sale of the farm. "It's rightfully mine, you ungrateful whelp! You're leaving here over my dead body!"

Thaddeus wrested the shotgun from the man, beat him into unconsciousness, and drove away in the wagon to pick up Martha.

Since that day he had never once raised his hand to a man in anger. Neither had he taken a drink of hard liquor or whored with other women. In fact, Martha was the only woman he had ever known carnally.

It wasn't from a religious upbringing that he had acquired his rigid moral values. He had never been inside a church, except for his wedding, before he came to Kansas, although he had read the Bible from cover to cover any number of times and considered himself a God-fearing man. But always in his mind was that old saying, "Like father, like son." He was constantly fearful that he would become like his father, and for that reason he exercised a stern

113

control over the hungers of the flesh. As a result, he came to view with suspicion anything that pleasured the flesh, or the emotions, or even the mind.

Martha had often teased him about it. "Thad, you're too unbending. It often makes me cry inside, the way you reject the few pleasures of life. You're like a rock, you work harder than any man I've ever known, but a man is supposed to enjoy the fruits of his labors. You smoke that old pipe, but I'm not sure you even enjoy *that*. You eat my victuals, but you never express pleasure. You might as well be that old iron cookstove, burning wood to keep a fire going."

"That's not so, Martha! I've often remarked on how good your cooking is!"

"Yes, but do you enjoy eating it, Thad? And when we lie down in bed at night, do you enjoy that?"

"You do have a way of embarrassing a man!"

"But do you enjoy it, do you find pleasure when we are joined together?"

"Martha, you are my wife. I love you."

"That is not what I asked you. Do you find pleasure with me?"

Goaded, he had said, "It is not right that a man should find pleasure in such things!"

"Then why do you suppose our Lord gave us the ability to feel pleasure in our bodies?"

"It is to test us. A man must have the strength to resist the temptations of the flesh."

Sadly she had shaken her head and turned away.

How many times since her death had he wished he could have found the proper words to tell Martha how much he had enjoyed the warmth and the love of their nights together? The feel of her small but fully rounded body fitted snugly to his, the hot pleasure he felt at his entry into her eager body. But the words to voice such delights were not in him. Would Martha now lie easier in the cold ground had he once, just once, let her know the pleasure she had given him?

Now, on the porch, Thaddeus came to his feet with a soft grunt. As the days, the months, the years passed since Martha's death, carnal thoughts and dreams had come increasingly to plague him. The blood ran hot in his veins, he well knew. Had he not lain with Martha almost every night of their life together, up until she had taken to her bed for the last time?

Not once had he taken a woman since Martha passed on. It wasn't from a lack of wanting. Almost nightly in his dreams nowadays, he pranced goatlike after naked women and all too often awoke to find himself lying in a puddle of his own semen. Other nights the wanting had such a grip on him that he couldn't sleep and would walk the fields until exhausted.

Was such a thing not shameful in a man past forty?

Thaddeus went about finishing his morning chores. He knew that some time during that porch reverie he had made up his mind—he was going to follow Seymour's suggestion and drive down south to check on the progress of the Cayne crew. He would have to run the risk of a hard rain or a hailstorm and let the wheat stand another two or three days before mowing. If Seymour Hooker's story turned out to be true and it appeared that Amanda Cayne wouldn't reach his place in time, he would turn it over to Seymour to harvest. However much it would go against his nature to go back on his word to Amos Cayne, he couldn't allow friendship to endanger his wheat crop. He was sure Amos would be able to understand that.

Perhaps his daughter would not. What kind of a woman was she? He could admire her pitching in and trying to help out her father in his time of trouble. Yet bossing a wheat threshing crew wasn't work for a woman. Going about his chores, he tried to recall what she looked like. He vaguely remembered seeing a young girl around the crew, but at the time he had paid little heed to her. There were too many things to do during harvest time for a man to concern himself with a child.

Finished with the outside chores, he tidied up the house, then changed into his one suit. Wrestling with the stiffness of a celluloid collar, he paused to smile at himself in the yellowed mirror. If there wasn't a woman involved, would he have bothered to dress up? Doggedly he went about putting on a tie and struggling into stiff, high-topped shoes, shoes he wore only on those times he attended church. Or a funeral. That gave him pause to think of Martha. He could almost hear her voice in his head, "Be tolerant with her, Thad. Even if she is a woman doing man's work, give the girl a chance to prove what she can do."

"All right, Martha," he said aloud. "For your sake, I'll give her the benefit of the doubt."

Finally he was ready. He packed the necessaries into a small bag and carried it, along with an armload of blankets, out to the pickup. He would sleep in the back of the pickup while he was gone, which wouldn't be longer than three nights at the most. He couldn't afford to be gone longer than that.

He drove a mile down the road to the Parker place to ask Bert Parker to tend his stock while he was away.

"Glad to, Thaddeus, any time. You know that." Bert Parker was a stocky, bustling man of sixty-odd. He looked at Thaddeus curiously. "But I thought you were about to start cutting?"

"I was, but I'm putting it off a few days. I'll stop and tell the boys I'm hiring not to come yet." Thaddeus hesitated, then decided to tell him the rest of it. The Cayne outfit was due to thresh the Parker wheat also, and Bert deserved some warning. He told the man where he was going. "So I'll find out the truth of it and let you know first thing when I get back."

Parker had been looking increasingly dismayed. "But if it's true I'm up shit creek without a paddle, Thaddeus! It's too late to make other arrangements!"

"Don't worry, Bert. If for some reason the Cayne crew can't make it on time, Seymour Hooker will harvest your grain with his combines. You have my word on it."

"But I thought you were against combines? The rest of us around here have been following your lead."

Thaddeus smiled feebly. "Maybe I've been wrong. I've been doing some thinking on it."

Thaddeus drove on, making a few quick stops on the way to inform the men he'd hired of the delay in plans. Finally he aimed the pickup south. He had quite a few miles to go, and it grew dark before he had covered half the distance. At nine he stopped at a roadside diner and ate some supper, then pulled off the highway a few miles farther on and made his bed in the back of the pickup.

He was awake at daybreak, as was his habit. It took him a few moments to realize where he was. When he did, he smiled to himself. He couldn't remember when he had spent a night off the farm. He shaved in a bucket of cold water, then drove on, stopping at the first open place for a cup of coffee and a stack of wheat cakes.

Then, pipe going, he drove on south. He stepped up the pace, impatient to get there. He rarely drove the rattling pickup over thirty. Now he pushed it past forty, and it bucked and groaned, as though annoyed at being forced out of its usual comfortable pace. Thaddeus noticed several harvesting crews as he drove along, some using combines and some threshers.

When he arrived in the vicinity of where Seymour Hooker had told him the Cayne crew was threshing, he stopped a couple of times to ask directions. Consequently, it was just short of the noon hour when he finally located the right farm.

Following directions picked up at the farmhouse, he drove down a rutted lane alongside a fence. He saw the blowers first, spewing wheat straw and chaff. Then he made out the threshing machines and the men busy around them.

He steered the pickup toward them, stopping well out of the way, and climbed stiffly out of the cab. He saw someone striding vigorously toward him. At first he thought it was a man. The figure wore pants, boots and a man's shirt. Then, as it neared him, he realized it was a woman in a man's getup. In addition, she was smoking a cigarette.

Thaddeus halted, appalled. Could this be Amanda Cayne, the person responsible for threshing his wheat crop? He half-turned to get into the pickup and drive away, but he was too late.

The woman said, "You looking for work?"

"No," Thaddeus said gruffly. "I'm Thaddeus Martin. You're to thresh my wheat. I drove down to . . ."

"Thaddeus Martin? I don't . . ." the woman said, frowning. Then her face cleared. "Oh, yes! Mr. Martin. You don't remember me, I'm sure. I'm Amanda Cayne."

She stuck out her hand and Thaddeus took it reluctantly.

"We're just about to break for the noon hour. Why don't you sit down and eat with us? We can talk."

8

Amanda Cayne wasn't a great movie fan, but she did go now and then. A few weeks before she joined the threshing crew she had seen a rising young star in a film. Thaddeus Martin reminded her a lot of Spencer Tracy; on a much larger scale, of course. But he had the same ugly-handsome face, a suggestion of a quiet inner strength and the stubbornness of character portrayed by Tracy. One thing was missing—the impish sense of humor that popped out now and then. At least humor wasn't evident on the surface of Thaddeus Martin.

Amanda recognized that this man didn't approve of her mannish attire, her smoking cigarettes, or her bossing a threshing crew. She perceived this at once, yet she also noticed that he tried to put a good face on it. He tried not to show his disapproval and she was quite sure this was not his usual way with strangers, men *or* women.

Thaddeus Martin had by far the largest wheat acreage on their threshing schedule. Losing him would be a near-disaster, so she tried to put him at ease. She softened the harsh edges of the personality she showed around the crew and tried hard not to smoke a cigarette while they ate lunch at a card table set up outside her tent. She forgot and lit up a couple of times. She had taken a puff or two before she caught the flicker of disapproval in his gray eyes. She smoked the cigarettes through to the end. Damned if she would kowtow to him that much!

She reflected on the differences between this man and Seymour Hooker. Seymour got a kick out of her occasional vulgarity, her wearing of men's clothes—"That tail of yours looks great in a man's pants, sugar," he would say—and he made no bones about the fact that he would dearly love to get into her drawers. The only thing he didn't approve of was her running the crew, and that sprang from purely business considerations.

All at once, Amanda realized what she was thinking and paused to wonder. Why on earth was she making comparisons between this man and Seymour? Seymour was far from her male ideal, if there was such an animal. And why the devil did she care what *either* man thought of her?

Deep in thought, she had lost the thread of the conversation. She snapped to attention and said, "I'm sorry, Mr. Martin. I didn't catch all that?"

"I was saying, ma'am, that I'll have to start thinking about making some other arrangements about my wheat if your crew can't make it in time."

"Oh, we'll make it, never fear."

His look was frankly skeptical. "It's my understanding that you're almost two weeks behind now."

"You've been talking to Seymour Hooker!" she said angrily.

"I've talked to Seymour, yes. He was up my way checking things in advance of his crew."

"And he just *happened* to drop in on you and just happened to mention that the Cayne crew was running behind!"

"He dropped in, yes. He does that once a year. We go back a ways, Seymour and me."

"He's trying to get your wheat to thresh, isn't he?"

"He's been trying to do that for years." Thaddeus smiled briefly. He took an old, blackened pipe from his pocket. "But I've done business with your daddy since he started threshing and . . ."

"And we have an agreement with you for this year."

"With him, yes, Miss Cayne. But I don't know if I need consider that agreement binding now."

"I'm his daughter, this is still the Cayne crew. All right, we're a little behind. There've been some problems, some breakdowns, bad weather, we're shorthanded . . ." She tossed her head. "What would you say if Daddy was in my place, running behind schedule and he told you he'd catch up?"

"Why, I'd go along with him, more'n likely." Thaddeus shrugged massive shoulders. "But it's hardly the same thing, the way I see it."

"Why isn't it? Because I'm a woman? A woman shouldn't be operating a threshing crew. Is that your thinking?"

Thaddeus made an uncomfortable gesture. "No, I didn't say that, although it is hardly a job for a woman, you must admit."

"I'll admit no such damned thing!" She swept on, ignoring his look of shock. "Just because I *am* a woman, you think I'll fall farther and farther behind! Well, I won't, you'll see. Just give me a chance, Mr. Martin."

"I'd like to, Miss Cayne. I'd surely hate to cancel out with your daddy laid up sick like he is, but I have my wheat to think about."

"We'll get to your wheat in time, I promise you. We've been picking up some time the last few days, working from as early in the morning as we can until dark." She hesitated, not sure how he would take what she was going to say. "To make absolutely sure, I'll skip some of the smaller farms before your place."

Thaddeus frowned. He caressed his cheek with the cold pipe bowl. "I wouldn't want to be held responsible for putting others in a bind . . ."

"Oh, don't worry, Mr. Martin," she assured him hastily. "I'll inform them in plenty of time for them to get somebody else. There're enough harvesting crews around to handle the extra work. Probably be glad to get it." She made a face. "They can always hire Seymour and his combines. He'd be delighted to do it. In fact, he and J.C. Fallon will never be content until they've got all the wheat in the country to thresh!"

"But, Miss Cayne, you skipping farms to get to me . . . that's going to cost you."

"Let me worry about that. And it won't hurt nearly so much as losing your wheat." She leaned forward, elbows on the rickety table. "Let me be frank, Mr. Martin . . . it's not only the money we might lose this year, it's what'll happen next year. You're the biggest wheat grower in the state of Kansas. How'll it look if I lose you? Next year, people will say that the Cayne crew couldn't make the Martin place, so why risk it? Let's use somebody else this year. We'd be lucky to get any wheat at all to thresh!"

"Well now, I'm not sure I'm so all-fired that important people would follow my lead. But I want to be fair. I want to give you every chance. So, if it's okay with you, I'll watch awhile, the rest of today, part of tomorrow maybe. Just to see how things are going. Now don't get all het up again . . ." He held up a hand. "I'd do the same with a man, a man I knew nothing about. Does that strike you as fair enough?"

"Fair enough, Mr. Martin." Amanda voiced a small prayer to herself. Let nothing happen while he's watching. No breakdowns of that falling-apart machinery. No wholesale desertions by the crew. She heard the tractors start up with a roar and she looked across the field.

125

She smiled to herself. The men were probably wondering what had happened to her. She usually started prodding them back to work a few minutes early. She glanced at her wrist watch. One o'clock on the nose. Maybe she did ride them too hard, maybe she should ease up.

She stood up abruptly and repeated, "Fair enough, Mr. Martin." She held out her hand. "Shall we shake on it?"

With a look of surprise he got to his feet and accepted her hand.

"They're starting up. I'd better get over there. Coming?"

"Not right now. I wouldn't want you to think I was looking over your shoulder ever minute . . ." He made an embarrassed gesture with the pipe. "I'll just sit here and smoke a pipe. I've found it ain't a good idea to smoke a pipe around threshing machines. Too much chance of a spark setting a wheat field afire." He smiled. "You've got enough problems without that. You go on. I'll be over directly."

Amanda nodded and started across the field. The men were already busy threshing when she reached them. Dudley Graham was busy at one of the tractors, poking around in the innards, but the tractor was running all right.

"Something wrong, Dudley?" she asked in some alarm.

He backed out from under the motor canopy, face lighting up with a smile. "Nothing serious." He began wiping his hands on some waste. "Just running a little rough."

Amanda cocked her head. "Sounds fine to me."

His smile died. "It may sound all right to you, but it's missing a little. That's the way you head off trouble with machinery, catch it when it starts acting up, not wait until it breaks down. If that had been done with your machinery before, you wouldn't have had so much trouble."

She started a hot retort, then checked her tongue. "Just so long as you keep them operating, Buster Brown, do it any way you want," she said curtly, and walked away.

Dudley Graham *was* doing his job, she had to admit that. He might be a hobo, but he was a magician with machinery, worlds better than the clod she'd had before. The breakdowns had been far less frequent during the week Dudley had been working for her and those breakdowns that had occurred were of much shorter duration. Amanda had suspected sabotage before, knowing that many of the crew would like to see her fail. She'd never had the slightest proof of this, and if it was still going on, it wasn't as effective.

Her first impression of Dudley Graham had been unfavorable, placing him in the category of the thousands of lazy, shiftless men who lived on freights these days. Whatever else Dudley was, he wasn't lazy. She had caught herself almost liking him a time or two. Yet he made himself difficult to like. He was touchy, with a thorny, almost sullen personality, and every time she let down her guard with him, something would touch him off and he'd turn on her with a snarl.

She dismissed Dudley from her thoughts. As long as he performed the job she'd hired him to do, she didn't have to like him.

For the next couple of hours, Amanda directed all her attention to seeing that wheat got threshed. She was everywhere at once, speaking sharply to any man she thought lollygagging. She was convinced that they would slack off if she didn't watch them every second. In the beginning her ignorance had been abysmal; they could get away with almost anything right under her nose. But she had quickly educated herself in every phase of threshing, so now she could spot a slacker in an instant.

Everything was going smoothly this afternoon, thank God for small favors. She was especially grateful for this when she saw Thaddeus Martin leaning against the fender of his pickup, watching. So smoothly was it going that the bundle wagons couldn't keep pace with the threshing machines.

Desperately shorthanded, Amanda needed at least two more men to drive bundle wagons. She kept an extra wagon handy, the mules already hitched up, in the shade of a broad oak at the edge of the field. When she saw that another wagon was needed, she hurried across the field and hopped aboard, clucking to the mules. She drove the wagon onto the field, down between rows of shocks, and began pitching bundles onto the rack. It was grueling, backbreaking labor, but this wasn't the first time she had pitched bundles.

After two hours of it, she was dirty and itchy and sweat-stained. She saw that several wagons were lined up now, waiting their turn at the threshers, so she could ease off for a while.

She drove the team and wagon back under the oak, and checked to see if the mules had water in the tub. She was tempted to splash herself good with the water, but she knew that some mules were finicky, refusing to drink water in which a human had washed.

She started back to the threshers, stopping at the water barrel, in the scant shade of one of the tractors. She drank two dippers of the tepid water, then wet her kerchief in a third dipper and swabbed her face. She lit a cigarette before remembering Thaddeus Martin. She sent a glance his way. He was sitting in the pickup cab now, the door open, feet on the running board. Apparently he was intent on the threshing, at least he wasn't looking at her.

Amanda smoked the cigarette down, dumped a half-dipper of water on it to make sure it was out, and walked toward the pickup, shaking her hair loose from the binding scarf and running her fingers through it with a sigh of relief.

It wasn't until she saw the man in the pickup staring intently at her that Amanda realized that holding her arms up that way was straining the fullness of her breasts against her shirt. Heat surged to her face and she dropped her arms. If he thought she was trying to use female wiles to bring him around . . .

129

Thaddeus seemed to become aware that he was staring at the same instant, and hastily looked away.

Amanda stopped at the pickup. "Everything running smoothly enough to suit you, Mr. Martin?" The words came out tinged with a sarcasm she hadn't intended.

His glance swung around. "Seems to be going along just fine. Don't really think it was necessary for you to pitch bundles just to convince me." He had removed his suit coat now, but he still had the tie on.

"I didn't do that just to show off to you!" Again she felt her face flush. "I wasn't even thinking about you. It's not the first time I've loaded bundles. There's not much I haven't done around the threshers, except tinker with machinery. I'm a poor hand at that."

"Rest of the men take kindly to you doing a man's work?"

Although his tone was noncommittal, Amanda was sure she detected a new look of respect in his eyes. Taking heart, she said tartly, "No reason they should object. I'm not taking bread out of their mouths. There was nothing my daddy wouldn't, or couldn't, do around a thresher when he was shorthanded. And I *am* shorthanded. A number of the men quit when they learned Daddy wasn't coming back, and I haven't been able to replace them. Most experienced threshermen are already working with other crews."

"Seems to me there're a lot of men looking for work, these Depression times."

"Most of the ones who've come around are hobos, no-goods, right off a freight, not worth half-wages. When a good man does come along, I hire him. If he'll work for a woman."

"And there's the rub, ain't it? If he'll work for a woman."

"I'm managing. And they'll come around in time."

Thaddeus's glance went past her. "Speaking of machinery, which you were a bit ago, strikes me that most of yours is in pretty bad shape."

"That's true," Amanda admitted. "Daddy had a bad habit of putting things off. The tractors certainly should have been replaced long ago. But I did hire a man last week, just off a freight, funnily enough, who's the best I've ever seen around machinery. He's keeping things in working order. Come along, I'd like you to meet him."

"Might as well."

Thaddeus climbed out of the cab, and they started toward the tractors where Dudley Graham was half-buried inside one again. Walking beside the wheat rancher, Amanda realized that he was indeed a big man. There probably wasn't much difference in height between Thaddeus and Seymour Hooker, but where Seymour was slim, Thaddeus was broad of shoulder, wide and thick through the chest, with muscles ridged like ropes under his shirt. She noticed his capable-looking hands, broad and powerful with stubby fingers. Hair grew like fur on the backs of his hands.

There I go again, she scolded herself, comparing him to Seymour! What has gotten into me today?

They stopped at the tractor. Amanda said, "Dudley . . . somebody here I'd like you to meet."

Dudley backed out of the tractor, facing around.

"Thaddeus, I'd like you to meet Dudley Graham. Dudley, this is Thaddeus Martin. Mr. Martin has the biggest wheat acreage on our schedule."

Thaddeus held out his hand. Dudley hastily wiped his right hand on some waste before extending it. "Happy to know you, Mr. Martin."

"Likewise, I'm sure. Miss Cayne here tells me that you're pretty handy around machinery. Think you can keep them running," he jerked his head, "until you get to my place?"

"I'll do my best, Mr. Martin." Dudley slanted a glance at Amanda. "They're pretty old and beat-up, but I think I can keep them limping along until the season's over."

Amanda glared at him. Damn him, he didn't have to say it like that! She curbed a hot retort when she saw the glint of humor in his eyes and knew he was baiting her.

Now his glance went past her and he said in a flat voice, "Looks like you're about to have company, Miss Amanda."

Amanda faced around. The sun was dropping toward the western horizon and she had to shade her eyes. It was Seymour in his new Ford. He stopped at the edge of the field, got out of the car, and came loping toward them.

Amanda felt a certain nervousness. Almost without thinking she lit a cigarette, crossed an arm over her breasts, and propped the elbow.

Seymour reached them, face creased in a broad grin. "Thaddeus!" He pumped the man's hand. "I see you made it!"

"You knew he would," Amanda said icily. "You went up there on purpose to put a bug in his ear, get him worried and send him hurrying down here!"

"Now, sugar," Seymour drawled, face innocent as a babe's, "why in the world would I want to do something like that?"

"Because you hope to get his wheat to thresh, that's why! You told him we'd never make it to his place in time. There's nothing too low of you and J.C. Fallon to pull when it comes to getting some of my customers for your lousy combines!"

"Well now, seems to me I was just telling the truth. Face it, Amanda, you ain't ever going to make it."

"That's what you *hope*! But I'll make it. We'll be threshing Mr. Martin's wheat, you wait and see!"

"Reckon it ain't exactly up to you to decide that, sugar. That right, Thaddeus? Now that you've seen how things are here, you're going to switch over to my combines. Right?"

Thaddeus Martin took his time about answering, watching the busy crew and the chaff-spewing threshers for a little. Finally he said mildly, "Guess I'll stick with Miss Cayne's outfit, Seymour."

133

"What!" Seymour's face darkened, veins swelling in his neck. "After seeing this broken-down outfit in action, seeing how far behind they are?"

Amanda was delighted at his discomfiture, but she managed to keep a straight face. Laughing at Seymour right now could be a mistake.

Still in that mild voice, Thaddeus said, "It strikes me that Miss Cayne has got things pretty well in hand. And I did give my word to her daddy."

"You must be out of your . . ." Seymour broke off, gritting his teeth. He glared at Amanda. He went on in an ugly, insinuating voice, "Oh, I get it. Miss Cayne here has got things pretty well in hand, has she? What things, Thaddeus? Must be you, can't be the threshing. Any fool can see that. She don't know beans about threshing. But she is right pretty, ain't she? But don't you go believing every little thing she promises. What *did* she promise you, Thaddeus?"

Thaddeus said, "I don't know as I quite get what you're saying, Seymour."

"Seems pretty plain to me. Like they say, any man can be a fool over a pretty woman . . ."

Amanda took two short steps and slapped Seymour across the cheek with her open hand. Quick as an uncoiling snake, he slapped her right back. The blow sent Amanda reeling back against Thaddeus. He caught her in strong hands. Ears ringing, she blinked against the hot sting of tears.

"You all right, Amanda?" Thaddeus said in her ear.

Amanda nodded mutely.

Thaddeus gently set her aside and confronted Seymour. "I don't hold with striking a woman, Hooker!"

"She's playing a man's game, ain't she? Besides, she hit me first." Seymour bared his teeth in a mirthless grin. "Tit for tat, I always say."

"I still don't hold with . . ."

"Fuck that noise, Thaddeus Martin! She's asking for it, lording it over everybody like some damned queen!"

Thaddeus's back went rigid with outrage. "Watch your foul tongue! There's a lady present!"

"What lady?" Seymour said coarsely. "If you're speaking of Amanda, she's heard worse. Probably used worse, if I know her."

Thaddeus's hands doubled into fists at his sides. "I haven't struck another man in anger since my eighteenth birthday, but if you don't apologize at once, I will, sir!"

"And the same goes for me."

To Amanda's amazement the last came from Dudley, who had also stepped in with his fists raised.

"For God's sake!" Seymour gaped at them. "Both of you? Has she got the pair of you buffaloed?"

Then he aimed a look at the scowling Thaddeus. His grin was obviously forced as he spread his hands. "Well, I can't fight both of you. Especially over something as picayune as this. Besides, I'm a lover, not a fighter."

He wasn't fooling Amanda for a moment. It was perfectly clear to her that he had suddenly remembered which side his bread was buttered on with respect to Thaddeus Martin.

Now Seymour turned his glance on her. With some of his old insouciant charm, he said, "I'm right sorry if I said something to ruffle your feelings, sugar. Reckon I got a little carried away there. You gonna forgive and forget?"

Amanda crossed her arms over her breasts. She smoked, maintaining a stony silence.

When the seconds stretched into a full minute and it was clear that she wasn't going to relent, Seymour spread his hands again. He nodded. "Well . . . so long, everybody. You know something, fella, I don't even know your name?"

"Dudley Graham."

"Dudley Graham, huh? Well, Dudley, I'll try to remember that."

Seymour's gaze remained on Dudley for a long moment, as though fixing his image firmly in his memory. Then he turned on his heel and started toward the Ford. A few steps away he paused. He aimed a vicious kick at a clod of dirt. And broke it into fragments, then strode on.

Amanda stood smiling to herself.

Dudley said disgustedly, "Ready to fight over you like a couple of dogs over a . . ."

Amanda whipped around, pinning him with her glare.

"Well, it's true, damnit! Now, if you'll excuse me, I have work to do if this chickenshit outfit is to stay together!"

9

Dudley was furious with himself. Behaving like some moony clodhopper, ready to lift his fists to defend the honor of Amanda Cayne. He didn't know as he cared much for Seymour Hooker, but what he'd said about Amanda came pretty close to the truth.

Bent over the tractor motor, he forgot himself in brooding and touched his knuckles to the fire-hot motor block. Cursing, he jerked back. He put his blistered knuckles to his mouth and sucked on them.

In a fit of childish frustration, he banged the wrench in his other hand against the offending motor block.

"Hey, sport, that's no way to treat that there motor. It's so old, it'll break into pieces, many more whacks like that one."

Dudley backed out and straightened up to look into Bud's grinning face. He glanced past the man to see that the threshing machines were shutting down.

"Yup." Bud grinned and spat tobacco juice. "All done here, wheat's all threshed. Best day we've had all season. Didn't expect to finish up here until tomorrow. Miss Amanda says since it's late anyways, we'll stay here until morning before moving out."

"Yeah, I noticed she put on a good show for our visitor." Dudley glanced across to where Thaddeus Martin's pickup was parked by Amanda's tent.

"Good reason for that." But spat. "Hell, he's the biggest wheat rancher in the whole goldarn state of Kansas. She lose his place and she's kaput, you can bank on it."

"I see," Dudley said absently, wiping his hands on a wad of waste.

Bud glanced around with a conspiratorial air. "How about a couple of snorts before supper, Dudley? I picked up a bottle of hooch last night."

"Sure, why not?" Dudley wasn't much of a drinker. A couple of drinks and he was as loose-witted as a goose. But a drink seemed called for right now.

Grinning, Bud jerked his head. "Over by those trees. I'll get the jug out of my bedroll."

Bud left, and Dudley shut down both tractors, the long pulley belts winding down with a great racket. Most of the men were washing up at the wash bench beside the cook wagon. There was a festive air about them. It was unusual for them to be knocking off before sundown. He had a hunch that many of them would sneak off into town after supper, even though it was the middle of the week and Amanda had given strict orders that there was to be no town carousing except on Saturday nights.

140

Dudley finished up and joined the men at the bench. He washed up, then trudged over to the grove of trees where Bud was already sitting back against a tree, sucking at a pint bottle of cheap whiskey.

Dudley dropped down beside him with a weary sigh, and Bud passed the bottle. It was raw, going down his gullet like a trickle of fire. It was all he could do to keep from gagging. He quickly rolled and lit a cigarette to kill the taste.

Bud tilted the bottle up without bothering to wipe the top and drank with a gurgling sound, his prominent Adam's apple bobbing.

"Powerful strong stuff," he said with a smack of his lips.

Dudley had to agree with that. Despite the God-awful taste, it was down, spreading heat in his belly and taking the edge off his weariness.

After a moment Bud passed the bottle back and Dudley slugged it again. He felt sweat break out on his face. He stared with heavy-lidded eyes toward Amanda's tent, just in time to see her emerge from it and climb in the pickup with Thaddeus Martin. Dudley felt a twinge of something in his gut. Jealousy? He was frank enough with himself to admit that it probably was.

First Seymour Hooker, now Thaddeus Martin.

His thoughts circled back to that acrimonious scene this afternoon. Didn't Amanda know that she had three men chasing after her? Of course, she had little cause to think he was after her. If she ever had an inkling, Dudley could visualize her sneer. A hobo right off a freight?

But didn't she realize the trouble she could stir up? Maybe she didn't care, maybe she was just a tease.

Yet if she had the brains of a flea, she should grasp what a potentially explosive situation it was. Dudley knew that he had absolutely no intention of fighting over her, but he could see Martin and Hooker going at it. Both were strong men, accustomed to having their own way. He sensed that Hooker was a man of strong appetites, used to getting what he wanted and apt to become violent when thwarted. Martin was quieter, more restrained, yet underneath was a powerful and stubborn will.

His musings were interrupted by a nudge from Bud's elbow. "Another snort, sport?"

"Sure."

He accepted the bottle and drank, knowing that he was getting looped and not giving a rat's ass.

Bud said, "Guy I got the jug from was selling some of these little beauties. You seen this one, Dudley?"

With a lewd smirk Bud held out a little booklet and Dudley took it before he fully realized what it was. It was one of the dirty little comics; in California they were called Tijuana bibles. Dudley had never cared for them, the sex depicted struck him as being gross, grotesque, and not at all erotic. But as a kid in high school he had, in the presence of the other kids, glanced through the well-thumbed booklets and snickered appreciatively.

Now, as then, he did the same, rather than try and explain to Bud or risk his scorn. The booklet extolled the fantastic sexual feats of Popeye and Wimpy, with Wimpy performing one particularly revolting episode involving salt and pepper and a burger routine.

And then, to his astonishment and disgust, Dudley felt himself erecting. Embarrassed, he tried to shift position to conceal his condition. From Bud's snicker, he knew that he was too late.

"Hot stuff, huh, Dudley?"

Dudley shrugged without comment and returned the booklet. He must be getting horny as hell to have that strong a reaction to such slimy crap.

As though reading his thoughts, Bud said slyly, "Some of us thought we'd slip off into town after supper and scout around for some pussy maybe. Care to come along?"

Dudley's glance went across the field to where Martin's pickup had been parked. He said, "Why not?"

The supper bell clanged.

"Want another little snort?"

"No, thanks, I've had enough."

Using the tree trunk to climb to his feet, Dudley started toward the cook wagon, weaving slightly. He ate ravenously. At least the hot food took some of the edge off the fuzziness, and he was reasonably sober afterward.

He put on his other pair of khakis and got ready for the trip into town. Now that he was sober, his enthusiasm for the sortie into town had waned. Any female a harvest hand could corner would likely be clapped up. But he couldn't very well back out now.

Fortunately he had received his first week's pay and he still had all of it, having skipped last Saturday night's trip into town.

The small town was only a few miles from where they were threshing, and a half-dozen of the harvest hands rode in on one of the grain trucks. The truck didn't even go all the way into town, pulling onto a graveled parking lot at a honky-tonk called Annie's Place.

It was a long, low room with tables and a bandstand at one end. There were only about a dozen people in the place when the Cayne crew came roaring in. Dudley saw no graceful way of escaping from Bud, so he sat down at a table with him.

The sign outside had advertised 3.2 beer only, yet when a buxom blonde came over to their table to ask, "What'll it be, boys?," Bud showed no hesitation. "Couple of shots of whiskey. I'll have a bottle of Coke with mine. How about you, Dudley?"

Dudley shuddered. "God, no! I'll have mine neat."

His gaze lingered on the swaying, well-rounded rump as the blonde strutted away. "That Annie?"

"Damned if I know."

"The way you ordered, I thought you'd been in here before and knew her."

Bud grinned. "No need to know the bitch. Most of these places serve booze. If she didn't serve it, what could she do but say no? At the worst order us out." He raked the room with his glance and spat on the floor. "And I've been ordered out of better places than this, believe you me!"

The drinks came, and Dudley drank his, a potion as potent as a mule's kick. Somehow another round was served before he knew it, and things became a little hazy after that. He sat with his shoulders hunched, brooding down into his drink, wondering what the hell he was doing here—in the state of Kansas, working with a threshing crew, and drinking in a honky-tonk with a man he had little liking for.

To the first question he knew the answer well enough. A freight train had brought him to Kansas. As for working with the threshing crew, it was a job and jobs were almost impossible to come by these days. The job was something within his experience, and he was good at it. And there was Amanda Cayne . . .

A strong hand clamped on his shoulder, hauling him upright in the chair. A sneering voice said, "Well, if it ain't the grease monkey! Amanda Cayne's grease monkey, ain't that right, Dudley? I have got the name right?"

Dudley stared up into the sarcastically grinning face of Seymour Hooker. He tried to blink away the alcohol fog. He said, "You've got the name right, yeah. But I'm nobody's pet monkey, Amanda Cayne's or anybody's!"

"Oh? You sure as shit could have fooled me. The way you hopped to her defense this afternoon, peckerwood, strikes me she has a leash around your neck." Hooker's sneer was like a slap in the face. "Or is it your pecker?"

Dudley staggered to his feet. He noticed that Bud had somehow disappeared. He lurched away from the table. "You're a foul-mouthed son-of-a-bitch, Hooker!"

"Foul-mouthed, maybe. But I don't cotton to peckerwoods like you calling me son-of-a-bitch. Only my friends and . . ." The man's grin widened, a slash of white across his face. "And my boss call me that. And you ain't either one."

"Well, I'm calling you that, so what are you going to do about it, son-of-a-bitch?"

"Knock the crap out of you," Hooker said gleefully. "You're not surrounded by the Cayne crew now."

"Then come ahead."

Dudley cocked his fists. A part of his mind hooted in derision, as he recalled pictures of just such poses assumed by John L. Sullivan. He hadn't had a fist fight since high school and that one he had lost handily, with a smashed nose that bled for two days. Besides, he was drunk and he was no match for this man even sober.

Hooker threw back his head and roared with laughter, and Dudley hit him with all his strength in the belly. Perhaps it wasn't strictly according to Marquis of Queensberry, but Dud-

146

ley wasn't so drunk that he didn't realize how slim his chances were. His knuckles felt broken, as though he'd smashed them against a washboard.

Hooker's mouth fell open, the breath whooshing out of him. He glared at Dudley in pained astonishment. "Why, you sneaky shitass!"

Dudley didn't even see the blow coming. But he felt it. Oh, did he ever feel it! It felt like Hooker had hit him alongside the head with a two-by-four. He reeled back, knocking over the table and chair where he'd been sitting, and careened into the wall.

Through blurred vision, he saw Seymour Hooker advancing on him. He tried to come off the wall swinging, but he didn't have a chance. Hooker hit him with a barrage of lightning lefts and rights, delivered like hammer blows. Pain exploded like a bomb in his skull, and he slid slowly to the floor to a sitting position, his back against the wall. He wasn't all the way out—he could still hear, as from a distance.

He heard an indignant female voice, "Don't you stomp that poor guy, Seymour Hooker!"

"But the peckerwood hit me first, Annie!"

"You came in here spoiling for a fuss, stud. I watched what happened. That poor boy couldn't whip a butterfly and you, you ain't ever lost a fist fight that I ever heard. Now you go on, get out of here, and I'll take care of him."

"But Annie, I thought maybe you and me, maybe we could get together later on. It's been a couple of weeks since I've snuggled up with you."

"And it may well be a couple of weeks more, if you don't behave."

"Aww, Annie."

"Go, go!"

Along about then Dudley's consciousness began to glide away from him, the voices above him receding as though down a long tunnel. For the next several minutes he slipped in and out of consciousness and was dimly aware of being partly carried, partly dragged, until he was finally stretched out on something soft. His clothes were removed over his weak protests, and his face bathed in cold water, while a deep, rich female voice clucked over him.

Then some fiery liquid was dumped down his throat, and he came out of it coughing and flailing the air with both hands.

"Easy, Charlie, easy."

"Name's Dudley."

"All right, Dud. Take it easy."

"Don't like Dud." A thought surfaced. "What happened to Bud?"

"I don't know any Bud."

"Guy at the table with me."

"Oh, that one. He ran like a cottontail when Seymour came roaring in. You'd've been smart to do the same."

Dudley managed to open his eyes. He was lying on a narrow bed in a rather primitive room, the furnishings stark and barely functional. A few pitiful efforts had been made to feminize it—wilted flowers in a vase on the dresser, freshly starched flowered curtains on the one window, a few bright throw rugs on the floor. One light burned dimly by the bed.

He focused on the woman sitting on the bed beside him. She was a large woman, with a friendly open face, a sunny smile and ample breasts spilling out of a low bodice. Dudley became conscious of the warmth of a well-fleshed thigh pressing against his. She had a dripping towel in her hand.

"I'm Annie Mae Delong, Dudley. Pleased to meet you."

"I got whipped, didn't I?"

"Yup," Annie said cheerfully. "Old Seymour whomped the tar out of you. But don't feel bad. Who hasn't he whipped? He'd rather fight than eat. Sometimes I think he'd rather fight than screw." Her grin was bawdy. "Although he'd deny that."

"I never did like fighting. In fact . . ." He turned his face away. "I'm something of a physical coward."

"No need to be ashamed of that. Anyway, you stood up to Seymour. Not many men would."

"I probably wouldn't have if I hadn't been drunk." To Dudley's chagrin, he discovered that he was crying, weak tears leaking from his squinched-shut eyes.

"Dudley?"

He didn't answer and desperately tried to stem the tears.

She took his head in gentle hands and turned his face toward hers. "Why, you're crying! Poor baby, does it hurt?"

"No, no," he gasped out. "It doesn't hurt that much."

"Why then?"

"I don't know, goddamnit! A man's not supposed to cry!"

"That's where you're wrong, baby. A real man needn't be ashamed to cry, if he feels the need of it."

She cradled his head on that warm, ample bosom, rocking slightly. And then, to his amazement, Dudley discovered that there was nothing between his cheek and the heated flesh of one breast. Mere inches before his eyes was a nut-brown nipple, erect as a thumb. Tentatively his tongue crept out and touched it. Annie stiffened, then relaxed with a soft sigh. Her palm cupped the back of his head and pressed his face closer. He took the nipple between his lips and suckled it like a babe.

He felt himself slowly hardening. His hands were busy elsewhere, burrowing under the loosened blouse. Craftily he ran a hand up under her skirt. She had on a pair of silk panties. She arched under the stroke of his exploring hand and Dudley felt a seepage of moisture. Annie moaned as her hand brushed across the bulge in his trousers. She unbuttoned the trousers and took his organ in her hand.

"Oh, my! That's a good-sized pecker you've got there, Dudley," she said huskily.

She dipped her face and kissed him. Her mouth slid down over the purple head of his cock.

Dudley groaned, fearful he would explode

then and there. The aches and pains, the humiliation of the beating, were forgotten, buried under the onslaught of pleasure.

And then, without his ever knowing how it happened, Annie was on her back, skirts tucked up around her waist, and he was kneeling between those spreading thighs. Her pubic pelt was a bed of thick moss.

"What's the matter, sweetness?" She grinned up at him, mouth loose and wet. "Seems to me you've gone this far, might as well continue."

Dudley made some incomprehensible sound, and Annie reached down to seize his cock with both hands. At the same time she arched her hips, and he went all the way inside her with the first thrust, driving in with such force he could feel the grinding of her pelvic bones against him.

"Go now, sweetness. Go, go, *go*!"

To Dudley, she was the earth mother, yet lover and eternal woman at the same time. She bucked and rolled and gyrated under him as he plunged into her again and again.

Annie's head rolled back and forth on the pillow. Her eyes were clenched shut, and she was biting hard on her lip.

Dudley came, and Annie muttered, "Oh, yes, sweetness, yes," pulling his mouth down to hers. He tasted the brassy flavor of her blood from the bitten lip.

She was still drumming against him when his spasms ceased. Then she made a keening sound, lifted him high off the bed, cleaving to him for a long moment, and went slack, falling away.

Dudley lay atop of her, sheathed in sweat. He was still inside her. He discovered a good reason for that.

He was still hard! He couldn't remember when that had ever happened to him.

Annie noticed it, of course. She raised her head to look at him. "Didn't you pop?"

"I sure as hell did."

"I thought so. Doesn't that pecker of yours ever go down?" He heard her raspy laughter. "Or has it been a long dry spell?"

"It's been a long dry spell."

"Not that I'm complaining, you understand. But let's not let it go to waste." With a sudden hitch she elevated her legs and locked them around his hips. "Go, sweetness, go!"

10

When Dudley awoke the next morning, he had his usual horrendous hangover—head pounding, mouth tasting like a monkey's cage, belly nauseous and bloated with gas.

He was lying on his back in a puddle of sweat, sun streaming through an uncurtained window, like heat through an open furnace door. He groaned. "Never again! Christ, never again!"

Then he grinned painfully, remembering how many times he'd said that in the past. Bits and pieces of the night before blew through his mind like confetti—the way he'd made an ass of himself over Amanda Cayne, and the humiliating fight with Seymour Hooker. Well, neither of them would ever plague him again. The threshing crew would already be on the road, without him, and he would no doubt be fired.

He moved cautiously and felt throbbing pain in the various places where Hooker's fists had pounded him. He remembered Annie Mae, and groped for her without opening his eyes. He was rewarded by a silken encounter with a breast that rose and fell under his hand. Annie muttered in her sleep and flung his hand off.

Memory of her last words the night before brought a smile to Dudley's lips: "Stay with me as long as you care to, sweetness. I like you, and I get lonely for a man around. I'm not a mattress pounder, you understand. I don't put out for money. Don't have to. I don't lay on my back for money like most honky-tonk girls. I do quite well, thank you, playing and singing, and taking my cut from the moonshine and beer sales."

Since Annie, at the time, had had his pecker in her hand and it was hardening for yet a third time, Dudley hadn't agreed or disagreed.

At the end of their third ardent coupling, Annie had gasped out, "My Gawd, yes, sweetness! Stick around for a while. For a little feller, and no insult intended, you are some ding-dong daddy!"

How many times since he had hit the road, sitting around a hobo campfire, had he heard men talk wistfully of finding a woman, a well-padded woman with a willing pussy and an income, eager to keep a man around to service that pussy? It was a freight rider's dream, and Dudley had to admit that he had daydreamed of just such a situation himself. Now that it was his, now that he could loll in it, he could not accept it. He knew that before the day was half over, he would be on the road, thumbing his way north, hot on the trail of the Cayne crew.

And so it came about. After a melancholy farewell to Annie, he hefted his suitcase, which had been dropped off at the tavern, and

154

trudged north out of town. There was no railroad going in the direction where the crew was headed, and Dudley jerked his thumb without a great deal of hope. Bitter experience had taught him that it was a rare motorist who would pick up a hitchhiker nowadays.

Therefore, he was surprised when the third vehicle he thumbed, a dusty pickup, stopped for him.

But when he had tossed his suitcase into the pickup bed and climbed into the cab, his surprise evaporated. The driver was Thaddeus Martin, shiny suit straining at the seams, his ropey, leathery neck bulging against the tight, high-button collar.

Thaddeus said, "I thought I recognized you. You're Amanda's mechanic."

Dudley stiffened at the possessive, then relaxed, laughing to himself. "That's right, Mr. Martin. I'm Dudley Graham."

"Got left behind, did you?"

"Not exactly. I quit, then changed my mind."

They rode along in silence for a little; the only sounds were the rattling of the pickup and the thrumming of the insects in the roadside ditch. Thaddeus, from long practice, filled and lit his pipe with one hand.

Dudley was sweating freely, the moonshine poison leaking out of his pores. He rolled his shirt sleeves up above the elbows, and propped one arm on the pickup window. With the heat and the sweat, some of the soreness was easing.

Thaddeus cleared his throat. "Mind telling

me why you quit? It's not my business, but I'm kind of curious."

"I don't mind. Amanda Cayne is not the easiest person in the world to work for."

"You mean, because she's a woman? I know most men balk at taking orders from a woman."

"That's not it. She'd be just as hard to work for if she was a man." Dudley paused, examining what he had just said. He smiled slightly. "That's not quite true, now that I think of it. The fact that she is a woman, and a pretty one, has a hell of a lot to do with it."

Thaddeus glanced over at him. "You look somewhat beat-up, Mr. Graham. A fight?"

"Not so much a fight as a plain beating. I was too drunk to put up much of a fight."

Thaddeus said disapprovingly, "A honky-tonk brawl, I suppose. Such drunken brawls, rowdiness of that nature, are what give wheat-threshing crews a bad name. From what I've seen of Miss Cayne, I would think she would frown on such antics."

Dudley did a slow burn. He looked directly at the other man. "It wasn't a drunken brawl, as such. *I* was drunk, true, but the other guy was sober, and it happened over your precious Miss Cayne!"

"I find it hard to believe that a lady such as Amanda Cayne could be the cause of a honky-tonk brawl!"

"If you want to think her a lady, fine and dandy. But she's also a troublemaking bitch!"

Thaddeus stiffened, his face flushing. "Now

see here, Graham! I won't sit still and listen to you blacken Amanda's name!"

"Come on, Martin." Dudley made his voice deliberately coarse. "Yesterday afternoon, I watched you and Seymour Hooker bristle over her like two dogs sniffing around a bitch in heat!"

Thaddeus sent a baleful glare in his direction, started to speak, then clamped his lips shut. After a cooling moment or two, he finally said, "It's true I lost my temper with Seymour, but it was because of his foul mouth before a woman. Besides," his mouth shaped a faint smile, "if I remember correctly, you stepped in also."

Dudley started to frame an angry retort, then checked himself, laughing ruefully. "You're right, I did, didn't I? But don't you see?" He spread his hands. "That only proves me right, and also goes to prove that I'm as bad as you and Hooker."

"I don't see it that way."

Dull anger stirred in Dudley and he snapped, "I don't give a good goddamn how you see it, Mr. Martin! And if you don't like what I'm saying, you can let me out here. I'll walk. I'm good at that."

"No need for that. Besides, we've caught up with the threshers."

He nodded his head forward. Glancing through the windshield, Dudley saw that they had indeed caught up with the slow-moving threshers and crew. Falling in behind, Thaddeus slowed the pickup almost to a crawl.

"Thanks for the hitch, Mr. Martin," Dudley said coolly. He jumped out of the cab and trotted alongside the pickup until he could heave his suitcase out of the back. He jogged on ahead.

As he drew abreast of Amanda's pickup, she glanced over at him, eyebrows elevating. "Well, Buster Brown! I thought you'd up and quit on me."

"Who told you that?"

"Why . . . I reckon Bud told me."

"Well, he was wrong, as you can see. Here I am."

She smiled suddenly, a pleasant smile. "I'm glad, Dudley. I need you. You're pretty handy to have around."

Dudley cursed himself for the warm glow that spread through him. Swept by a sudden impulse to needle her, he said, "I got roaring drunk last night and got into a fracas."

She frowned, then shrugged carelessly. "I don't approve of that, but I suppose what you do during your time off is no business of mine."

Surprised by her mild reaction, he blurted, "Don't you want to know who I had the brawl with?"

"Not particularly, no, but I have a feeling you're itching to tell me."

"It was Seymour Hooker, and we were scrapping over you, Miss Amanda."

Abruptly ashamed of himself, Dudley put on a burst of speed, spurting on ahead. Amanda gave an angry toot of the horn. He ignored it, hurrying on.

Two vehicles in front of Amanda was another pickup, three men riding in the bed.

One of the men waved a hand. "Hey, Dudley! Thought we'd seen the last of you. Hop in. Here, give me your suitcase."

After a moment's hesitation, Dudley hoisted the suitcase high. Bud Dalmas took it from him, then gave him a hand over the sideboards.

Dudley dropped down beside Dalmas, and said through gritted teeth, "Some asshole buddy you are, telling Amanda Cayne I'd quit."

Bud Dalmas grinned. "Thought you had. Drunk as you were and in the tow of that honky-tonk dame, I thought we'd never clap eyes on you again. That's some prime pussy, hey, sport?" He gave his silent laugh. "You look a mite peaked. Give you a good ride, hey?"

Dudley's anger thickened. "I won't listen to any of your foul mouth, Dalmas! Even if Annie is a honky-tonk girl, she is a woman, and entitled to some respect. In fact, she's more a lady than some I know who call themselves one!"

"All right, sport, all right! Don't get your bowels in an uproar." Dalmas held up his hands in mock fright, and spat tobacco juice over the side.

Not about to be sidetracked now, Dudley plunged on. "And there's another thing . . . some friend you are, fading away like that, leaving me at the mercy of Seymour Hooker."

Bud stared. "You think I was going to back you up against Hooker and his crew? You're

159

out of your pumpkin. Shit, he had a half-dozen of his hardcases with him. They would have whacked me around good. 'Sides, it wasn't my fight." His Adam's apple bobbed. "No, sirree, Dudley. You get liquored up and tangle with that buzzsaw, you're on your own!"

"Fine. That's fine with me. I didn't ask you to buddy with me. It was all your idea. So just consider it quits between us." Dudley picked up his suitcase. "You stay out of my way, and I'll stay out of yours."

Suitcase hugged to his chest, he vaulted from the slow-moving vehicle.

Amanda stared after Dudley Graham, seething. Although she might not approve of the members of her crew drinking and tavern brawling, she knew she couldn't keep a rein on them during their off hours. Besides, they needed some relaxation, and the tank towns they passed through offered little in the way of entertainment aside from honky-tonk women and liquor.

But brawling over her was something else again, and she wasn't going to stand still for it. The thought of her name being bandied about in a honky-tonk made her skin crawl.

All of a sudden, she pulled out of line, speeding the pickup down the wrong side of the narrow, blacktop road. Drawing up alongside the lead pickup, she leaned over to shout, "Jack?"

Jack Rollins poked his head out. "Yes, Miss Amanda?"

"I forgot to do something back in town. You

go on ahead and set up at our next location. I'll catch up with you tonight, or early in the morning. Okay?"

"All right, Miss Amanda. You take care now."

Amanda drove on ahead until she came to a crossroad. She whipped the pickup around in a tight U-turn and headed back the way they had come. She was moving fast when she met the caravan again, hitting the horn with the heel of her hand as she drove past.

Fishing a cigarette out of the pack, she lit it with a kitchen match, smoking in angry puffs. She was still furious with Dudley Graham, but she knew well who the target of her anger should be.

Even though it was Sunday, she found Seymour Hooker and his combines finishing up the last dozen acres of the farm where they were threshing.

Seymour was operating one combine himself. When he finished a swath and turned, he saw her pickup parked at the edge of the field, with Amanda leaning on the fender, smoking.

He gave her a wave of his hand, and stopped the combine. He got down stiffly. His leg gave way, and he almost fell. His old wound was acting up. They were short a man, and he had been herding the combine all morning. Catching at the combine for support, he made a ceremony out of lighting a cigar, taking his time until the stiffness in his leg eased up. Then he went swinging toward her, trailing smoke, careful not to limp.

"Hi, sugar. Didn't expect to see you for a spell. I thought you'd moved on."

Without straightening up from the pickup fender, Amanda looked at him levelly. "I did start on, but I've come back, as you can see."

"Anything wrong?"

"That depends. Dudley Graham told me that the pair of you had a fight . . . over me. Is that true?"

"Aww, sugar." Seymour assumed an injured air. "I owed the peckerwood one, mouthing off to me like he did. Fact is . . ." He blew smoke, grinning. "It wasn't what you'd call a fight. He was crocked, and I don't think he's much with his dukes, anyway."

"That's something to brag on?" she said icily. "Seymour Hooker, known far and wide as a brawler beyond compare, beating up a smaller man and a drunk one to boot?"

"He had it coming," Seymour said stubbornly. "Drunk or sober, he had it coming. Want to bet it's awhile before he talks back to me again?"

She made a sound of contempt. "To me, a man who has to prove his manhood by using his fists every time he feels he's insulted has not grown up!"

He didn't take offense. Instead, he grinned lazily, drawling, "I have a bunch of hardnoses working for me, Amanda. It's my brag that I can whip any of 'em. Now what would they think if they heard I'd let a smaller man than me talk back and get away with it? Nope, I have to keep their respect, and to do that I have to stomp on anyone who sasses me. Size ain't got a thing to do with it."

"I've talked back to you, like right now. Maybe you'd better stomp on me or lose the respect of your," she motioned to the men, "your hardnoses out there."

"Aw, now you're funning me, sugar. You're a woman. I don't go around stomping women."

"But you bandy my name about in honkytonks!" she snapped. "I don't care how many men you stomp, Seymour Hooker, just so long as it's not over me."

"Oh, that's what got your nose in the air. I thought you were sore 'cause I'd pounded on this Graham feller . . ."

"I don't give a damn about Dudley Graham!"

"Is that so?" He peered closely at her. "I'm glad to hear it. I reckon maybe I was feeling a little jealousy there."

"Jealousy!" She stared. "Since when have I given you reason, or the right, to feel jealous of me?"

"Right has little to do with it, sugar. You know I'm soft on you, Amanda. I thought I'd made that clear enough."

"Seymour . . ." She spread her hands in a helpless gesture. "I've told you that I don't have time to play boy and girl games. I have a threshing season to finish up."

"You don't *have* to finish it." He drew on the cigar, blew smoke. "Sell those old beat-up, out-of-date machines. I'll finish your farms for you."

"You'd like that, wouldn't you? And what will I do?"

"Well, you could . . ." He grinned. "You could marry me."

"I'm not ready to get married, and when I do get around to considering it, you'll be way down at the bottom of the list."

"May not be any list, sugar, you wait too long," he said, still grinning. "I've seen a few women try to cut it doing a man's work. They all ended up dried-up old maids, with shells as hard as an armadillos."

Her lips tightened. "I think I have a ways to go before becoming an old maid. And it'll be a cold day in hell, Seymour Hooker, before I'll marry you. Being an old maid is a better choice!"

She wheeled about, got into the pickup, and started it, racing the motor.

Seymour leaned on his hands on the window, and said cheerfully, "I don't give up that easy, Amanda. I'll keep trying . . ."

She jammed the gearshift into low and drove away, almost knocking him over. Seymour stood smoking, musing after her and grinning slightly. He said aloud, "Always did like a dame with spunk, and Amanda's sure got spunk!"

11

Dudley found himself working longer hours than ever, but it seemed that no matter how hard he worked, he kept falling behind. The ancient tractors and threshers were disintegrating before his eyes. There were several times when he was mystified as to the causes of the frequent breakdowns. Not even the dilapidated condition of the machines was a satisfactory explanation. It seemed to him that perverse demons inhabited the machines, coming out of their hiding places at night to do their dirty work, since almost every morning one, or more, of the machines would have to be tinkered with before it would operate with any degree of efficiency.

The fact that this enraged Amanda and brought her wrath down on him didn't help any. She grew more irritable and short-tempered every day as they fell further and further behind schedule. Dudley understood her plight and tried to be tolerant, yet it wasn't always easy.

One morning a telegram was delivered to her in the field where they were threshing. She was reading the wire when Dudley came up behind her.

"Shit!" she said explosively, and crumpled the telegram up, tossing it onto the ground. Dudley cleared his throat, and she whipped around, glaring. "What do *you* want?"

"The tractor pulley on the number-two thresher parted a little bit ago, Amanda . . ."

"Well, fix it! It's what I'm paying you for, isn't it?"

"It can't be repaired, it'll have to be replaced."

"Take my pickup and go into town for one. Here . . ." She tossed the keys to him, then half-turned away to take a thin roll of bills from her pocket. She counted off several and thrust them at him. "That should be enough. And don't stop off at a honky-tonk and get soused again. Okay, freight rider?"

Dudley tightened up, but managed to retain a grip on his temper. "There's another thing . . ."

"Well?"

"I think that pulley was half-sawed into with a knife. Then, when tension was put on it this morning, it snapped. The thing is, the belt's so old and half-rotten, it's hard to be sure."

She frowned at him. "You mean somebody may have done it deliberately? Now why would they do that?"

He shrugged. "You can answer that better than me."

"But who would do a thing like that?"

"I can think of one guy who might. Seymour Hooker."

166

"Seymour? Seymour may play rough, but I can't see him sneaking around in the dark. If he was going to do something like that, you can bet he'd do it right out in the open."

Dudley shrugged again. "You asked me, I told you."

Elbow propped on the arm across her breasts, she tapped a thumbnail against her teeth, studying him speculatively.

Dudley couldn't keep his gaze from straying down to the thrust of her breasts. Did she realize that her arm across her breasts that way pushed them out provocatively against the shirt? From some of her actions, he wouldn't put it past her to do it deliberately.

She said suddenly, "You've got it in for Seymour, haven't you, Dudley? Because he beat you up?"

Dudley felt heat rise to his face. "If you mean I don't like the man, you're dead right. But it's not just the fight, I'm not that sore a loser. I didn't like him before that. Hell, Amanda, you know he would stop at nothing to see you fold, and everybody knows his reputation . . ."

"I don't listen to gossip, Buster Brown. Your job here is to keep the machinery running. You tend to that and let me worry about Seymour." She half-turned away, then swung back. "And don't sneak up behind me again like that, hear?"

Seething, Dudley stared after her retreating back. Finally he sighed and started toward her pickup, which was parked at the edge of the field. His glance happened upon the crumpled-up telegram on the ground. He looked up and saw that Amanda's back was still to him. Without breaking stride, he bent and scooped up the wire, holding it clenched in his fist until he was in the pickup.

. There, he smoothed it out flat on the steering wheel, and read the brief message: "Amanda Cayne: Since your father is no longer running crew I figure agreement no longer holds Stop Am letting Hooker combine wheat Stop Don Barnes Stop."

Dudley laughed shortly, remembering his clash with Amanda a few minutes before. Chalk up another in Seymour Hooker's column! He could understand her anger on reading the telegram. But why in God's name should she fly to Hooker's defense?

Women, who could understand them? And that went double for Amanda Cayne.

He snorted, started the pickup, and drove toward town.

Hearing her pickup start up, Amanda turned, looking after it. She was already sorry she had been so hard on Dudley. She was always so prickly around him. Sometimes he gave her a reason, true, but not today. He was right about Seymour wanting to drive her out of business, although she couldn't see him skulking around at night sabotaging the equipment.

And the telegram informing her that he had taken another farm from her . . .

She sighed, pushing a hand distractedly

through sweat-matted hair. The wire and its bad news had triggered her temper, but that was still no reason to vent her spleen on Dudley Graham, who had so far proven to be a useful, hard-working employee.

Amanda's glance went to the threshers. One was standing idle; the hands who usually operated it were lounging in the shade. How long could she continue, with Dudley holding the machinery together with baling wire?

Hearing another laboring motor, she turned. A pickup had turned into the field from the blacktop road. Shading her eyes against the lowering sun, Amanda saw that it was Thaddeus's ancient vehicle. So long as she retained his vast acreage to thresh, she wouldn't consider the season a failure. Hands in her pockets, she waited for him.

He stopped a few yards away and climbed out of the cab. He was still wearing the shiny suit, celluloid collar, and tie.

"Miss Cayne. How are you today?"

"I'm fine, Mister Martin." She smiled brightly. "Seems to me we know each other well enough by now for you to call me Amanda."

His gray eyes held her with a sober gaze. He nodded. "All right . . . Amanda. In exchange, you will call me Thaddeus."

"I'll be happy to, Thaddeus. Or Thad, if you like."

He blinked once, as if in reflex to ancient pain. "I'd rather you didn't. Only one person ever called me that. No offense, I hope."

"No offense, Thaddeus."

His glance went past her and he frowned slightly. "Only one thresher working, I see."

Amanda went tense. Of all the times for him to drop by! She said lightly, "Nothing serious. A broken pulley belt. Dudley's gone into town for a replacement. We should have a spare on hand, I know, but I've been so busy . . ." Careful, Amanda, you're over-explaining! "It'll be threshing again shortly."

He nodded. "That's good."

Anxiety drove her to ask, "You're not thinking of using Seymour's combines, are you?"

His eyes widened. "Good Lord, no! Did I say something to give you that idea? If I did, I'm sorry. After watching you and your men these past few days, I think yours is the hardest-working crew I've seen. You could use new equipment, sure, but you work hard enough to overcome that. I still think threshed wheat is better than combined wheat. Haven't changed my mind about that. In fact . . ." He was smiling now. "I'm going home in the morning. I have to get my mowing and stacking done, ready for you. I intend to stop in on some of my neighbors, who are wavering, and reassure them about you, Amanda."

She let her breath go with a sigh. Close to tears, she said simply, "Thank you, Thaddeus. You won't be sorry."

"I'm sure I won't be." He hesitated, looking uncomfortable. "The reason I stopped by, I thought you'd be kind enough to have supper with me this evening. I won't be seeing you again for ten days or so."

"I'd love to, Thaddeus." She motioned to herself. "Just give me time to have a bath and change. I'm all sweaty and sticky."

She was astonished to see him turn a beet red. I made what he considers an indelicate remark! Dear God! I'm going to have to watch every single word I say around him!

The town ten miles from where they were threshing was a slightly larger replica of the last one, but it had a hotel with a decent dining room. Amanda was in a yellow jersey dress, the hem striking her well below the knees, and she had on silk stockings and white, high-heeled shoes. Although she wouldn't have admitted it to anyone, wearing feminine attire gave her pleasure.

Thaddeus's approving look gave her even more pleasure. "You look much better in a dress, Amanda. I know, I know!" He held up a staying hand. "It's not practical around threshers. I'm hopelessly old-fashioned. Women in the kitchen, never in pants. As Martha would say," his smile was wry, " 'Times change, Thad, and you have to change with them.' "

She glanced over at him. "Martha?"

"My late wife," he said in clipped tones. A shutter seemed to slam shut across his face, the gray eyes almost hostile.

The pickup rattled down the main street of the town. Although it was just a little after dusk, many of the storefronts were dark— boarded up, Amanda saw. And the benches in front of others held men talking idly, with something hopeless and defeated about their postures. There were a number on the hotel veranda, and they scarcely glanced up as Thaddeus and Amanda entered the hotel.

Thaddeus made a sound of contempt. "Lazy louts, the whole lot. You can find them sitting here, doing nothing, almost any hour of the day or night."

"That judgment's a little harsh, don't you think, Thaddeus?"

"No, I don't. You probably don't see men on the road every day like I do. They stop at my kitchen asking for handouts. In the beginning I'd offer to give them a meal, if they'd do some chores, chop wood, something like that. And even that was make work, I didn't need their help. But you know what happened most times? They'd run like jackrabbits! A few even called me names for asking them to work. So I stopped feeding them. Now I turn them all away."

"I still think you're being unfair, Thaddeus. Some are like that, sure, but not the majority. Those men out there . . ." They were crossing the hotel lobby now. "They're not hobos, freight riders. Most of them live here in town."

"It amounts to the same thing. They'd rather live off the government without working, leaning on a shovel all day."

At the entrance to the dining room they were met by a waitress who escorted them to a table with a red, checkered cloth. There were only a half-dozen people in the dining room.

At the table Amanda continued the discussion. "It's no doubt true that a great many people, ground down by this Depression, have lost their pride. I used to think like you, but I've changed my ideas a little since Dudley Graham went to work for me. He was a freight rider, but he is a good mechanic and he works himself to death. I wouldn't tell him this, you understand, but I doubt I'd still be operating without him."

"An exception. Like they say, the exception only proves the rule."

Thaddeus made a dismissing gesture, as though everything had been said on the subject as far as he was concerned. It was so peremptory, such a typical male attitude when discussing weighty matters with a female, that Amanda's temper sparked. Then she subsided as she realized her error. Oh, he likely didn't give much weight to a woman's opinion, but basically, like so many men weathering the Great Depression reasonably well, Thaddeus's ideas were set in concrete. Her father's thoughts about the men idled by the Depression were much the same, even though Amos Cayne, before his stroke, had been slowly going under himself. However, her own ideas, Amanda had to admit, had been almost as rigid, until Dudley had come along. She had never known the economic pinch of the Depression, and probably never would, even if she was unemployed.

She smiled wryly to herself. It was one advantage women had over men in these trying times, pretty women certainly: they could always find a man to support them. It was a galling thought, perhaps degrading, but it was a fact of life.

Even with this man, she thought, looking across the table at Thaddeus Martin. He had come down prepared to dispense with her services, and had she been homely, he would have done so. He would likely deny it vehemently, but Amanda knew it was true. *Touché*, Seymour, you hit it on the button again.

With the thought of Seymour Hooker, she suddenly longed for a drink, something she rarely indulged in. It was probable that the dining room served liquor to the customers, but she knew it would be a mistake to ask Thaddeus to order some for her.

There were no menus. On the wall behind them was a blackboard, listing the night's offerings: pot roast, beef stew, chicken-fried steak.

"What'll you have, Amanda?"

"Pot roast, I believe. I have enough stew and fried steak from the cook wagon. Any kind of a roast takes too much time for the cooks, it seems."

"Pot roast it is for me, too." He smiled. "I'm not a half-bad cook, and I'm known at home for my stew. I've always got a pot of stew simmering, for whoever might drop in."

"The same pot?"

"Same pot, adding a few ingredients from time to time."

With the pot roast came ears of corn, string beans, goblets of milk, and hot cornbread. It was simple fare, but very tasty and filling, and Amanda ate heartily. One thing that both sur-

174

prised and amused her—since joining the
threshing crew, she had acquired a trencher-
man's appetite. Before, she had always lost her
appetite in the heat of summer. Now, not even
hundred-degree weather could dampen her appetite.

They finished off with ice cream and slabs
of apple pie. Replete, Amanda leaned back with
a sigh of content, lighting a cigarette. Noticing
Thaddeus's quickly erased frown of disap-
proval, she said lightly, "What would your
Martha say, Thaddeus? Change with the times?
More and more women are smoking cigarettes,
Thaddeus."

"I know, but I guess I'm too old to change
much. I don't suppose I'll ever entirely accept
some things women do nowadays." His smile
was wry. "But for your sake, I'll try. Be patient
with me, Amanda."

"At least you're honest about it. Most men
aren't, and of course I'll be patient." She blew
smoke. "But I hardly think I'm that important
in your life, Thaddeus. A couple of weeks and
I'll be gone. And the way things are going, who
knows if I'll be back next year?"

"You're that important to me, Amanda," he
said.

The intensity of his voice startled Amanda,
and she stared at him with her mouth open.

Then he slapped his hand down on the table
and got to his feet. "It's late, we'd better be
off."

He came around to help her up. She waited
until he'd counted out the exact money for the

bill. He hesitated for a moment before finally leaving a dime for the waitress.

Not a big tipper, Thaddeus Martin. But then who could afford to be these days? Amanda was sure that the dime sprang from a frugal nature, not stinginess.

Outside, they found a Model-A touring car parked directly behind the pickup. The top was down, and six youths lounged in the seats. A chorus of whistles shrilled out at the sight of Amanda, and one youth lifted a bottle in a brown paper bag. "Like a snort, toots?"

Thaddeus's hand tightened on her arm, and she saw him glaring at the boys. He muttered, "Young whelps. Drinking, and not even twenty, none of them. Liquor is a tool of the devil, and that man in the White House had to make it legal again. Thank the Lord we had the good sense to keep Kansas dry."

"Doesn't seem to have prevented that bunch from finding a bottle," Amanda said dryly.

"There's always a way, if you have that turn of nature," Thaddeus said—somewhat cryptically, Amanda thought.

He helped her into the cab. The whistles sounded again, as Amanda stepped onto the high fender, skirt hiking up to reveal a length of silken thigh. Thaddeus slammed the door and glared over at the Model A, hands on hips.

Amanda, aware of the amused glances of the men on the hotel veranda, murmured, "Please, Thaddeus, let's go. This is becoming embarrassing."

Thaddeus crossed around to get behind the

wheel. He started the pickup and looked back through the window. "They haven't moved. I can't back out, they're blocking the way."

He tapped the horn and received an answering toot, derisive, mocking.

Thaddeus, face reddening, veins swelling in his neck like ropes, stuck his head out the window. "Move out of the way, you insolent young pups, so I can back out!"

Catcalls erupted, and before Amanda realized what was happening, there were three youths on each side of the pickup cab. One boy on her side vaulted up onto the fender, his face close to hers. His breath was rank with the odor of cheap whiskey. "Hi, toots, why don't you come along with us and have a good time? Dads over there is too old for a doll like you."

Amanda felt a shiver of fear. She tried to roll up the window. Too late. The youth planted both hands on the glass, preventing her from rolling it up.

There were two of them on the fender on Thaddeus's side. One, gripping the door, swung back and forth, chanting, "Old dad is mad, is old dad. Mad because we won't move, old dad, or 'cause doll baby there won't drop her panties for you?"

An inarticulate roar erupted from Thaddeus, and he exploded out the door like a bomb. The swinging door knocked the chanting youth off the fender. He landed against the car in the next parking slot, with a yelp of pain. The other one managed to jump aside in time.

The pickup cab was so high Amanda could

only get an incomplete picture of what was happening—thumping sounds, groans, shouted obscenities. The boys on her side were gone, running around to the front of the pickup to aid their companions.

Six against one! The odds were prohibitive, even for a man of Thaddeus's bulk. Forgetting her own fears, Amanda flung open the door. She saw that the men on the veranda were up off the benches, watching avidly, their eyes alive for the first time.

"Please," Amanda said, "won't you help him?"

One man took a pipe from his mouth and spat over the railing. "Ain't none of our beeswax, lady. Best not to mix in another man's fight. A stranger, at that. Them boys now, they live around here."

"But six against one? Oh! Thaddeus was right about you," she said furiously. "None of you are worth spit!"

She ran on around the pickup, and saw at once that she need not have worried. Thaddeus was giving more than a good account of himself. The youth he'd knocked against the car was sitting on the pavement, moaning and clutching one shoulder. A second one had backed off, and was holding a nose dripping blood. Two more were in full flight, and Thaddeus had the remaining two in his grip, one big hand around the neck of each. As Amanda watched, he brought their heads together with a cracking sound, then let loose of them. They crumpled to the pavement and lay still.

Thaddeus stood over them, shoulders slumped, head lowered.

Amanda touched him on the shoulder. "Thaddeus?"

He turned a dazed face to her. "I don't know when I've been so mad. That's the first time I've struck another person in anger since I hit my father."

"My God!" Amanda said in awe. "Six of them!"

Thaddeus drew a shuddering breath and gazed around. "Do you suppose any of them are badly hurt?"

"I don't think so, Thaddeus. Mostly injured pride, I'd say." She smiled at him. "They had it coming, you did real good."

"Did I?" He focused on her and his voice went cold. "It's like your man Graham said . . . fighting over you like dogs fighting over a bitch in heat. You seem to bring out the worst in men."

Stung, Amanda recoiled. "That's not fair, Thaddeus!"

"Perhaps not." He sighed gustily. "But I think it's a good thing that I'm going home."

12

For our days later another telegram came for Amanda. For once everything seemed to be working all right, and Dudley, taking advantage of an idle moment, was leaning against a tractor wheel, building a cigarette, when he saw the bicycle coming up the lane. Spotting the Western-Union uniform, he wondered which wheat farm was canceling out this time.

Amanda, who had been near the number-one thresher, saw the approaching bicycle at about the same time and advanced to meet it, shoulders squared, as though determined to meet trouble head-on.

She stood for a time with her back to the threshers, continued to stand long after the Western-Union boy had pedaled his bicycle out of sight, with only a thin plume of dust marking his passage, like brown exhaust smoke.

Finally Amanda faced around, her gaze sweeping across the area until it rested on Dudley. She lifted a hand, beckoning, and Dudley went to her reluctantly, loath to share her bad news. Maybe this was the final straw and she'd have to close down. Astonishingly, Dudley felt deep sadness at this prospect. He had to wonder if it was for the demise of the Cayne threshing crew, or for the fact that he would be forced to move on, never to see Amanda Cayne again.

"This wire," she waved the telegram, "is from Wichita Falls. My father had another stroke . . ."

"I'm sorry, Amanda," he said automatically.

"The wire doesn't say how bad it is, but he is still alive. I'd better drive down and see for myself. They might not tell me the truth on the telephone, good *or* bad. We're about finished here, it'll take a full day to move, and there's a Sunday in between, so I'll only miss about a day and a half. I want you to take over, Dudley, while I'm gone."

He felt a lurch of dismay. "Why me? I'm your newest hand, and what I know about wheat threshing, you can put in your left eye."

"It's not always what you know, Dudley, but how you use what you know that counts." Her gaze was direct. "Besides, you know machinery, and I've decided that's the most important thing with this outfit. Something you need to know about threshing, ask Jack."

"He's your foreman. Why not leave it in his hands?"

She was shaking her head. "Not really my foreman. He's never wanted to run things, anyway. Don't worry, he won't resent you taking charge. He'll be relieved."

"But the others might resent taking orders from me. What you once called," he smiled sourly, "a freight rider."

"I think you've got what it takes to ride herd on them. It's your chance to prove yourself, Dudley. As for calling you a freight rider, I haven't changed my mind about that. Maybe some day I will." She smiled. "I suppose that's up to you. I'll be leaving shortly, so it's all in your pocket, Buster Brown."

Dudley stood without moving, watching her stride toward the tent, his dismay growing heavier. Damn her anyway, why should she dump all that responsibility on him?

"It's a chance to prove yourself, Dudley." Where had he heard those exact words before?

His thoughts jumped back two years, back to another time when responsibility had been dumped on him. . . .

He was back in California and young, just twenty. More precisely, he was in Orange County and working at his first real job, in the orange groves which covered much of the area south of Los Angeles.

His father had died three years before, and Dudley had been living alone with his mother. They were not starving, since his mother had been the beneficiary of an insurance policy on his father's death, but that money, invested, gave them only enough to live on. His mother, a small, intense woman, had never worked in her life, and had no skills that would enable her to get employment in these days of mass unemployment. Yet they were more fortunate than most—an uncle, his father's brother, owned a vast acreage covered with orange trees.

At crop-picking time, Dudley was hired to oversee the harvesting of the oranges. He had worked as a picker for his uncle all three years since his father's death, yet he was surprised at being placed in such a position of responsibility, at his age.

Bart Graham, a bluff, hearty man, grinned at the expression on Dudley's face. "Don't sweat it, boy." He clapped his nephew on the shoulder. "All you have to do is keep a close eye on these Okie drifters and see that they put in a good day's work. I know, they're on piece work, paid according to the amount of oranges they pick. But they tend to lollygag, if you don't watch 'em, and I want my crop picked before the oranges rot on the trees. Also, see to it they don't eat more than they pick. Poor bastards, most of 'em are starving. But it ain't my place to feed 'em."

The Okie exodus from Texas and Oklahoma was not yet in full tide, since the dust storms were only beginning and had yet to lay waste the land soon to become known as the Dust Bowl. But the Great Depression had made its mark, and the old jalopies were heading west, loaded down with migrants and their household goods. The tales of the Land of Opportunity, untouched by depression, oranges hanging on trees like nuggets of gold, had found many believers.

Here, they found it hard to grasp the unpleasant fact that the tales were false, that California also felt the weight of the Depression. Yet there was work to be found, backbreaking

184

labor paying barely a living wage, and they continued to come. The animosity between the fruit growers and the migrants had not as yet become so bitter, since the growers were happy to have a supply of cheap, readily available labor. However, the tide was swelling, and the more farsighted of the growers realized that it would roll over them in the end, like a flash-flood roaring out of the California canyons following heavy rains.

As for Dudley, he knew little of the Okies, only what he had read in the newspapers and what Bart Graham had told him. He was proud as a peacock that he, twenty-year-old Dudley Graham, should be put in such a position of responsibility, without, at the time, grasping the scope of it.

This was the first year that his uncle had hired the migrant workers, and always before he'd employed an experienced man to direct the pickers at their labors. Dudley questioned him about this, for the first time wondering if his Uncle Bart was stingy.

As if reading his mind, Bart Graham said, "No, boy, I ain't being tight-fisted, no matter how it might look." He sighed. "The truth is, I'm about at the edge. The goddamned Depression is hitting me hard. With the price of oranges what it is, the pennies I can save is about my margin of profit. The banks have lent me all the money they'll let go. I'm caught by the short hairs, boy. I know the local people need the seasonal work I've been giving them, but I can't afford them anymore. The Okies work cheaper. I had to let Charlie go. The guy who's been in charge of the sorting, crating, and shipping. Couldn't afford him, though, and I'll have to take over his duties myself. Same reason I'm hiring you to oversee the picking. Admittedly, I'm paying you less than a foreman's wages, but I can't afford more. You're young, no wife and family to support. You'll have to do. It's your chance to prove yourself, Dudley."

And so, the first day the picking began, Dudley was there. Uncle Bart had even let him hire the pickers. "You'll have to be the one gets along with them, boy. So you hire 'em. You don't have to be particular. First ones show up are the first ones hired. No way of knowing beforehand if they're good workers. If they're not, fire their asses. Plenty more out there."

Signs had been posted along Highway 66, promising jobs picking oranges. They were already there, five families, when Dudley bicycled out to the orange grove at sunup. They were a scroungy-looking lot, clothes tattered and worn, gaunt with hunger, and Dudley had never seen such a disreputable collection of automobiles—sagging on broken springs, tires bald as eggs, household belongings piled haphazardly, with solemn, urchin faces peering out at him from unexpected places. He couldn't understand how the cars, pickups and trucks had survived the long trek here.

He was even more astonished and dismayed to learn that it wasn't just the males who clamored for work. The women and children of each family wanted to pick. Dudley steeled himself against the round, sunken, wistful eyes, the beseeching faces of the women and children, and said in a too-loud voice, falling far short of authoritative, that he could only hire men and boys, none under thirteen.

Voices rose, hammering at him, and he finally relented, understanding the need voiced in one man's plea. The man was tall, rawboned, and talked with an Okie twang. He looked tubercular enough to be on his deathbed. But he was virile, as was evidenced by the ten, stair-stepped children, with ages from sixteen down to the infant suckling on the wife's scrawny breast. The man's name was Ira Rogers. Rogers said, "I can't see, young feller, what difference it makes to you. You just want your oranges picked, I reckon. So if the women and young'uns only pick a basket a day, you get that many more of your oranges picked, and we'uns get paid for the basket."

Dudley spread his hands in resignation and that opened the gate. Yelling, they poured into the grove. It took most of the first day to get them sorted out. It was obvious to Dudley that, since most of the oranges had to be picked from stepladders, the children and many of the women wouldn't be able to do much actual picking. He got the five families separated, directing those capable of it onto the stepladders, then ordered the women and children to pick those oranges they could reach standing on the ground, also instructing them to handle the loading of the baskets.

There was a mutter of protest at this, and

Rogers, who seemed to have become their spokesman by some means Dudley couldn't fathom, said, "That ain't the way we figured it, young feller. We figured we'd all, even the young'uns, pick from the ladders."

"It can't work that way, don't you see?" Dudley said in exasperation. "That's why I've divided you up into families. Each family pools the oranges it picks and you'll be paid by the family at the end of the day. From there, you divide it up any way you like." The man's face took on a mulish look. Suddenly, Dudley was shouting. "Goddamnit, that's the way it'll be! I'm the boss here, get that through your thick skull!" Then he sighed, modulating his voice. "Look, it's risky enough on those stepladders for a grown man, the ground being so soft and uneven. Do you want your women and children falling and breaking an arm or a leg? I'm doing this for your own good!"

"Seems everybody is always telling us things for our own good," Rogers said softly. "It ain't arms and legs we have to fret about, it's hungry bellies."

"I realize that, and you'll be able to fill your bellies. But there is no way women and children will work on those stepladders. My uncle has no insurance to pay for doctors, and I'm sure you don't, either. Now I don't wish to sound mean, but that's the deal, take it or leave it. You know there're hundreds more out there looking for work."

They took it, of course—which made Dudley feel guilty—since they had no recourse.

Once settled in, they worked hard enough. Of course, they had little choice there, either. At the piecework wages they were being paid, they had to work their tails off to earn enough to buy food for each brood.

They didn't, contrary to Bart Graham's warning, eat more oranges than they picked. They ate a few in the beginning, and the children still ate the ones picked up off the ground, but those were not saleable anyway.

And Dudley knew something that his uncle did not, having learned during his own days of picking. For a while a picker is inclined to eat the oranges, but the fruit soon loses its attraction. Even an empty belly soon rebels at the puckery taste of the oranges.

Things went very well, and Bart Graham complimented his nephew on a job well done. Dudley was happy and couldn't help puffing up with pride.

It took a week for that pride to be punctured.

His downfall was so stereotyped as to be hilarious; it had its roots in Adam's biblical fall from grace.

Among the Rogers brood, the second oldest, at sixteen, was Cora Lee. She was thin, scrawny, with breasts not much larger than the oranges she handled. The first few times Dudley's glance passed over her, she scarcely registered on his consciousness. But slowly, she swam into focus. He finally decided that it had to do with her eyes—large, round, brown orbs, seemingly as depthless and expressionless as Little Orphan Annie's of the funny papers. But soon, they exerted a magnetic pull on him. Each and every time he was in her presence his gaze was drawn to Cora Lee and he would find her staring at him, a secretive awareness in those eyes. And each time she smiled, a slow curving of lips surprisingly full considering her general skinniness.

Dudley wasn't a virgin, not in the technical sense, but his few fumbling experiences scarcely qualified him as a sexual expert. So embarrassing had his few encounters been—so much time and effort expended for only a few moments of pleasure—that he was tempted to shy away.

Yet, his awareness of Cora Lee's aura of sexuality grew until he began getting an erection in her presence. She, he soon realized, was aware of his condition. Once, as they stood close together while Dudley explained how to pack the oranges more carefully, she turned into him and stroked his semi-erection through the material of his trousers. A hot spark ignited in her usually expressionless eyes. Her mouth curved in that knowing smile, and her tongue came out to circle her lips, leaving them moist and glistening.

Speechless and red as fire, Dudley wheeled and plunged away. Her low laughter, like a blatant invitation, pursued him.

However, Dudley would never have made the first move—or so he told himself, repeatedly, later.

Cora Lee, apparently confident of her conquest, decided the issue, during lunch hour on the seventh day of picking.

Dudley usually ate his lunch early, while the others worked. Then, while they ate, he would range ahead, examining the next trees to be picked. On this particular day, he ranged farther than usual, moving out of sight and sound of the migrant workers. He had recently started smoking, something neither his mother nor Uncle Bart knew about. Since he knew they would not approve, he smoked in secret. Now, he leaned against an orange tree, rolling a cigarette, a trick he was becoming expert at. He put the Bull Durham cigarette in his mouth and struck a match.

"Whyn't you roll one for me, hon?"

Dudley jumped, almost dropping the cigarette. He spun around. Cora Lee stood close to him. She wore a single, loose garment, legs and feet bare. Smiling, she shook her head at him in rebuke, bobbed curls dancing. "You sure are a hard feller to get alone, Dudley."

Breathing hard, he snapped, "Why should you want to get me alone?"

"Now Dudley, you ain't dumb. You know why. You want to get in my pants, it sticks out all over you. And something else sticks out, too
. . ." Her knowing smile was as ancient as time.

Before Dudley could divine her intention, she had tweaked his organ between thumb and forefinger. It throbbed and grew, and Dudley groaned, sweeping Cora Lee into his arms. She felt thin, as fragile as a bundle of sticks, her sharp bones poking him in several places. Yet

191

there was a wiry strength about her, he quickly learned, as she coiled around him. Her mouth was hot, lips opening under his.

All the other girls, even those he'd laid, had kept their lips clamped shut. Not so Cora Lee. Her lips parted and she drove her tongue into his mouth—Dudley's first French kiss.

Without his being aware of how it happened, they were rolling over and over on the ground.

Cora Lee chuckled. "You ain't getting into my pants, hon . . . 'cause I ain't wearing any!"

She hiked her dress up, then took Dudley's hand and placed it on the jut of her pubic mound. Dudley reared up and stared at the brown pubic patch. All his other sexual adventures had taken place in the dark, and this was his first glimpse of a woman's genitals, of the pink-lipped aperture, into which entry gave a man such pleasure.

His entry into the place of pleasure was accomplished mostly through the efforts of Cora Lee, who yanked his penis almost brutally, taking him inside her with an adroit roll of hip.

Her response was fierce, wanton; she matched his every move with small cries designed to goad him on. He'd never encountered such abandon, such intense sexual response. A small part of his mind marveled at this—no one had ever told him that a girl could thoroughly enjoy sex. But his senses, his whole body, were so engaged, that he ceased to think and only existed in pure sensation.

At the moment of Dudley's orgasm Cora Lee,

as though perfectly attuned to his sexual nuances, sensed it and rose, her pelvis drumming at him. A keening sound burst from her, and her nails raked his upper arms and shoulders.

Her body left the ground, supported only by her head and shoulders and feet, forming a bridge holding him off the ground. She shuddered and Dudley could feel her vaginal muscles contract, milking his cock.

"Oh, Jesus!" he said, as a final spasm of ecstasy seized him.

He must have blanked out, or at least been mindless for a few moments, because the next thing he knew he was on his back on the ground. He sat up. His trousers were in a tangle around his ankles, like hobbles. If he had stood up, he would have fallen flat on his face. He felt a burning sensation along both upper arms. His shirt was ripped, the exposed flesh welling blood.

He glanced at Cora Lee. She lay in a wanton sprawl, her dress still tucked up around her waist. Her eyes were closed, her chest heaving. His gaze strayed to the pubic mound, then jumped away.

He was dazed, thoughts disoriented, yet he had never felt more alive. His nerve-ends still thrummed, as though reverberating from his orgasm. And he was having another sensory reaction—he was getting another erection.

Cora Lee's low laughter jolted him. "Sorry, hon. We haven't time for another piece now. Pa will begin to wonder where I am. He knows I like to screw, and he still whips my tail, he gets riled enough."

She sat up, pushing the dress down and giving her head a shake. She brushed the dirt out of her hair, then stood up to dust the back of her dress. Since it was the Southern California dry season, no rain had fallen for months and the ground was very dry.

Meanwhile, Dudley had scrambled to his feet, busily pulling up, buckling up, and buttoning up.

Cora Lee gave him a measuring look. "You do it good, Dudley. You come out here at this time tomorrow, I'll be here." She was gone, bare feet kicking up dust.

An unsettling thought occurred to Dudley after she'd disappeared into the orange trees. If she made a habit of this, maybe she was clapped up or syphilitic? He remembered the horror stories he'd heard—a man's pecker rotting and dropping off, et cetera. He shuddered and swore to himself that this would be the first and last time. True, it was the first time he'd really enjoyed sex, the most pleasurable few moments of his life, but it wasn't worth the risk. And if Uncle Bart caught him . . .

Dudley shuddered again.

But he learned something—a man's cock has a will of its own, and resolutions made immediately after sex are short-lived.

As noon approached the next day, he felt the heat building in his groin. He tried to push all thoughts of Cora Lee from his mind. It was useless—at noon he hurried toward the spot where they'd met yesterday.

He arrived breathless to find Cora Lee waiting. "I thought you weren't coming, hon."

Without a word he reached for her. They grappled, then were rolling on the ground, and then he was into her, pumping.

This time, when it was over and they rolled apart, Cora Lee didn't rush away.

"Why don't you roll me one of your cigarettes, Dudley?"

Making the cigarette, he said, "I thought you were afraid your father might catch us?"

"Not all that much. He's whomped on me before, and I lived through it." She stretched, grinning. "I figure after you've rested for a bit, we'd knock off another little piece. That, I reckon, is worth a whomping." She accepted the cigarette, puffed on it twice, then glanced down at his lap. "From the looks of that thing of yours, I reckon we don't have to wait any longer."

She threw away the cigarette, and reached for him, drawing him on top of her. With a shift of her hips, she took him inside her.

For four days they rutted away the noon hour in the dirt of the orange grove like the healthy young animals they were—Cora Lee wasn't diseased, Dudley learned in time.

On the fifth day Dudley—deaf, dumb and blind in his orgasm—was lifted bodily from Cora Lee and hurled aside into the dirt. Dazed, he reared up on his hands and knees, staring up, his organ still spurting.

Bart Graham loomed over him. Eyes blazing, he said in a choked voice, "I give you a chance to be somebody, give you some responsibility, and look what happens! Screwing the help when you should be seeing to it they're working! I want you off my property, you young pup, and never set foot on it again. And don't think I won't tell your mother about this! Think what this is going to do to her, learning that her only child would rather screw than live up to his responsibilities! Now get your butt out of my orange grove."

Dudley was already on his feet, pulling up his trousers. Cora Lee was long gone.

"And just in case you don't shag ass," his uncle said. "I'm going to tell that girl's father. He'll likely come after you with a two-by-four!" He took several bills from his pocket. "Here's your week's wages. By rights I shouldn't give you a thin dime!"

He flung the bills into the dirt, then stood, hands on hips, until Dudley had his clothes more or less arranged, had scooped up the money, and was on his way out of the grove.

Dudley's mind was made up before he ever reached home. He knew that his mother was spending the day shopping; for this he was grateful. In his room he threw some things into an old suitcase and fled the house, not even leaving a note for his mother.

He knew he was taking the coward's way out, but he simply couldn't face his mother after what had happened.

Dudley hit the road, joining the swelling

band of nomads—riding box cars, hitchhiking, and when all else failed, walking. He slept in freight cars, hobo jungles, and empty buildings. He ate when and what he could, which was far from three square meals a day, and was reduced to foraging in garbage cans on occasions. He begged from house to house, offering to work for a handout. Due to his pride, it took awhile for him to force himself to do this; in fact, it took three straight days without a bite to eat. He was turned away more often than not. He took what work he could find, a day here and an hour there, but a steady job was not to be found.

He wasn't on the road a month—the time it took for his one week's wages to melt away—when he knew he had made a terrible mistake in leaving home. Yet his pride, and the deep shame he felt, wouldn't permit him to return.

Whenever he could spare a penny for a postcard, he sent one to his mother, with scribbled, lying words about how well he was faring. There was never any return address for he had no address. He couldn't even use General Delivery, since the cops always hustled him out of town; he was never allowed to stay in one town long enough for a reply from his mother to reach him.

By accident he discovered his talent for repairing machinery, when he chanced upon a motorist stalled by the side of the highway one day. At home, Dudley had been handy at repairing things, but since his family had had no automobile, he had never tinkered with one. Now he found that he seemed to have been born with an instinctive knowledge of the innards of an automobile. The car, an ancient Model T, wouldn't start.

The owner, a middle-aged, leathery farmer, was fuming when Dudley walked up. "Dadblamed machine! Never had any such trouble with a horse and buggy. Dadblamed thing's always dying on me!"

Dudley delved under the hood. It took him about fifteen minutes to discover that an ignition wire had frayed and parted. He spliced it together, and told the farmer to get behind the wheel and advance the spark. Dudley seized the crank and spun it. The motor backfired once, like a mule breaking wind, and caught.

The good deed earned Dudley a five-mile ride down the highway, a hot supper, a goodnight's rest in the barn on a pile of fragrant hay, and breakfast in the morning.

After that, things went a little easier for him. As his knowledge of machinery increased, he could pick up a few dollars from time to time. The age of the automobile was still comparatively new, and a great many people were at a loss when their car or truck refused to function. Even so, there weren't a great many jobs to be found for an expert mechanic. In most of the small towns throughout the Southwest and the Midwest, blacksmiths or filling station operators did their best to repair automobiles. The big cities had garages, but the full-time mechanic jobs were already filled, and no man in his right mind gave up a job in these hard times.

Dudley not only became a good mechanic, but he learned how to survive on the road—how to scrounge for food and clothing, how to dodge small-town cops and railroad bulls, how to drift down to Florida or Texas in winter so he wouldn't freeze sleeping out-of-doors. One place he did *not* go was California; he hadn't set foot in his home state since his hasty departure.

Now, staring after Amanda Cayne, Dudley considered the irony of hearing the identical words that had preceded his downfall before: "It's your chance to prove yourself, Dudley."

Goddamnit, he should have told her to go straight to hell.

No! He squared his shoulders. Now *was* the time to prove himself, if he was ever going to get off the road. Despite its many hardships, life as a hobo—a freight rider—had a strange fascination. Dudley had met a great many drifters who bemoaned their fate, yet he instinctively knew that they would have it no other way.

Was he like that? Now was the time to find out, to prove himself to Amanda Cayne, *and* himself. Also, he realized something for the first time. Despite the backbreaking labor, he liked being with the threshing crew. It had the same nomadic flavor as the life of a freight rider, plus a little spending money in his pocket and the satisfaction of a job well done.

He turned away toward the threshers, determined to prove himself once and for all.

There would be, he supposed, some resentment toward a man of his age and inexperience being placed in charge, even if only for a few days. But if such resentment existed, it was well-hidden. And after thinking about it, he concluded that the harvesters probably resented less taking orders from him than from a woman.

Jack Rollins certainly didn't resent it. "By god, I'm glad she left you in charge, Dudley. I just ain't cut out to be a boss." He leaned forward with a conspiratorial air. "Anything you ain't sure about, or if'n I see some yahoo doing something wrong, we'll have a quiet chat, so's they won't know I'm having any say."

"Thanks, Jack. I appreciate it."

The only static came from Bud Dalmas in the form of a snide remark. "Sure this job ain't too big for your breeches, Dud? Or maybe . . ." He spat tobacco juice and laughed soundlessly. "Or maybe it's what you got *in* your breeches that got you promoted in the first place. That right, bo?"

"Let's get one thing straight, Dalmas," Dudley said through gritted teeth. "I'll listen to no dirty digs at Amanda. One more such remark, and you can pack your bedroll, collect your pay, and be on your way. Whether you like it or not, she did leave me in charge."

"Whooee, excuse me all to hell! I didn't know you thought Miss Amanda was one of the Lord's little angels. Last time we talked, you didn't seem to have such a high opinion of her."

Dudley longed to punch him in the mouth,

and weirdly, Dalmas seemed to expect it, yet he simply stood, grinning hugely.

"Just remember, this is the last and only warning," Dudley said tightly.

"Oh, I ain't likely to forget," Bud Dalmas said. "A warning like that, coming from such a fierce bugger as yourself."

By God, Dudley thought, he *is* trying to goad me into hitting him! Why? It made no sense.

He turned on his heel and stalked away.

The next morning one of the tractors sputtered and died not long after they started threshing. It took Dudley an hour to discover that sugar had been poured into the gas tank. It was noon before he had the tank and the clogged lines cleaned out so the tractor would run again. With one thresher down for half a day, they had fallen further behind schedule.

That night Dudley lay awake until after everyone had fallen asleep. Then he got up from his pallet on the ground and eased quietly over to stand against one of the threshers. It was a moonless night, but there was enough light from the stars to show him the mounds the sleeping men made. He kept his gaze pinned on them. Before long he was dying for a cigarette, but he fought back the urge.

His vigil paid off shortly after midnight, just when he was beginning to think he had been wrong. A figure rose off the ground and slunk toward the other thresher. The man had a can of something in one hand.

Dudley plastered himself against the side of

the thresher, waiting. He saw now that the man was carrying a squirt can, used to oil the working parts of the thresher; the top had been screwed off.

Dudley stepped up behind the man. "I thought it was you behind the breakdowns, Dalmas, thought it for some time."

With a startled cry, Bud Dalmas spun around.

Dudley held out his hand. "Give me the can."

Silently the man handed over the squirt can. Dudley poured a little of the oil onto his fingers and rubbed them together. The oil was grainy with tiny, hard objects. "What have you got in here? Gravel? A couple of hours in the gears and bearings and the thresher would be down for the season, perhaps permanently." He made his voice hard. "Who're you working for, Dalmas? Who's paying you?"

"Go take a flying fuck for yourself, bo."

"Dirty-mouthed to the end, huh? Who, damn you? Seymour Hooker? Yes, my guess would be Hooker. You're walking, tonight, but you could make it easier on yourself if you'd leave me with a name."

"How could that make it any easier?" Dalmas said in a sneering voice. "What more can you do than fire me?"

"This."

With all his strength Dudley hit the man in the mouth. Bud Dalmas flew back against the side of the thresher, his head thumping against metal. He slid slowly to the ground and was still. After a moment Dudley went to one knee and placed an ear to the man's chest. He was still breathing. Dudley went for the man's bedroll, dumped it beside him.

In the morning Bud Dalmas was gone.

13

"We're pushing her closer and closer to the wall, J.C.," Seymour said into the phone. "I'll tell my man over there to speed things up a little. Won't be long now."

"Shitfire, Hooker, you've been saying that for weeks now." The reedy voice from Dallas was angry. "I hear things, Hooker. People are always calling me up and passing on interesting gossip."

Seymour went tense. "Such as?"

"Such as, you been chasing after her. If you've gone sweet on Amanda Cayne, I'll have your ass. I know you're a tail-chaser. Wouldn't have you around if you weren't, a man your age. But if you allow it to interfere with business . . ."

"I haven't gone soft on Amanda, J.C. Sure, I've squired her around some. She's a good-looking doll. I wouldn't mind at all getting into her breeches. But I haven't gone sweet on her, J.C. My word on it."

The distant voice was quiet for a long moment. "Okay, Hooker. How long before she's due to thresh this Martin's place?"

"Two weeks, ten days."

"I warned you, remember? If she's able to thresh Martin's wheat, goodbye Seymour Hooker!"

Seymour hung up, a sour taste in his mouth. He hated to talk about Amanda as if she was some chippie he was chasing; she was due more respect than that. But he knew the best way to pacify J.C. Fallon was to allow him to believe that she was no more than a piece of tail.

The trouble was, Amanda meant more than that to him now. The realization had been slow in coming, and painful when it arrived, but he finally had to admit to himself that he was gone on her. Of all the broads he had ever known—and God knew there had been plenty—Amanda Cayne was the first one he'd ever thought of in any terms except hopping in and out of bed.

Yet, J.C. was right. It never worked, mixing business and pleasure, or business and love—whatever that was.

Climbing into the V-8, he fired a cigar and sat smoking, staring through the windshield, squinting against the glare of the sun.

He knew that he had to concentrate on driving Amanda out of the threshing business. If he didn't succeed, it was his ass, and if a man didn't protect his own ass, first and foremost, he was a fool. Any personal feeling that he had for Amanda would have to be shoved to the back burner until the harvest season was over.

He made a face and threw the half-smoked cigar out the window. Until recently he had never smoked more than three or four a day. Now he was burning up a dozen or more. He figured that had to be a gauge of his emotional state.

Slamming the car into gear, he roared out of the filling station, the tires smoking. He drove fast out of town, the car devouring the three miles to the farm where the combines were busy at work. He parked at the edge of the field and watched.

Watching, his discontent abated somewhat. He always derived great pleasure watching these combines at work—giant insects devised by men that gobbled up the wheat, digesting it, then spitting it out as a product that would soon become food for men's bellies.

Seymour snorted at the fancy. Yet, it was true, damnit! Why wouldn't these wheat farmers, old fogies all, grasp the fact that combines were *here*? Why couldn't they realize that the old threshing machines were as obsolete as those prehistoric monsters? What were they called? Dinosaurs, that was it!

A cough at his elbow distracted him, and Seymour looked around into the face of Bud Dalmas.

"Dalmas!" he said harshly. "What the devil are you doing here? Haven't I told you not to come near me, where people might see us together?" He broke off with a double take, staring at Dalmas's scabbed-over lip. "What the holy hell happened to you?"

"Dudley Graham gave me this. Caught me when I wasn't looking." Gingerly Dalmas touched the scab, wincing. "We don't have to tippytoe around anymore, Mr. Hooker. Graham knows . . ."

"You asshole!" Seymour shoved open the door, forcing Dalmas to step back. He loomed angrily over the man. "What do you mean, he knows? Knows what?"

Dalmas didn't look at him. In a whining voice he said, "He caught me trying to fix one of the threshers for good and all."

Raging, Seymour snarled, "And you told him you worked for me! You cowardly bastard, you peached on me!"

"Nah, Mr. Hooker." Dalmas backed a step, Adam's apple bobbing in fear. "He already guessed, I swear! Never did care much for you, that Dudley."

"I don't believe you." Seymour raised a fist, then dropped it in a weary gesture. "Ah, hell! You're not worth skinning my knuckles on. Get out of my sight."

"But you owe me, Mr. Hooker!"

"Owe you what?" Seymour laughed sarcastically. "I owe you a mouthful of knuckles, is what I owe you."

Dalmas spat tobacco juice defiantly. "You promised to pay me money to do your dirty work for you."

"I didn't pay you to fuck up, and you fucked up."

"I did the best I could," Dalmas whined. "I want my pay."

Seymour's rage erupted. He seized the man by the shirt front and swung him around, slam-

208

ming him against the Ford. He bent Dalmas back over the hood and shook him from side to side, then rammed a knee hard into his crotch. Dalmas yowled, and a mist of tobacco juice sprayed Seymour's face. He released Dalmas and stepped quickly back out of the way.

"You don't get a thin dime from me. If you don't haul ass this minute, I'm going to whack on you until you'll have to crawl away from here!"

Dalmas slid off the fender to the ground, clutching at his groin. He turned a pain-wracked face up. Tears leaked out of his eyes, yet the eyes were as baleful as a rattlesnake's. He croaked, "You're going to be sorry for this, Mr. Hooker. You'll see "

"I'm already sorry, sorry I ever knew you." Seymour jerked a thumb over his shoulder. "Now beat it! Move your carcass!"

Bud Dalmas got to his feet and moved off, creeping, half-bent over. Seymour lit a cigar and leaned on the fender, staring after Dalmas until the man disappeared up the lane.

His thoughts were bleak, J.C. Fallon's words sounding in his head: "If she's able to thresh Martin's wheat, goodbye Seymour Hooker!"

And now he was back where he had started. Worse off, in fact. Where before he'd had a man, fuck-up though he might be, in Amanda's camp, now he had no one. And if that pecker-wood, Dudley Graham, could convince Amanda that Seymour Hooker was behind the sabotage attempts, she probably wouldn't ever speak to him again.

It had been a desperate measure, putting his own man in her crew, and the sneakiest thing he'd ever done. But he hadn't really known Amanda that well then, hadn't been gone on her, so her opinion of him had never mattered all that much. Now, now it was different, it mattered to hell-and-gone!

He straightened up, throwing the half-smoked cigar away, grinding it out under his foot. Always a man of action, he felt a need for action now. He gazed out at the whirring combines. Should he send one of his men over to Amanda's camp, seeking a job, to replace Bud Dalmas? The trouble was, he had a small crew—combines required a smaller crew than threshers—and he couldn't spare a man. Besides, Amanda had seen his crew in Annie's Place that night, and would more than likely recognize anyone he sent over. He decided it was too risky.

But at least he could drop in on Amanda, a friendly visit, and get firsthand her reaction to discovering that all this time she'd had a viper clasped to her bosom—in a manner of speaking.

He got into the Ford, backed it around, and sent in careening down the bumpy lane.

Of course he could give up the game, tell J.C. to go fly a kite, and let Amanda go her way undeterred. Yet that wasn't his way. Disregarding the fact that he would be out of a job if he did that, it was the game that mattered, the competitiveness of it. Seymour seldom gambled, not for money, yet he loved the gamble when his own livelihood, maybe even his life, was at

210

stake. He had never been in a situation where his life had been in danger, not really, but he knew himself well enough to realize that it would give him a hell of a boot, win or lose. He had heard stories of men in hazardous occupations who claimed that they got their rocks off, came in their pants, when face to face with death. Seymour had often wondered if that would happen to him.

So, the game would go on. Nothing personal, Amanda. Hope you understand that!

He threw back his head and laughed aloud.

14

Amanda was tired and cranky. She had driven almost nonstop all the way back from Wichita Falls, spurred by apprehension, wondering if she had made a mistake by turning the crew over to a young freight rider like Dudley Graham.

Part of her mood, she realized, was the result of what had happened in the hospital in Wichita Falls.

Remembering all the horror stories she'd heard about strokes, remembering how close Amos had come to being permanently paralyzed after the first one, she hadn't known what to expect. But what she actually went through, she could never, never have anticipated . . .

At the sight of her in the doorway, his face had turned red and he had raged, "So you finally got here, did you? Your poor father could be dead and in the ground for all you give a good goddamn!"

"I'm sorry, Daddy. I got here as soon as I could. It's a long drive down from where we're threshing."

"Threshing, what do you mean, threshing? It ain't threshing season now. If it was, don't you think I'd goldanged be there? The threshers are in the yard for the winter." He had been propped up in bed when she rushed into the room, seemingly no more seriously impaired physically. "You probably been out fucking some boy. I know you modern females." His eyes were narrow and mean.

Amanda could only stare, appalled. Was this the man who had always been so gentle with her? The man she'd once seen flatten a thresher hand with one blow when the man had said, "Shit," in her presence?

A doctor had come into the room behind her; she glanced at him in bafflement. He shrugged slightly, a motion indicating helplessness. She said slowly, "Daddy, I've been operating the threshers since your stroke. Don't you remember?"

"Don't remember nothing like that," Amos said peevishly. "Don't know nothing about any stroke."

He turned his head aside to look out the window. Amanda looked again at the doctor, in silent appeal. A finger to his lips, he motioned her out into the corridor.

But before they could take a single step, Amos's head swung around and he rasped, "Who's the gent with you, girl? One of the guys you're fucking?"

"There's no need for language like that, Mr. Cayne." The doctor moved forward with authority. "You're a very sick man, and you shouldn't upset yourself, or your daughter."

"Ain't so sick I can't see what's in front of me," Amos said. "All's wrong with me is a touch of grippe."

"No, Mr. Cayne, you've had a stroke."

He touched Amos on the shoulder, and at the touch Amos's belligerence left him, escaping like air from a balloon. He peered around the doctor at Amanda. He said piteously, "Don't leave me in here, Amanda! You don't know what they're doing to me. I ain't crazy!"

"Of course you're not crazy, Mr. Cayne," the doctor said soothingly. "You'll be fine."

"They're torturing me, Amanda!" Amos cried. "Don't go way and leave me."

Amanda, near tears, said in a choked voice, "I'm not going to leave you, Daddy."

At a loss for what more to say or do, she took a step toward the bed. The doctor held up a hand, stopping her. Looking at her father, she saw the reason. Amos Cayne was fast asleep. The transformation from foul-mouthed truculence to deep sleep within the blink of an eye was bewildering. The doctor took her arm, and they stepped out into the corridor. With a shrug of his shoulder, he indicated a small waiting room down at the end.

Amanda had her cigarettes out by the time they reached the waiting room. She put one in her mouth and held out the pack. The doctor took one, cupping his hands around a match for her. Amanda inhaled deeply and blew smoke.

"I'm Dr. Anderson, Miss Cayne. Your father

215

is in my care. I'm sorry you had to go through that in there. If I could have seen you first, I would have warned you."

"What's wrong with him, Doctor? I've never seen him like this! The first time, being partially paralyzed, was bad enough. But this!" She shuddered.

"Unfortunately, medical science still has a great deal to learn about strokes." He sighed. "I understand from your father's medical history that the first stroke did leave him paralyzed and impaired his speech for a time. This time it destroyed a part of his brain, a not uncommon occurrence."

"But the way he talked to me! My father has never used language like that in his life."

"Irritability and loss of memory are symptoms of brain damage. Anticipating your next question, he may become better with the passing of time. On the other hand, he may not. Sadly, there is little we can do to change his condition. You must face that."

Amanda said slowly, "Should I stay for a few days? Would that help?"

Dr. Anderson hesitated. "You have a job, someplace you're needed?" At her nod he continued, "My advice would be to leave now, don't even see him again. Not at this time, I mean. Don't misunderstand me, Miss Cayne, I'm not being cruel. It'll be the best thing for both of you. You'll only have to go through the same thing each time you visit him. When he improves, *if* he does, your father will be ashamed if he remembers how he acted. Leave now, Miss

Cayne. Leave an address, a phone number, where I can contact you."

"That's not possible. I'm running a wheat-threshing crew; we move every few days."

"Then call me here, at the hospital, every day. I'll keep you current on his condition. Now," his smile was kind, "just go, Miss Cayne."

She had gone, almost fleeing, feeling a vast relief. And guilt.

And that, Amanda supposed, was another reason she was in a lousy mood—she was feeling guilt at having deserted her father. But what good could she have accomplished there? And if the threshing crew went under through her neglect, the Caynes, father and daughter, would have to go on relief.

Her anxiety mounted with each mile she drew closer to the farm where they were threshing. Where she *hoped* they were threshing.

She drew a sigh of relief when she drove up to the field, seeing the threshers fuming wheat chaff. It was late afternoon, and she saw that they were close to being finished.

She parked the pickup. She saw Dudley Graham coming toward her and went to meet him. "Is everything okay, Dudley?"

Something in her voice must have betrayed her anxiety, for he bristled. "Everything's fine. Why shouldn't it be?" He swung a hand about. "Even a blind person could see that."

"Okay, don't get your hackles up." Relaxing

a little, she lit a cigarette. "Anything happen while I was away?"

"One thing." He looked straight at her. "I fired a man."

"What gave you the right to do that?"

"You did," he said tightly. "When you left me in charge, I took that to mean I had the right to hire and fire."

"With good, experienced help so hard to get this late in the season . . . who was it?"

"Bud Dalmas."

"He's been a thresherman for years!"

"I had a good reason to fire him."

"I'm not sure I want to hear it." Her shoulders slumped. "So now we're shorthanded."

"No, we're not. I've already hired somebody to replace him."

"Who?"

"A freight rider," he said challengingly.

Amanda held her temper in check with an effort. "You *did* take a lot on yourself, didn't you, Buster Brown?"

"He's a good man, working his ass off. I'll be responsible for him."

"A fat lot of good that'll do, if he doesn't work out. All right . . . why did you fire Dalmas? Aside from the fact that I know you didn't like him. I didn't like him either, but that's no reason to can him."

"I don't like him, I won't deny that. He's a foul-mouthed, dirty-minded cretin. But I didn't can him just for that. I caught him trying to pour gravel into the gears of one of the threshers. In the middle of the night. If he'd've succeeded, scratch one thresher, probably for good. Wasn't that reason enough to can him?"

"If it's true . . . okay, okay!" She held up a hand as his mouth tightened. "I accept your word for it. But why? What did he have to gain? I never abused him, so he'd have no reason to get back at me."

"We've talked about this before. You didn't believe me then, you probably won't believe me now, but here goes . . . he's working for Seymour Hooker."

"We're back to that, are we?" She sighed. "Did Bud admit that?"

For the first time Dudley seemed unsure of himself. He tossed his head. "As much as."

"But he didn't out-and-out admit it, did he? And why should Seymour pay him to . . . I know, I know, to put me out of business, so he'd get the harvesting contracts for his combines. Well, I flat out don't believe it. Seymour is ruthless in his business dealings, true, but not sneaky. If he wanted to sabotage a thresher, he'd likely come barging in in broad daylight, with a sledgehammer . . ." At the sound of a car motor she faced around and saw Seymour's V-8 coming down the lane toward them. She crossed one arm over her breasts. "Here he comes now. We'll ask him, straight out."

Dudley laughed shortly. "You think he's going to come out and admit it?"

"With Seymour, you never know. He's hardly what you'd call predictable."

They fell silent as Seymour Hooker braked the Ford, slewing it sideways at the last instant to escape its own dust—most of it anyway. Seymour got out and came toward them with that cocky stride.

His face split in a broad grin. "Sugar! How you? It's been a few days."

"I've been away, down to Wichita Falls. Daddy had another stroke." Now why did I tell him that? He probably couldn't care less. She could almost feel Dudley's scornful gaze on her, and knew what he was thinking: *You're stalling, Amanda!*

Seymour said, "Aww, hell, I'm right sorry to hear that. How is old Amos?"

"Seymour, I came back to learn that one of our threshermen, Bud Dalmas, was caught trying to dump gravel into the gears of one of the threshers."

"Well, I'll be dogged! Why would the rascal do a thing like that, you suppose?"

"Was he following your orders, Seymour?"

"*My* orders?" Seymour rocked back and forth on his heels. His face assumed a hurt look. "Sugar, I'm wounded to the quick. How could you think a thing like that of me?" His hard glance settled on Dudley. "Course, I can guess the source. You put that bug in her ear, peckerwood?"

"You see, Amanda. I told you he'd deny it."

"Of course I'm denying it, you peckerwood, because it ain't true!"

Dudley snorted in derision. "Why else would Dalmas try a stunt like that, if not for money from you?"

"Maybe he's got a hard-on for Amanda . . .

excuse the language, sugar," Seymour said without looking away from Dudley. "Why would I be behind something like that?"

"To put this outfit out of business, that's why!"

"Whatever I may be, I don't play a game underhanded. You know something, peckerwood? You're beginning to rile me." He smacked a fist into one palm. "I've a mind to send you screaming to the dentist."

"Go ahead," Dudley said. "I'm not falling down drunk this time."

Seymour bellowed with laughter. "You think you can stand up to me, drunk *or* sober?" He took a threatening step.

Amanda snapped, "Now stop it, you two! Stop acting like a couple of kids!"

Seymour relaxed, smiling benignly at her. "Right, sugar. When did fists ever solve anything? But I do think you owe me an apology. Do *you* think I'm responsible for what this Dalmas, whoever the hell he is, did?"

Amanda flicked a thumbnail against her teeth. "I'm thinking . . ." She studied Seymour's innocently smiling face, then let her breath go with a sigh. "I reckon I believe you. If I can't, who can I believe?"

"Shit!" Dudley said explosively. "I should have known you'd swallow his line. Well, it's on your head, lady." He turned and stalked off toward the threshers.

"Thanks for your vote of confidence, sugar. Appreciate it."

Amanda, who had been staring after Dudley,

transferred her gaze to him. She said dryly, "Don't overdo it, Seymour. I'm not all that sure I believe you myself."

His face took on that hurt look again. "But you told the peckerwood . . ."

"I know what I told him!" she snapped. "Since he had no proof, what else could I say? So don't put on that whipped-dog look for me. I'm going to be watching more closely from now on. If there are any more unexplained breakdowns, I'm going to be damned suspicious. So just consider this a parole, not a pardon, Seymour. If nothing else happens, fine. If something does, watch out!"

"Oh, I'll watch it, never fear," he said easily, smiling. "You scare me, that you do, sugar."

"I'll just bet!"

"And now, sugar, now that I've driven all the way over here, why let the opportunity go to waste? Will you let a parolee on his good behavior take you out to supper?"

It was on the tip of her tongue to turn him down. But the weight of the depression she'd been feeling crashed in on her again, and she didn't want to be alone. An evening with Seymour Hooker was always entertaining, even if she had to spend much of it fending off his sexual overtures. She said, "We won't be going to a honky-tonk?"

Seymour held up his hands. "No honky-tonks, Amanda. My word on it. There's a pretty good café in town."

Remembering, Amanda spoke without think-

222

ing, "I hope nothing happens like last time when I went to supper."

"That right?" Seymour said suspiciously. "You been going to supper with another gent? I'm hurt, sugar."

"It was Thaddeus Martin, the night before he went home."

"Old Thaddeus, huh? Reckon there's no need for me to be jealous there. What happened?"

She told him about the young punks and the fight.

Seymour frowned thoughtfully. "That surprises me, Thaddeus Martin mixing it up. I never heard of him fighting anybody." He cocked an eye at her. "Sounds like he may be gone on you, Amanda. Maybe I should be a mite jealous at that."

She said tartly, "If you're going to act up like this, forget the supper!"

"No, no!" He shook his head vigorously. "Not another word, I swear."

The supper wasn't too bad, but Amanda was a little fuzzy-headed afterward. Seymour had brought along a flask of gin, and she had drunk one too many. But it had helped to drive away the residue of depression still hanging on after the visit with her father. She didn't even protest when Seymour turned off the main road on the way back to camp, and headed down a narrow dirt lane.

In a blurred voice she said, "Where we going? Some Lover's Lane you've stumbled onto? I'm warning you, Seymour . . . it will be a waste of your time."

"Nothing like that," he said in an aggrieved voice. "It's early yet, and I found a nice little lake down here a ways last week. Full moon and all, I thought it might be nice. Trust me, sugar."

Amanda, too relaxed to be contentious, gave a resigned shrug. It was easier to go with the flow. So far Seymour had been on his best behavior; maybe he would remain so.

It was too much to hope for; she should have known better.

About a mile down the lane was a small lake, almost pear-shaped, with quite a lot of water, glinting silver under the full Kansas moon. Amanda was surprised that the summer heat and near-drought hadn't cause it to shrink down to a mudhole.

There was a huge oak spreading its branches on the south bank of the lake. Across the water, a scattering of milk cows dozed on their feet, chewing cuds in slow motion.

Seymour braked the Ford and started to get out.

"What's the matter with right here? I can see what scenery there is just fine from the car."

"Come on, Amanda. Be a good sport. It's a nice night." From the back seat he took a folded blanket.

Amanda said caustically, "That your pussy blanket, Seymour?"

Seymour reared back in shock. "That's not

nice language to hear from a lady! I've never heard you speak like that, Amanda."

"I don't feel much like a lady tonight." Before the words were out of her mouth, she wondered if it hadn't been the wrong thing to say under the circumstances.

"Visit with your daddy upset you, did it?"

His voice oozed sympathy, and Amanda had to smile behind her hand. The pitch was on. All of a sudden, she thought, why not? Why the hell not? She wasn't a virgin by far, and she hadn't been with a man since she took over the threshing crew. Sex, good sex, was supposed to release tension, the little death of orgasm brought a few moments of forgetfulness, and God knows she had plenty to forget.

And, she admitted to herself, she was curious about Seymour. He was brash, often downright crude, yet there was a roaring vitality about him that occasionally left her breathless, her heartbeat accelerating.

What kind of a lover was he? She often wondered about the kind of a lover a particular man would make; she supposed most women did. This was a good time to find out.

He was around at her side of the car now, the blanket folded over one arm. He opened the door and offered his hand. She'd worn a skirt and blouse tonight, and she was amused to notice that, after one quick look, he averted his glance when her skirt hiked far up her thighs as she got out.

"What's the matter, Seymour?" she taunted. "You're missing the show. That's the reason you got this car, isn't it? So you could see all the way up to a girl's crotch?"

"Aww, sugar." Then he gave a shout of laughter. "Yeah, you're right. That was one reason I bought this model. Never could fool you, could I?"

"Oh, I don't know," she said lightly. "For all I know, you may have fooled me many times. You may have fooled me about Bud Dalmas. Dudley may be right."

"Now Amanda, if you're going to take that attitude, you might as well get your tail back into the car. You acting this way, you're spoiling things for us."

"What things?" she asked guilelessly. "We're just here to enjoy the scenery, right?"

Without waiting for a reply she strode over to stand under the tree. She lit a cigarette and stared calmly out at the water. The ground under the great oak was moon-dappled.

She looked around when she heard the scuffle of his footsteps. His face had a sullen cast. "You going to sulk now, Seymour?"

He exploded, throwing the blanket to the ground. "Goddamnit, I'm not sulking! I'm plain sore, that's what. You do try a man's patience, Amanda!"

"You're right, Seymour. I *am* being a bitch. It's just that . . ." She broke off with a rueful shrug. "Never mind. But you are right, and I apologize. I'll behave. Scout's honor. Okay?" She touched his hand. "Forgiven?"

His features remained hostile for a long moment, then slowly relaxed into a smile. "Forgiven." He stooped to spread the blanket on the ground, then straightened up and motioned. "Sit, sugar, and take a load off."

Amanda sat on the blanket, raising her legs to rest her chin on her knees, tucking her dress around her ankles.

"It is nice here, I'll give you that." She sighed. "I can almost forget my troubles."

"I been telling you how to get out from under all those troubles."

Amanda motioned wearily. "Are you going to start that song again? You never give up, do you?"

"What kind of a life is it for a woman, Amanda? Ask yourself that question. And what can it come to in the end? Say you make it through the season. How about next year? You keep telling me, telling yourself, that you're holding things together for your daddy, so he can take the threshers out next season. Face it, sugar, he ain't never going to be able to hit the road again." When she made a sound of protest, he held up a hand. "I know, putting it that way sounds cruel, but the truth often is cruel, it's the way of the world."

"About Daddy, you may be right. But how about me? If I can limp along, finish out the season, make a little profit, I can come out next year in better shape. I find that I like the threshing business."

"You see, that's it right there, you liking it. It's changing you, making you hard, trying to play a man's game like you are. It might turn you into a ball-buster. No, Amanda, it's no life for a woman."

"And what is? As if I didn't know your answer already."

"Find a man, marry him, settle down and keep house, raise a passel of kids. That's the life God picked out for women."

"That's what I've heard all my life, first from Daddy, then from every other man I ever met."

"It's the truth, and it won't ever change. You can depend on that, sugar."

"They said women would never get the vote, but it happened."

"And look what happened when they did, look at this Depression."

"Oh, for God's sake! Are you blaming the Depression on women getting the vote?" She began to laugh helplessly. Recovering, she gasped out, "One thing's for sure. *You* will never change. This home and marriage you think I'll settle for . . . you have a candidate in mind?"

"Yep. Me," he said gruffly.

Taken completely by surprise, never dreaming that Seymour Hooker would consider marriage to any woman, she peered at him. He was serious, this time he was really serious!

"I'm in love with you, sugar."

With a groan he swept her into his arms. Still somewhat in shock, Amanda put up no resistance. The touch of his mouth on hers was tentative, exploratory, as though he was afraid she'd rebuff him.

His mouth sent heat coursing through her body, and she went limp and pliant in his arms, returning his kiss with a growing urgency.

Bolder now, his hand pushed her skirt up until he could cup her mound. The heel of his hand rotated, and she reacted to the friction, surging against his hand. He half-turned, one leg thrown over hers, the stone-hard length of his erection throbbing against her thigh.

He unbuttoned her blouse, his hand searching for a breast. A snarl of frustration came from him when he couldn't solve the mystery of the brassiere.

"Wait a minute, hon."

Rolling away from him, Amanda quickly removed blouse, skirt, brassiere, panties, and stockings. Seymour had stripped to the skin also.

Amanda gasped as her hand closed around his organ. "My God, you're big!"

"I'll be careful, sugar," he said with heaving breath.

"Did I ask that? Did I?"

His cock filling her hand had made Amanda ready, and he was unmistakably ready. She fell back onto the blanket, never once relinquishing her grip. "I want you inside me, Seymour! Hurry!"

He kneeled between her thighs, weight resting on his hands on each side of her head. Amanda guided him inside of her, at the last moment arching her hips. He filled her, filled her completely. She shuddered, crying out.

He began to move, still tentatively, surprisingly gentle for such a big man. Amanda raised her head to look down at the juncture of their bodies. There was enough moonlight to show his cock moving in and out with his rhythmic lunges. Watching this was incredibly erotic, exciting her even more.

She said, "I'm not a doll, Seymour. I don't break so easily. You're a man, show me what a man can do."

She locked her legs around his hips. Goaded, Seymour drove at her. With glad cries of delight, Amanda corralled his plunging body between her thighs.

Seymour's tempo increased, racing out of control. He slipped out of her with a curse. Muttering, Amanda fumbled for him, guided him back inside. The feel of his slick, pulsating organ after the few seconds absence brought her close to orgasm. She drummed her pelvis frantically against him, and her pleasure broke with a suddenness and intensity that was almost painful.

Crying out, she rose and clung to him.

"Aww, sugar! Ahh!" Seymour shouted.

Her own spasms subsiding, Amanda lay still, holding him inside her as shudder after shudder wracked his big frame. Finally, with a gusty exhalation of breath, he grew still, then rolled off her.

In a moment she heard his low chuckle. "One thing you'll have to admit, Amanda . . ."

Amanda's body, so long deprived, was still a riot of sensation, her problems momentarily forgotten. She said, "What's that?"

"All that talk before about a woman working or getting married, women getting the vote, there's this to remember . . . a woman has to be different from a man for what just happened to happen. I guess the Lord knew what He was doing."

"*Vive la différence*," she said drowsily.

"What?"

"*Vive la différence*. That's French for . . ."

"I know what it means, goddamnit!" he said, outraged. "You think I'm ignorant?"

15

Seymour was happy as a stinkbug. He sent the Ford speeding down the highway like an arrow. He was singing tunelessly at the top of his voice, a voice that someone once said would scare crows a mile away.

"I'm a ding-dong daddy from Dumas, and you oughta see me do my stuff . . ."

He broke off, shouting, "I am, by God!" And struck the steering wheel with the heel of his hand. He always felt good the morning after a great piece of ass, but never this good! Besides, Amanda wasn't just another piece of ass, she was *his* woman. True, she hadn't exactly said so, but then she wasn't a woman to give herself to just any man. She was playing it cagey, afraid of losing her independence. She'd come around before long.

But he couldn't risk another fuck-up like Bud Dalmas. If Amanda ever found out about *that*, it would be Katie bar the door! Nope, no more sabotage. From now on he'd have to use persuasion to woo the farmers away from her. She would understand and even respect that.

That was where he was headed now—to make another stab at getting Thaddeus's wheat to thresh.

There was only a little more than a week left before Amanda was due at the Martin place; that wasn't a hell of a lot of time. He'd tried just about everything with Thaddeus, and hadn't managed to shake him loose, but he had been saving a last card. Now he was going to offer to thresh Thaddeus's wheat at far less than the going rate per bushel, so low a man'd be a fool not to go for it, especially in these hard times.

Old J.C. should be happy to get the Martin acreage, even at a loss. If Seymour, after feeling him out, decided that Fallon would balk at he cut-rate price, he figured he'd still be ahead in the long run if he made up the difference out of his own pocket.

At least I don't have to drive so damned far this time, he thought, as he wheeled the Ford down the lane leading to that unpainted house rearing up as if it had grown out of the ground. With a splatter of gravel against the undersides of the fenders, he braked the car to a stop. Getting out, he saw Thaddeus down at the barn, tinkering with a mower.

He moved toward him. Thaddeus had turned at the sound of the Ford, and now stood with hands on hips. The expression on his face wasn't exactly a welcoming one.

"How you, Thaddeus?" Seymour said breezily.

Thaddeus Martin frowned. "I'm just fine, Seymour. What are you doing up this way again so soon?"

"Just thought I'd drop in for a chat, since I was already up this way and all."

"That didn't answer my question . . . What are you doing up here?"

"I like to touch bases with my people, now you know that."

"I'm not one of your people."

Seymour put on his injured look. "Maybe not in a business way, but I've always considered you a friend. Can't a guy stop and shoot the breeze with a friend?"

"We both know why you're here, Seymour, so why waltz all the way round the mulberry bush? Nothing you can say will change my mind." Thaddeus's mouth set stubbornly. "Amanda is threshing my wheat, no more's to be said about it."

Seymour smiled craftily. "Not even if I offer to halve the bushel rate she's charging?"

"You'd go that far?" Thaddeus blinked. "Did J.C. Fallon authorize you to cut prices?"

"I'm in charge in the field. What I say goes."

"Of course he didn't. Much as I know he'd like to harvest my wheat crop, from what I've heard of him, he's too much of a skinflint to do that. No, you're making it up out of your own pocket. That's low, Seymour, even for you."

Stung, Seymour retorted, "What's low about it? It's just good business practice. These are the days of cutthroat competition. Hell, go along any Main Street, any town nowadays, you'll find stores practically giving away merchandise to drive their competitors into bankruptcy!"

"That's their concern, not mine. No, I'll have no part of it."

"Thaddeus, you're cutting your own throat." Seymour made his voice wheedling. "Damnit, man, think of the profit for you. Fact is, the price of wheat what it is today, you'll be lucky to break even, time you pay for the mowing *and* Amanda's going rate. Don Moore now, the farm adjoining yours, he's seen the light, and letting me have his wheat to combine."

"That's Don Moore, not Thaddeus Martin. I happen to think that a man's word is worth more than profit, and I gave my word. No, Seymour, I'll not listen to you." His voice hardened. "You're trespassing, Hooker. I want you off my property."

Seymour gaped at him. "Man, we're old friends. You can't order me off just like that!"

"I am ordering you off. I consider our friendship at an end. Either you go willingly, or I'll run you off. I'd be within my rights." Thaddeus crossed his arms over his chest, his features as unyielding as granite.

Seymour longed to make a taunting remark about his being hooked on Amanda, but he held his tongue, sensing that it would be a mistake.

"All right, I'm going." He held up his hand. "I can't believe my ears, but by God, I don't have to have a house fall on me to know when I'm not wanted." Suddenly his temper boiled over, and he shouted in Thaddeus's face, "From this day on, you can go to hell, Thaddeus Martin, for all of me!"

Thaddeus was unmoved. "If I do, I'll likely find you there, waiting for me."

Seymour turned on his heel and stomped to the car. He threw gravel turning the Ford in a narrow circle. It was growing dark when he reached the main highway.

He took out a cigar and chomped savagely on it, then struck a match to it. He couldn't remember when he had been so mad and frustrated. Floorboarding the gas pedal, he sent the V-8 roaring down the highway much too fast. Fortunately there was no traffic. The headlights bored twin tunnels into the night.

Now what the hell was he going to do? He was caught between a rock and a hard place. It looked like he had lost Thaddeus's wheat; J.C. would flip his lid.

And old Thaddeus gone on Amanda! How about that?

A harsh bark of laughter came from him. Was he sore because Thaddeus refused to let him combine his wheat, or jealous because of Amanda? Well, hell, it could be equal parts of both, couldn't it?

With a start he suddenly realized that he was driving like a madman. He began easing his foot from the floorboard when a flicker of movement to the right snagged his attention. Coming onto the highway from a side road was a truck without lights. Seymour hit the horn with one hand, and slammed on the brakes. The horn blared, the tires squealed on the asphalt— far too late.

The truck struck the Ford broadside, just behind the door on the opposite side. The V-8 skidded across the highway. Seymour desperately tried to straighten it out, and then he realized that the truck was not slowing. It was still coming. He risked a glance to his left and saw a deep ditch.

Then the world tilted crazily, and the Ford was turning over, once, twice. He was tossed about like a doll. His head struck something hard, his skull exploding with pain. Then all was still and he dimly realized that the car had come to a stop, upside down. Dazed, his thoughts moving like cold molasses, he tried to move and slumped back.

The motor was still running, and the thought of fire sent a jolt of adrenalin through him. Frantically he tried to scramble around to reach the ignition. But it was dark, and everything was topsy-turvy . . .

Again, his head struck something. The pain was excruciating and he heard a moan that he knew came from him.

Consciousness began to slide away from him. Just before he went under completely, Seymour thought he heard the crackle of flames. . . .

Bud Dalmas got down out of the cab of the stolen truck and moved to the edge of the highway to stare down at the overturned Ford. One headlight was still burning, slanted up at a weird angle.

Even as he watched, flames spurted out from under the hood, probably from a broken gas line.

Dalmas gave his silent laugh, and sent a stream of tobacco juice toward the wrecked car. So much for Mr. High-and-Mighty Seymour Hooker and his fancy pussy wagon! Grinning gleefully, he watched the flames spread. Soon Seymour Hooker would be burned like a piece of bacon. That would teach him to hire a man to do a job, then refuse to pay what was due!

He cocked an ear, listening for Hooker's screams. He heard nothing but the sound of the flames, like radio static. He felt a stab of disappointment. Maybe Hooker was unconscious and couldn't feel anything.

Dalmas sucked in his breath as he saw distant headlights up the highway. He danced from one foot to the other in frustration, his glance jumping from the burning car to the approaching headlights.

Goddamnit all to hell, shit!

Dalmas jumped into the truck and began straightening it out. It wasn't easy; apparently the collision had screwed up the front-end alignment. But when he finally got it straightened out and headed down the highway, in the opposite direction from the approaching car, it seemed to run all right. He barreled along toward the nearby town where he'd left his old jalopy, a beat-up Model A he'd bought with most of his remaining dollars. Consumed by a vengeful rage against Seymour Hooker and Dudley Graham, Dalmas gave little thought to the future. Tomorrow would take care of itself. First things first. He had needed transportation so he could trail Hooker around, looking for his chance.

Today had been the day. When he had followed Hooker in this direction, Dalmas knew that the man could only be headed for one place—the Martin farm. And when Hooker was finished there, he would be heading back to his combines. So Dalmas had found a truck, parked on a street in the town up ahead—and with the keys still in it! It had been easy enough to back into that little-used side road and wait for Hooker's fancy V-8 to come speeding along.

And then—whammo! No more Seymour Hooker!

Dalmas laughed aloud, a cackle this time, not his usual silent laugh.

Now he saw the cluster of lights ahead, the small town where he'd stolen the truck and left his jalopy. Likely the truck hadn't even been missed.

An idea came to him, and he laughed again. If he could park the truck in the same spot, wouldn't the guy who owned it have a head-scratching time when he came out in the morning and found the front end smashed in! It tickled his fancy, and he decided to risk it. Small risk, probably. When these clodhoppers went into the house, they hardly ever came out before morning for anything less than a twister.

One down, one to go. With Seymour Hooker taken care of, Dudley Graham was next. Watch it, Dud, you asshole! You're next!

16

As a youngster, Seymour had often attended tent revival meetings, it was a fertile ground for pussy hunting. But it always entailed patiently sitting through a fiery, hellfire-and-brimstone sermon, and most of those revivalist preachers could paint a vivid picture of hell. As a result, Seymour often had nightmares of hell.

He was in hell now.

Crackling flames danced around him like gleeful demons. Everywhere he looked—nothing but flames, and smoke. The very air he breathed seared his lungs, and he could smell roasting flesh. It took him a moment to realize that it was his own flesh cooking. The pain seemed distant, just an unpleasant warmth, secondary to the pounding pain in his head.

Still only half-conscious, he had sense enough to grasp the fact that he had only seconds before he would be burned alive. He tried to move and pain drove into his skull like a dull spike, wrenching a groan from him. For a moment he was tempted to give up, just sink back, let the devil's open arms welcome him.

"No, goddamnit! You're not going to get Seymour Hooker just yet!"

He fumbled under him and, miracle of miracles, his hand closed around a door handle.

It resisted stubbornly. In a last desperate burst of strength, Seymour flung himself against the door. It held for just a moment, then sprang open, and he was falling. Blessed, cool air laved his face and he gulped at it greedily. He hit soft ground and rolled several feet downhill. And that was a good thing, he found, when he finally raised his head. The Ford was burning fiercely now, and he would have been caught in the inferno if he'd lain where he had fallen. Also, the rolling had snuffed out several places where his clothing had been afire. His head throbbed abominably, his left arm, the one he'd landed on, ached, and his scorched flesh pained; but more than anything, Seymour felt sadness sweep over him as he looked at the blazing Ford.

The best car he'd ever owned, and it was finished—without even four thousand miles on it.

If he ever got his hands on the son-of-a-bitch who had banged into him . . .

A thought drove through his pain-fogged mind. It hadn't been an accident! The driver of that truck had been lying in wait for him, for Seymour Hooker and his Ford. There weren't that many of this particular model out there on the highways yet, and the way the truck kept coming, there wasn't a shred of doubt—it had been intentional.

Outrage pumped through Seymour and he

242

tried to get up. Pain slammed into him with sledgehammer force, and he fell back. As blackness swirled around him, he heard car doors slam up on the highway, and excited voices coming closer. . . .

He awoke to a white world—blinding white sunlight pouring through a window, antiseptic white walls, and white bed linen.

At least, with all that white, it couldn't be hell. Seymour grinned, started to raise his head, and grunted as pain went through his skull. Before his head dropped back, he caught a blurred glimpse of the bulky figure of a white-haired man in a black suit—but wearing a white smock.

"Just take it easy, Mr. Hooker." A hand lifted his wrist, a finger on the pulse.

"A hospital, right, Doc?" Seymour's throat was raw, raspy.

"That's right. I'm Dr. Moran. You're a very lucky fellow, Mr. Hooker."

"I don't feel so damned lucky. I hurt in several thousand places, and the last thing I remember is seeing my almost-new Ford burning to a crisp."

"About your car, I don't know. But you're lucky *you* weren't burned to a crisp. From what the people who brought you in told me, you were thrown clear. Otherwise, you would have been incinerated along with the car."

"Wasn't thrown clear," Seymour croaked.

"What?"

"Not important, Doc."

"Do you remember what happened? No other

vehicle was observed at the scene of the accident."

Seymour thought of the truck ramming into him, and he wanted to tell the doctor to call in the cops so he could spill out his venom. But he doubted they would believe it had been done on purpose. He didn't even know the make of truck, much less the license number. Besides, he had always taken care of his own messes, and by God he would this time!

"Some hit-and-run driver broadsided me, Doc," he mumbled. "I was so taken by surprise I didn't get a good enough look at the bastard to do any good."

"The other car should be damaged, so the police may find it."

"I wouldn't bet on it. Doc, how badly am I bunged up?"

"You have a sprained left shoulder, a large bump on your head that could be concussed, I can't be sure for a couple of days, and you have several burned areas. Not first-degree burns, however."

"Real lucky, huh, Doc?" Seymour said dryly.

"I would say so, yes. You could be dead right now, or have first-degree burns. Now *that* would give you some discomfort."

"How long will I have to stay here?"

"At least forty-eight hours, until I can make sure you don't have a concussion."

"I'm in the wheat-harvesting business, Doc. I have combines to run."

"I shouldn't think you'd be indispensable.

Don't you have anyone to take charge for a couple of days?"

Seymour thought of Rooster Cockrun, and smiled. Rooster was the man nominally in charge of the combines in Seymour's absence, but only for one reason—he could whip the others. In recruiting his crew Seymour had used two yardsticks: a man had to be willing to work hard and long hours; and he had to be a hardcase, willing to fight at a whistle. Aside from those requirements, he hadn't been particular, and he knew that some of them had criminal records, but he figured he could ride herd on them.

Rooster Cockrun had a long record of assault and battery behind him. He was a runty man, wide as a barrel, with hair as red as a rooster's comb—the reason for his nickname. He also had a hair-trigger temper, and Seymour knew he couldn't be trusted to run the crew for very long. But it seemed there was little choice now.

He sighed and said, "Has anyone from my crew been notified about me being in the hospital?"

Dr. Moran shrugged. "Not to my knowledge. We knew nothing of your business. The identification you carried gave us your name and some address down in Texas. That was all."

"Then would you do me a big favor, Doc? My combines are down south a ways. Would you notify a man by the name of Rooster Cockrun? Tell him where I am? I'll give you the phone number of the farm where the men are working."

"In return you'll stay in this bed until I've checked you out thoroughly? I know your kind. You're just liable to walk out the first time my back is turned. Not that I'm concerned for your welfare, but I haven't lost a patient for two months. I don't wish to spoil my record."

Seymour tapped a thumbnail against his teeth. "That's a record? Two months without losing a patient?"

"For me it is," the doctor said with a grave countenance.

Seymour bellowed laughter. "I like you, Doc. You're my kind of people. Okay, it's a deal. You get Rooster up here to me, and I'll behave."

"Rooster? Now that's an intriguing name. I'm afraid to ask how he got it."

"Three reasons, Doc. He has red hair, he's feisty as a banty rooster, and he'll hump anything that has a hole anywhere near the right location."

Rooster Cockrun strutted into the hospital room at noon the next day. His step faltered as he approached the bed. "Boss? By damn, it *is* you! I thought that sawbones was talking through his asshole. Seymour Hooker bunged up and in the hospital! Hard to believe."

"Believe it, Rooster." Seymour grinned. "I was blindsided, in a manner of speaking. Some guy in a truck whomped into me. No accident, it was deliberate. The thing that hurts the worst is the Ford. It's finished, kaput, burned up."

Rooster's long face looked disturbed. "Hell,

boss, I am sorry. That was some beautiful heap. No idea who rammed into you?"

"Not the slightest."

"How about that pissant you whipped in Annie's Place? Works for the Cayne bunch. Graham, something like that. Think maybe he could be getting back at you?"

"That's a thought. It never occurred to me. Naw, I don't think he'd have the balls for that."

"What balls?" Rooster snorted. "It don't take any balls to hide and then come barreling at a man with a truck. It has to be somebody knows you, boss, if it was done deliberately."

"That could cover a broad field, Rooster," Seymour said with a smile. "I ain't exactly known as a man who makes friends. Enemies now, I got plenty."

"My money's on somebody from the Cayne crew, and my pick'd be this Graham feller. I could get the boys together and go over after dark and teach that whole bunch a lesson."

Seymour wasn't really listening. "You wouldn't accomplish much . . ."

"It'd put them out of business. That's what you been aiming for, ain't it?" Rooster was like a dog on a leash, straining to be turned loose to hunt.

Seymour regarded him fondly. "Appreciate the thought, Rooster, but I'll take care of that little matter in my own way, in my own good time. And I think you're wrong about Dudley Graham. He don't care much for me, but I don't see him doing this."

* * *

Rooster Cockrun had no god but Seymour Hooker. First place, Seymour was the only man who'd ever hammered Rooster into the ground with his fists. Second place, he was the first man to give him a job without digging back into his past, asking all sorts of upsetting questions.

He worshipped Seymour Hooker and would gladly put his life on the line for him. He'd had two great seasons working Seymour's combines, with all the boozing, fucking and brawling he could handle. He figured that he owed Seymour, but so far had found no way to pay him back.

Leaving the hospital, Rooster was humming happily to himself. He had figured out a way to square accounts. He was sure that Seymour was wrong about this Graham fellow; he had to be the sneaky pissant who'd landed Seymour in the hospital and ruined that beautiful Ford. Rooster had been almost as proud of that machine as Seymour himself.

Now all he had to do was get the boys together for a little talk. It wouldn't take much convincing; they were always spoiling for a fight, and they all felt about Seymour the way he did.

Late tonight, armed with axe handles, baseball bats, whatever was handy, they'd pay a little visit to the Cayne camp and bust a few skulls, plus putting two threshers out of commission. If this Graham wasn't the guy, they'd put Amanda Cayne out of business, so it wouldn't be a waste.

The fact that the Cayne crew outnumbered them two to one didn't faze Rooster in the least. They'd have the element of surprise on their side, and one of Seymour's boys was as good as two of the Cayne bunch any day.

Grinning hugely, Rooster smacked a fist into his palm before getting into his old Chevy and driving away from the hospital.

And so, shortly after midnight, Seymour Hooker's crew descended on the Cayne encampment, like a band of renegade Indians, yelling and screaming, brandishing axe handles and baseball bats. Rooster, in the lead, was in his element.

He didn't catch on that anything was amiss until he skidded to a stop by the first bundle of blankets, and brought the axe handle whistling down. Expecting it to whack into a mass of flesh and bone, he almost lost his balance when the axe handle sank into something soft and struck the ground. With a grunt Rooster stripped away the top blanket.

It was empty, the damned bedroll was filled with nothing but another rolled-up blanket!

From the moment Dudley heard about Seymour Hooker being hospitalized, he had a strong premonition of pending trouble.

Amanda scoffed when he went to her with his fears. "Dudley, you're really something, you know that? I think you have some kind of a fixation about Seymour, I really do. Why on earth should he send his men around to jump us just because a truck ran him off the road?"

"The first thing he'll think is that it was me."

"But that happened a half-day's drive from here! You were here the night in question. I know that for a fact and I'll tell him so, if he thinks differently. I'll take time off tomorrow and drive up to visit him in the hospital."

He set his lips stubbornly. "He doesn't know that at present, and I'd be much surprised if he believed you anyway."

Amanda rolled her eyes in exasperation. "So what do you expect of me, Buster Brown? Go into town and tell the law? You know how that would go. They'd sneer at me. Townies want nothing to do with threshing crews. We're gypsies, on a level with carnies."

"You don't have to do anything, Amanda. Just stay in your tent until it's all over. If I'm right, you shouldn't be around, anyway. All I want is to have the men hide in wait tonight. We'll stuff their bedrolls so they'll seem occupied. When Hooker's crew shows up, we won't be caught with our pants down."

"*If* they show up. And if the men stay up all night, they'll be in fine shape to work tomorrow."

"They won't be up all night."

"They'll laugh at me, Dudley."

"Not you. I'll be giving the orders. If anyone looks the fool, it'll be me. I'm right, Amanda. I have this feeling!"

"Funny, Buster Brown," she said dryly. "I never knew you had a crystal ball."

Dudley's temper slipped. "If I'm wrong, you

won't have me around to annoy you any longer. I'll walk!"

"No, Dudley." She looked at him intently. "I don't want you to walk. I need you. You go ahead, do what you see fit." She touched his cheek with her fingers and walked away.

He watched her go away from him, her rare gesture of affection leaving him as soft and warm inside as a toasting marshmallow. He made an angry sound in his throat and turned away.

After supper he motioned everyone around him. "I'm expecting a visit tonight from Seymour Hooker's crew. To those of you who don't already know, Hooker was run off the highway last night by a hit-and-run driver. He's bunged up and in the hospital. If my hunch is right, he's going to lay the blame on us. You know the bad blood between our outfit and his . . ."

"If Hooker's got a hard-on for anybody, Dudley, it's you," said a voice from the rear of the group. "After that honky-tonk set-to the pair of you had."

It was dark and Dudley couldn't see who had spoken. A clamor of voices rose, telling whoever it was to shut up.

Jack Rollins said, "There's bad blood, we all know that. And even if it was just Dudley he's after, he's one of us. But there is something to consider, Dudley . . . they're a bunch of hardcases. They've got a bad rep up and down the wheat belt."

"But we outnumber them, and we'll have an advantage, if my plans works. They sneak in, expecting to catch us by surprise. But if we're laying for them, it'll be our surprise, not theirs. Now . . ." He paused , looking them over. "I'm not ordering you to take part. I only want volunteers, those of you willing to fight. Some of you will probably end up with a few bruises, maybe a broken nose or two."

Not a man backed off. In fact, when the idea finally took hold, they were all eager to have at the Hooker crew. Dudley armed them with whatever weapons he had at hand. There were more pitchforks than anything else.

One man hefted his pitchfork, the tines gleaming wickedly. He jabbed the air with it. "One of these rammed into a man's gut and he'll lose all taste for it."

"No," Dudley said sharply. "You could kill a man with that, certainly maim him for life. I don't want anyone seriously hurt. In the first place, you know how the town law looks upon us. A local sheriff would be delighted to arrest one of us for murder. So, just use the handle end."

Dudley concealed some of the men behind the threshers and the tractors, and some in the edge of the trees coming down to the field. He stationed himself behind a tractor wheel only a few yards from the rows of bedrolls. He surveyed the area with satisfaction. Extra blankets had been rolled up into the bedrolls, and it looked remarkably like men were occupying them.

He settled down to wait. It was a long wait, and as time dragged on, he began to think he

252

had been wrong. He had told the men to forego smoking, and to be as quiet as possible. From time to time he heard mutters of complaint. He ignored them, but he had to wonder how many of the men had dozed off.

Then he saw a shadowy form approaching the edge of the field nearest the highway. Then another and another. Suddenly going tense, Dudley waited.

Suddenly the man in the lead waved an axe handle over his head and loosed a rebel yell. The others echoed him.

Still Dudley waited, waited until the first figure—short, squatty, moving with a cocky strut reminiscent of Seymour Hooker—had reached the first bedroll and brought his axe handle down. When the man bent down to strip away the top blanket, Dudley jumped out into the open, waving his pitchfork high as a signal to his men.

He ran directly at the squatty man, dodged down low and to one side to avoid the swinging axe handle. All around him Dudley heard grunts, shouts, and the thumping sounds of wood against wood, as the two groups came together.

Coming up out of his crouch, he jabbed the short man in the belly with the pitchfork handle, then danced aside. Again, the axe handle swung at him. Dudley countered with the pitchfork. The shock of wood meeting wood jarred his arms all the way up to the elbows.

For a few minutes they danced in and out, sparring with the wooden implements. It reminded Dudley of swashbuckler movies he'd seen in which two men fought with cutlasses. He soon realized that he was at a disadvantage. He couldn't grip the pitchfork by the end, and therefore he couldn't get enough power into his swings, and also he was in constant danger of being pronged by the tines of his own weapon. About all he could do was parry the other's thrusts, and not very effectively. He was always on the defensive, and couldn't take the fight to his opponent.

Evidently the short man suddenly realized his advantage, for he began to press. Each time Dudley attempted to block the axe handle, the other knocked the pitchfork contemptuously aside and charged, yelling.

Dudley kept backing away, desperately seeking an opening. Then he found himself cornered, backed up against a tractor, pinned in between the two wheels. With a triumphant shout the other man brought the axe handle swishing down with such force that it knocked the pitchfork aside and a glancing blow landed on Dudley's shoulder, which immediately went numb.

He had to do something, or be pounded into the ground like a fence post.

He reversed the pitchfork and jabbed the prongs at his attacker, stopping inches from his chest.

The man halted, then backpedaled a few steps. "Hey now! That's no fair, you pissant! You could kill a man with that!"

"You should have thought of that before jumping us," Dudley said grimly.

He advanced, holding the shiny tines before him. The other man backed up again and Dudley kept coming. Suddenly he feinted a lunge at the man's face. His antagonist yelled in fright. He threw his hands up to shield his face, dropping the axe handle. He stumbled back, almost losing his balance.

Dudley brought the thick metal part of the pitchfork, where the tines fastened onto the wooden handle, against the back of the man's head with all his strength. The other grunted, stumbled a few steps, and fell forward on his face. Breathing hard, Dudley stood over him, ready to hit him again, but he didn't move. Dudley straightened up slowly and took his first good look around.

The fight was over, the Hooker men in full retreat. A few were out cold on the ground, and the others were being chased away.

Dudley saw Jack Rollins coming toward him.

Grinning, Rollins said, "It's all over but the shouting, Dudley."

"Any of ours badly hurt?"

"Don't think so. A few lumps and bruises, that seems to be about it." He looked down at the figure face down in the dirt. "Looks like you took good care of this one. Wonder who he is?" Rollins rolled him over with the toe of his boot, then struck a match, bending down. "Hey, I know this sucker! That's Rooster Cockrun, Hooker's top hand."

"Okay, Dudley," Amanda said from behind

them, "you can trot out the I-told-you-so's now."

Dudley faced around. Amanda stood looking down at the man on the ground, an arm under her breasts.

"You were right and I was wrong," she said. "I'm driving up to pay Seymour a little visit in the morning. I'll have a few choice words to say to him about this little business, you can bet your boots on that!"

17

"Amanda . . . sugar, I swear to you by God above . . ."

"I didn't think you believed in God."

". . . it wasn't my idea! That goddamned Rooster!" Seymour hit his forehead with his hand. "I'll kill the bugger, by God I will." He looked at Amanda pleadingly. "Sugar, you've got to believe me!"

He reached out for her hand, Amanda stepped back, and he fell back onto the bed with a groan.

"Why should I believe you, Seymour? Why should I believe *anything* you say? They were your men, Jack Rollins recognized the one called Rooster."

"I ain't denying that, but he did it on his own."

"How many times have you told me that your men do nothing but what you tell them?"

"This time they didn't. Rooster thought he was doing it for me, I'm sure, but by God he'll be sorry . . ." He broke off, staring past her. He sat up, motioning angrily. "Come in here, Rooster! Right now, you peckerwood!"

Rooster Cockrun, who had been about to enter the room, but had skidded to a stop at the sight of Amanda, came on inside hesitantly. He gave her a wide berth.

"Come on over here," Seymour growled.

"How you feeling this morning, boss?" Rooster asked brightly.

"Better than you, I bet." Seymour snorted laughter. "I understand you got your head bashed in last night, and no less than you deserve. Now you tell Miss Amanda here how that fracas came about, or I'll get out of this bed and stomp on you!"

"I don't know what you mean, boss." Rooster tried to look innocent and failed miserably.

"Don't put on the dumb act. Did *I* tell you to jump her crew? The truth now."

"No." Rooster sighed. "No, you didn't."

"Didn't I tell you I'd handle it my own way, that I didn't think it was this Graham peckerwood, or any of Amanda's crew?"

"You told me."

"Then the whole thing was your idea, right?"

"Right, boss. But I thought that somebody should do something."

Seymour motioned him quiet, looking at Amanda. "You see? What'd I tell you?"

"Why should I believe him, any more than you? You two could have cooked up this lie between you, for all I know."

"You sure are a hard woman to convince, sugar. Look . . . two things. First, I haven't seen Rooster since yesterday. Ask anybody in the hospital. No phone calls, either. Ask about

258

that, too. Second, if I had something like last night in mind, I'd've been in on it. You know me well enough to know," he grinned, "that I wouldn't miss a free-for-all like that for the world."

For the first time Amanda relaxed, even smiling slightly. "That, yes, I can understand. That's the Seymour I know. But then . . ." She frowned, motioning. "You're confined here to a hospital bed."

"But I would have postponed it, you see, until I was better able." He added hastily, "If I had something like that in mind, I mean."

"Okay, I suppose I believe you. But I don't know how many times I've said that these past few weeks, and I'm getting sick of saying it." She shook her head. "And I can just see myself trying to convince Dudley that those men weren't following your orders."

"Who gives a damn what that peckerwood believes?" Seymour said cheerfully. "As long as you do, sugar. That's the main thing."

"Well, no real damage was done. It would seem that your own men suffered the most. But that's because Dudley had the foresight . . ." She glared at Rooster Cockrun. "I hope you don't try that stunt again. For your information, Mr. Rooster, Dudley Graham couldn't have driven the truck that hit Seymour. He was in camp that night, a half-day's drive away."

"It won't happen again," Seymour hastened to assure her. "Rooster knows that I'll tear his arm off and beat him over the head with it. Right, Rooster?"

"Right, boss," said a chastened Rooster Cockrun. "I'd better run along now, see that the men don't fu . . . loaf off."

"Yeah, you do that, Rooster," Seymour said dryly. "I'll probably be back some time tomorrow. The doc promised to let me out of jail, if my noggin's all right."

Rooster ducked his head, mumbled something to Amanda, and hustled out of the room.

"I'll be going now, too, Seymour," Amanda said. "We're moving tonight and I have to be there."

"Don't run off, sugar. Stay and talk to me. A man gets lonesome in here, nobody to talk to." He pulled a mournful face, and tried to take her hand.

She stepped back, laughing. "I saw a couple of very pretty nurses down the hall. Wouldn't surprise me if you don't get one in that bed with you, if you haven't already."

"Amanda, I wouldn't be unfaithful to you. I'm not that kind of a guy," he said righteously.

She stared. "Unfaithful to me? To *me*? What's it to me if you are?"

"You can say that after all we've been to each other?"

"Seymour, you're incredible." She shook her head in wonder. "One moonlight romp on a blanket and now I'm your girl!"

"Well, ain't you?"

"I am not! I belong to no man. How many times do I have to say that to you?"

"You'll come around in time, sugar," Seymour said complacently. "I'm sure of it."

"Oh! You are an impossible man!" She started for the door, but paused in the doorway, looking back. She smiled slyly. "I'm sorry about your V-8, Seymour. That's going to put a crimp in your style, isn't it?"

"Always another where that one came from, Amanda," he yelled after her.

She hadn't been gone ten minutes when the telephone beside the bed rang. The hospital operator said, "There's a long-distance call for you, Mr. Hooker."

Seymour closed his eyes. "From Dallas?"

"Why, yes, how'd you know?" she said in a surprised voice.

"I'm a mind reader, honey. Put old J.C. on." Fallon sure did have a pipeline here. He likely knew about it, Seymour thought, before I even pulled myself out of the Ford!

In a moment the reedy voice of J.C. Fallon said in his ear, "Looks like you screwed up good, Hooker."

"It wasn't my fault, J.C. Some booger ran into me . . ."

"Don't matter. You're out of commission."

"Not for long, J.C.," Seymour said quickly. "The doc says I'll probably be out and running by tomorrow."

"That's not the main reason I'm calling. You made a last try at this Martin feller and came a cropper."

Seymour took the phone from his ear and stared at it in astonishment. This was by God too much! The phone to his mouth again, he said, "How could you know about that?"

261

That sound like dry leaves rustling came over the line. "That's for me to know and you to find out, Hooker. The point is, I'm right, ain't I?"

Seymour sighed. "Yeah, you're right, you hit it on the head. He's just too stubborn to reason with." Belatedly, in a flash of intuition, he realized that J.C. had probably been guessing, and now he'd just confirmed that guess. He tried to think back to all the other times when the old man had come up with startling insights. Had he always been fishing, waiting for me to open my big mouth? Seymour wondered. If so, that makes me some kind of a blabber-mouthed idiot!

He sat up straighter as he caught the thread of what J.C. was saying. "What was that you just said, J.C.?"

"I said . . . I reckon it's about time I took a more direct hand in things."

"How you going to do that?" Seymour asked, not really caring, as he realized with both relief and surprise that Fallon wasn't going to fire him.

"You just listen to what I have to say and you'll find out . . ."

Seymour listened with grudging admiration for the old fox. He interrupted once, "But that's going to cost, and it ain't going to be all that easy to do, J.C."

"If I change over all those wheat farmers to my combines, I'll come out way ahead, next year and the years after. And don't worry about my being able to swing it, Hooker. I got more clout than you ever knew. Now suppose you just shut up and listen."

Seymour shut up, and listened.

Thaddeus didn't hear about what was up until the week before the Cayne crew was due to arrive at his place. He was busy supervising the mowing and stacking, and keeping a worried eye on the weather. The weather was a critical factor from now on. Hail or rain could destroy the wheat in the shocks. Even a relatively mild rain would mean that the wheat would have to be spread out to dry, hopefully, and then shocked again.

But the weather held good—dry and hot—and the long-range forecast predicted no rain for the next week.

They had been working on the last section of his wheatland, and Thaddeus was reasonably satisfied. The only thing that could go wrong was if Amanda failed to arrive on time. A day late, even two or three days, wouldn't matter, but any longer than that could mean disaster. Disaster not only for Thaddeus but for many of his neighbors, those he'd been able to hold in line for Amanda's threshers. At the last report Amanda was pretty much on schedule, so it seemed likely she would make it.

The mowers and shockers stopped work at sundown. They would be able to finish up in three days at the outside. After they left, Thaddeus got into the pickup and drove back to the house. It was dusk now, and he was washing at the pump out back when he heard a car drive up. Shirtless, he toweled himself dry and walked around to the front of the house. His visitor was Bert Parker.

"Hello, Bert. How are you?"

"Fine, I guess, Thaddeus. The cutting about done?"

"Coming along. Another couple of days." Thaddeus wiped sweat from his face.

"Good. They're due at my place next. You heard from the Cayne bunch?"

"They're on schedule. They'll be here, Bert, don't fret it." Thaddeus took out his pipe and began to tamp tobacco into the bowl.

Bert Parker seemed unduly nervous, shifting from one foot to the other, and Thaddeus knew he had something else on his mind. Thaddeus didn't push him.

Finally Parker blurted, "You going to the Grange meeting tonight, Thaddeus?"

"What meeting is that, Bert? I knew nothing about any meeting."

"Well . . . I guess they didn't notify you, you not being a member of the Grange and all."

"You know I'm not a joiner." He snorted. "About all those meetings are good for is a lot of bellyaching, card and pool playing, and bootleg liquor." He peered at Parker closely. "What I can't understand is why you *think* I should be going, Bert. Like you say, I'm not a member."

"Well . . ." Parker cleared his throat, looking off. "Way I get it, the meeting's of interest to all us wheat farmers."

"That so?" Thaddeus said, interested in spite

264

of himself. "Now why should that be, you suppose?"

"I ain't sure, that's what has me worried. None of the farmers seem to know. I tried to talk to Jethro Carter. He's head of the Grange this year, you know."

"What did he say?"

"He just said it'd be in my best interest to be there, then clammed up."

"How'd they notify the Grange members, you know?"

"Oh, I got a little note in the mail, just saying there was a special meeting tonight, that was all it said. Thing that puzzles me," Parker was frowning, "is that I understand several farmers who ain't members of the Grange, like you, Thaddeus, also got notices."

A quiver, like a chill, went down Thaddeus's spine. He said slowly, "Now that *is* odd. They got notices and I didn't. Why is that, you suppose?"

Parker said eagerly, "Why not come along tonight, find out what it's about, Thaddeus?"

Thaddeus frowned at him. There it was again, the looking to him for guidance, for leadership. It was a role he had never sought and didn't want, yet it was always being thrust upon him.

"I'll think on it, Bert. Stay for a bite of supper?"

Bert Parker gave a start. "No, thanks, Thaddeus, the old lady is looking for me back. Sure hope you show up at the meeting tonight."

"We'll see," Thaddeus said curtly. "What time is the meeting supposed to start?"

"Eight sharp, I'm told. You go, you could ride in with me," Parker said hopefully.

Thaddeus just shook his head. Visibly disappointed, Parker got into his car and drove away.

Thaddeus already knew that he would be thoro; he sensed that something was up. The fact that he was the only farmer in this part of Kansas not invited made the whole thing suspect. But he didn't want to go with Bert Parker, and Bert was gossipy. If he knew Thaddeus was going, he'd broadcast it and Thaddeus wanted to sort of sneak in. There had to be a reason why he wasn't invited, and his showing up unexpectedly might rattle a few people.

The meeting of the local Grange was held in what had once been a saloon. Now it stood empty most of the time, except for the Grange meetings and an occasional meeting of the war veterans of the area. Aside from the fact that Thaddeus wasn't a joiner—in his opinion the things accomplished by men banding together, for whatever reason, were usually bad—he knew that bootleg liquor was sold on the premises and he certainly didn't approve of that.

The building was situated a half-mile out of town, sitting all alone, the nearest house several blocks away. It was a low, L-shaped structure, in need of paint, and had a large, graveled parking lot along one side. When Thaddeus drove into the lot a few minutes past eight, it was already filled with cars and trucks, and there were several horses tied off at the hitching rack behind the building.

The long section of the L was the meeting room—rows of folding chairs and a podium at the far end. There was a preacher's pulpit on the podium. The front door stood open, and Thaddeus was relieved to see that there was no one at the door. The room was two-thirds full, and the meeting was already in progress. Thaddeus was able to slip in unnoticed and he took a seat in a back row.

Jethro Carter, a middle-aged, balding man with a face that always reminded Thaddeus of a fox, stood at the pulpit. Carter had sold his farm earlier in the year and moved to town to open a feed store.

Spectacles perched on his short nose, Carter was reading from a sheet of paper. It took Thaddeus a few minutes to realize that it was some government bulletin telling of the need for terracing farmland to prevent the topsoil from blowing away in the dust storms.

The crowd was restless—scuffling feet, impatient coughs, neighbor whispering to neighbor. Clearly the men weren't interested in the bulletin.

"Aww, shit, Jethro," shouted a voice from the front. "You know we ain't interested in that stuff, we ain't in the Dust Bowl here. Whyn't you get down to the reason this meeting was called?"

Other voices rose in agreement. Jethro Carter stopped reading, peering over his glasses. "Well, if that's the feeling of all the members present . . ."

A clamor of voices sounded. As they quieted down again, a single voice said derisively, "And that goes for us nonmembers, too, Jethro!"

General laughter caused Jethro Carter to shift about uncomfortably, color rising to his face. He made batting motions with his hands. "It was thought that what was said here to-night would be of interest to *all* wheat growers, whether Grange members or not."

"Then what are *you* doing here, Jethro? You ain't a wheat farmer anymore. You sell cow shit for a living!"

The barbs were getting to Jethro Carter. Face a deep red now, he snapped, "I'm coming to that, if you're willing to listen, instead of mouthing off!"

"We'll listen, when you have something to say."

The man at the podium looked away from his tormentor and doggedly plowed ahead, "I would like to introduce Jim Perkins. As you know, many of the grain elevators in Kansas, especially in this area, are owned by Perkins Elevators, a company founded by Jim's grandfather." As a slender, well-dressed man of forty stood up, facing the audience, Jethro Carter said, "This here is Jim Perkins. He has a few words to say to you."

The introduction was greeted by a frigid silence, as though all the wheat farmers present sniffed bad tidings coming up.

Perkins took Carter's place at the pulpit.

Smiling pleasantly, he looked out at the up-turned faces. "I'm happy to be here, gentlemen. I'll be brief in what I have to say, so please give me your kind attention."

The silence still held, but it had a hostility now, a hostility almost visible.

Undaunted, Perkins's smile remained in place. "I'm sure that most, if not all, of you know that we in the grain-elevator business have long been unhappy with threshed wheat, preferring combined wheat. Combined wheat is superior, and makes superior product . . ."

"Says you!"

"That is what I say, yes, and I have been in the business all my adult life." The smile was wilting at the edges now. "But this opinion I do not hold alone. Others are of a like opinion."

"Why don't you get to the point, Perkins? We ain't much interested in your opinion. Give us the bad news. I'm sure you have some in store for us, else you wouldn't be up there spouting off."

"I'm afraid I do have some bad news, of a sort." Now the smile was gone, as though the speaker considered what he had to say next a matter of utmost gravity. "We have decided, at Perkins Elevators, to accept only combined wheat from this day forward . . ."

Angry voices interrupted him.

After a moment he held up his hand. "Please do me the courtesy of hearing me out. Now, you all know how low the price of wheat is this year. We simply cannot afford to handle an inferior product. We could even be stuck with it."

"Why'd you wait until this late in the season?"

"The decision was made just recently. And, I might add, the decision wasn't mine alone. We have a board of directors, you know."

"But we've already made arrangements for threshing! What are we supposed to do, if nobody'll take our wheat?"

"Ah, now that's the good news!" The smile was back. "Mr. Hooker, would you like to say a word?"

From the front row, Seymour Hooker bounced to his feet. "I surely would."

Smiling, at ease, he started toward the podium. As recognition swept through the meeting room, cries of indignation went up. Still smiling, Seymour stood at the pulpit, not fazed at all. He let the indignation run its course.

In his seat in the back, Thaddeus tightened up, anger swelling his neck. He forced himself to wait.

When relative quiet had descended once more, Seymour said, "I'd reckon most of you know me. Now I'm here to tell you that you got nothing in this whole wide world to worry about. If Perkins here wants combined wheat, that's what we'll give him! I can have another batch of combines up here on the next freight train. You have my promise on that. Your wheat'll be harvested. All you have to do is see me after the meeting and give me your names and the location of your farms . . ."

"But we've already made arrangements for

270

threshing! I sure as hell have, the Cayne crew is threshing my wheat!"

Other voices joined in, voicing the same protest.

Seymour waved his hands. "Way I get it, none of you signed anything. A verbal agreement ain't binding in court."

"We gave our word to Amos. Leastways, I did."

"Circumstances have changed. Poor Amos is laying up in a hospital bed down in Wichita Falls. His girl's running the show now. Seems to me that changes things around." Seymour was solemn now. "Times are hard, you all know that. A man has to look after himself first, look after his wife and kids. You heard Mr. Perkins. What are you going to do, let your wheat rot and blow away?"

Thaddeus stood up. "I'd like to ask a question." His voice carried like a trumpet call, and heads swiveled in his direction. A murmur came from the crowd.

After a flash of astonishment at Thaddeus's presence, Seymour's face became as expressionless as a wiped slate. He said, "Ask away, Thaddeus."

"The question is for Mr. Perkins . . . who's behind this move of yours, Mr. Perkins?"

At the sound of his name, Jim Perkins, sitting on a folding chair behind Seymour, started. He got to his feet and came forward uncertainly. "Who are you, sir? I don't think I . . ."

"Thaddeus Martin."

"Ah yes, Mr. Martin! I've heard of you. It's a pleasure to finally meet you."

"More of a surprise, I'd imagine, since I wasn't supposed to be here tonight. Wasn't even supposed to know about this meeting."

"Oh, I'm sure that was just an oversight on somebody's part, Mr. Martin."

"I'm sure, and I think I know who," Thaddeus said dryly. "Could I have an answer to my question, please? Who is behind this?"

"Weren't you here, Mr. Martin? I've explained that our board . . ."

Thaddeus made an impatient motion. "You think we're fools here? Your company, no company, would make such a drastic change at this time of the year. Look at the ill will it's going to cause, or don't you care?"

"Of course we care, but there's no cause for ill will," Perkins said huffily. "No one will suffer for it."

"How about Amanda Cayne? Won't she suffer? And there are other threshing crews. This puts them out of business, too, as I'm sure you're aware."

"Have to move with the times, Thaddeus," Seymour interjected. "This had to happen some time."

Thaddeus eyed him angrily. "Who asked you to stick your oar in?"

Seymour flushed. "Now see here, I didn't come here to be insulted!"

"Just why *did* you come here, Hooker? You must have known about this beforehand."

"Well . . . yeah, sure, I knew." Seymour

moved his shoulders, as though his shirt was suddenly too tight. "They were nice enough not to want anybody hurt by this. So they came to me to make sure I could handle the extra wheat."

"You sure it wasn't the other way around?"

Seymour's gaze sharpened. "Now what do you mean by that crack?"

"What I mean is this . . . I don't think they'd make a decision like this so sudden without some kind of heavy pressure. I think you supplied that pressure, Hooker."

"Now see here, Martin," Perkins blustered. "Our company doesn't bend to pressure . . ."

Seymour cut him off. "Let him spit it out." His eyes were dancing, and he was grinning broadly. "You flatter me, Thaddeus, you purely do, thinking that I've got that kind of clout."

"Oh, not you personally. But J.C. Fallon has." Thaddeus saw the smile die, and he knew he'd hit on the truth. "They don't call him Jesus Christ for nothing. He came to you, didn't he, Mr. Perkins? Or called on the phone. I understand he never leaves that house of his in Dallas. He must've come down on you pretty hard. But then he's known for that. What did he do, threaten to force you out of business if you didn't go along? Scared the pee-wadding out of you, did he?"

Perkins's small mouth opened and closed in a rapidly paling face. "Now see here, mister! Nobody can accuse me of taking orders from this Fallon, whoever he is!"

"Oh, you know who he is, all right," Thaddeus said calmly. "Everybody has heard of J.C. Fallon. That shows you're lying through your teeth right there, denying any knowledge of him."

Equally calm, Seymour said, "You have no proof of any of this, Thaddeus. Wouldn't matter a hell of a lot, anyway. You heard what the man said. He's no longer going to accept threshed wheat. Nothing you can do about it now."

"Now that's where you're wrong, Hooker. Perkins doesn't own every grain elevator in the country. There're others in Nebraska, up in South Dakota. I'm sure they'd be glad to take our wheat."

Seymour squinted at him. "That's a hell of a long haul, cost more than your damn wheat is worth, so what good will they do you?"

"There's always a way." Beginning to enjoy himself now, Thaddeus crossed his arms over his chest. "There are a lot of trucks standing idle nowadays. I'm sure the truckers would jump at the chance to haul our wheat. I don't think even J.C. Fallon can scare them all off."

"Man, don't you listen?" Seymour glared at him. "That'll cost you more than the wheat's worth!"

"In money, perhaps, but the satisfaction of beating you and Fallon will be well worth it."

Seymour stared at him a moment longer, then shrugged. "Okay, if you're that much of a damned fool, go ahead. Keep your precious word to Amanda and lose your ass." He grinned unpleasantly. "Maybe you can afford such a stunt, Thaddeus, but the others here can't. They need to show a profit to make ends meet."

"I think they can afford it all right, since it won't cost them a red cent. If they don't go back on their word to Amanda and the other threshermen, I'll see that their wheat is hauled for nothing." He raised his voice. "You all have the word of Thaddeus Martin on that."

Scattered applause broke out, and then the men were on their feet, applauding and cheering lustily.

Seymour stood glaring down at them. A voice rose above the din, "So take your damned lawn mowers and stuff 'em, Hooker!"

Seymour flushed a dark red at this ultimate insult—calling his combines "lawn mowers." Thaddeus grinned at Hooker's discomfiture. He'd had no such a quixotic gesture in mind when he'd come here tonight, but it had seemed the right thing to do, even though he knew it would cost him the profit from his wheat crop, and much more. He could afford it. The years of bumper crops and frugal living had made him relatively well-to-do, even in depression times. What else could he do with it, now that Martha was gone? He had no living relatives to inherit. If it would help his neighbors, and Amanda, it would be worth it.

Of course, he thought as he locked stares with Seymour Hooker, the greatest satisfaction came from thwarting this man. He was a little puzzled by that; he could remember few times in his life when he had felt such rancor toward a fellow human being. This feeling toward Hooker was of recent origin, which made it even more puzzling.

Sadly, he realized that many of those cheering him now were doing it out of respect for his generous gesture, since their wheat was already slated to be harvested by Hooker's combines anyway, and several of the others, Thaddeus suspected, would back off once their initial enthusiasm cooled, and go over to Hooker's combines. Yet a few of them might take him up on the offer.

But even a few would mean a victory, and even if *he* was the only one sticking with Amanda's threshers, it would still be a victory, for he knew without vanity that his acreage would be a prize plum for Hooker's combines. Quite likely, he was the prime target of this whole shabby trick.

He was pleasantly surprised when the wheat ranchers began flocking around, assuring him of their gratitude, and promising full cooperation.

All at once, Thaddeus noticed that the men on the outer edge of the semicircle before him were falling quiet, and then they parted. Seymour Hooker came striding up, like Moses through the parting of the Red Sea.

Hooker skidded to a stop, and thrust his angry face forward. "You're a turdhead, Thaddeus Martin, an ornery turdhead!" he shouted. "And you're letting that split-tail lead you around by the nose!"

Thaddeus's anger burst through all restraints, and without warning he lashed out with his fist, striking Seymour squarely on the nose. Seymour reeled back, blood squirting.

His hand came up, touching his nose. He looked at the smear of blood on his hand and roared, "Why, you pissant!"

He charged, the crowd moving hastily back out of the way, forming a rough-edged square. Thaddeus was waiting, his hands doubled into fists. They came together, fists striking like hammer blows. Cries of encouragement sounded around them, with by far the most cheering for Thaddeus.

They stood toe-to-toe, slugging it out, no finesse, no ducking or dodging, each absorbing the punishing blows and retaliating in kind. For the first time in his life Thaddeus took joy in fighting. It seemed to him that bitterness and frustration had been festering in him for days, and each blow landed let a little of it escape.

And he was invincible, he knew it in his heart of hearts. Seymour was younger, certainly a more seasoned brawler, but at this moment in time Thaddeus was unbeatable. He had the strength of ten, for right was on his side!

Martha's voice, a distant hooting sound, echoed in his head: "And who decided that you are right, Thad? God Almighty?"

Thaddeus snorted laughter and waded in, through a barrage of hard blows from Seymour's hammering fists. He connected with a solid right, all of his weight behind it, high on Seymour's cheek.

The blow sent Seymour stumbling back. He fell, knocking over several of the wooden folding chairs. They splintered like kindling under his weight. Still conscious, he blinked up at Thaddeus towering over him. He grinned crookedly, tried to get up, and fell back again.

A look of awe in his eyes, he mumbled through a split lip, "Sumbitch, you whipped me! You whipped me good!"

Some of the tension leaving him, Thaddeus said, "I want to hear you say you're sorry for what you said about Amanda!"

Seymour blinked again. "What? What are you talking about, Thaddeus?"

"What you called Amanda when you said she was leading me around by the nose."

"Oh, that! Hell, I didn't mean anything by that. Okay, okay, I'm sorry! I take it back. You satisfied now?"

Thaddeus relaxed, already feeling shame, about letting his temper rule him like that. What would these men, his friends and neighbors, men who looked to him for leadership, think of him brawling like a Saturday night honky-tonker? He looked around at the faces and saw only admiration, and that made the shame even worse.

He looked at the man on the floor. "I'll only be satisfied when you're out of Kansas, and I'm quit of your dirty tricks to get my wheat for your combines."

"Thaddeus, let me tell you something, something that just came to me clear as can be."

Seymour took a deep breath, wincing. "You can take your fucking wheat and burn it, for all of me. I no longer give a good goddamn. Now put that in that pipe of yours and smoke it!"

18

The wheezing cackle of laughter coming over the phone all the way from Dallas prompted Seymour to take the receiver away from his ear and stare at it. He couldn't credit his hearing.

He finally returned it to his ear. "J.C.?"

The laughter came to a stop, and some of the old sandpaper rasp was back in the voice. "What is it, Hooker?"

"So, where are we now?"

"We're nowhere, that's where. He's beat us, has this Martin feller."

Seymour held his breath, waiting for the axe to fall.

Again, the wheeze of laughter sounded. "I purely admire a man who can beat me."

"I'm sorry, J.C. I did every damned thing I could."

"I know that, so stop whining, man!"

"I'm not whining, goddamnit!" Seymour snarled. "Why should I whine? I'm fired anyway."

"Who says?"

"You did. You told me if I didn't get Thaddeus's wheat for the combines, I was through."

"That's what business people call giving your employees initiative." The wheeze of laughter again, softer now, as though Fallon's quota of laughter was used up for the year. "Cheaper than paying a bonus."

"Then we just give up on Thaddeus Martin?"

"I was never one to waste my time beating on a dead horse, even one that balked on me. This Martin feller is a dead horse, far as I'm concerned. Go ahead with the elevator scheme, try to get as many of the wheat ranchers to go along as you can. We have to look ahead to next season now. If we get enough of them to switch to combines, there won't be enough left to pay the Cayne outfit to take their threshers out next year. Nor the other threshermen, neither. Then this Martin feller won't have any choice but to swing over to us."

"Makes sense," Seymour said. Then a thought came to him. "Course, knowing Thaddeus, I wouldn't put it past him to buy his own combines."

"You think he'd go to that expense?"

"It's possible. He's a stubborn coot. This offer of his to truck his wheat, and that of the others, out of the state to other elevators is going to cost him a bundle. Besides, with all the wheat he grows, it might not be a bad investment, him buying his own combines."

"Let him. I can't hardly lose either way, so long as he buys his combines from a factory I own stock in."

Seymour had to smile. The old fox had it figured four ways from Sunday. Keeping any levity out of his voice, he said, "Okay, J.C., I'll proceed along those lines."

"You do that, Hooker." Again, the dry chuckle. "And next time, pick on some booger more your own size. Beat up on you pretty good, didn't he?" Bang went the phone on the other end.

Seymour stared at the phone a moment before hanging up. The sly old bastard! Nothing slipped past him.

Wincing from the bruises Thaddeus had left on him, Seymour left the filling-station building, stopping just outside to glare at the battered pickup squatting at the lone gas pump.

Walking over to the pop cooler, he thought of the night before. If he hadn't still been banged up from the accident, Thaddeus wouldn't have been able to beat up on him so easily, make no mistake about that!

He laughed aloud suddenly. Making excuses, are you, Seymour? Don't want to admit that old Thaddeus is better with his dukes? Goddamnit, he *was* making excuses!

Still grinning, he popped the top from a cold bottle of Nehi and swallowed half of it in a gulp. His glance strayed again to the pickup, and the scowl came back. Since the V-8 had been wrecked, he'd been driving around in the pickup, a utility vehicle.

What the hell! It looked like he wasn't going to be fired, so why not buy a new V-8?

The thought brightened his day. He finished the Nehi, and walked over to the pickup with a jaunty step. Paying the pimply youth for the gas and bottle of Nehi, he rattled away in the pickup. On his way back to where his combines were working, he had to pass close to Amanda's threshers, so he decided to detour by and see her.

It was nearing sundown when he reached the field where the threshers were. He parked the pickup and climbed out unnoticed, reflecting wryly that they always knew when Seymour Hooker had arrived by the sound of his V-8. He lit a cigar and started to lean against the fender, then winced, straightening up. The metal of the fender was like a roaring stovetop, the heat coming right through his trousers.

It was hot, damned hot. Good wheat-harvesting weather. It was also very dry; he shuddered to think what a chance fire could do to a wheat field right now.

The air was as still as a mirror, the chaff spuming out of the threshers and falling on the men working around them. Most of them had their shirts off, the chaff sticking to their sweaty hides like blown confetti. The thought of that chaff working down into their trousers made Seymour itch all over. Combines produced chaff, true, but they were in constant motion, moving ahead of most of it, unless there was a strong, following wind, whereas the threshers were stationary. What a hot, backbreaking, itchy job it was working around threshers! Why would a man do it? The answer was obvious—these days a job was a job, and thank the good Lord you had one!

He saw that Amanda had spotted him and

was heading in his direction. Dudley Graham, busy with a tractor motor, also saw Seymour, and he hastened after Amanda. Like a tail-wagging puppy dog trotting after its master, Seymour thought.

"Hi, sugar. How you?"

"Don't hi me, Seymour Hooker!" She stood with arms akimbo, eyes smouldering. "I heard what happened at that Grange meeting last night!"

"So, you heard." He shrugged. "Since it was a public meeting, I figured everybody would know." He grinned crookedly. "You can't say I went at it underhandedly, now can you?"

Dudley Graham arrived in time to hear the last remark. "Well, *I* think it was underhanded."

"Nobody asked what you thought, peckerwood," Seymour said in a flinty voice. "This is a private conversation between me and Amanda, so butt out."

"You going to make me?"

"It'd be my pleasure." Seymour took a step toward him.

"Now stop it, you two!" Amanda placed a restraining hand on Dudley's arm. "Why must the pair of you act like two kids whenever you get together?"

"Talk to your boy about that, sugar. I didn't invite him over."

"I should think you'd had enough of fighting." A glint of malice showed in her eyes. "I understand Thaddeus got the better of you last night."

Seymour smiled. "Yup. Old Thaddeus beat up on me pretty good."

"Well, I don't approve of fighting, but it was no more than you deserved."

"Now why do you say that, Amanda?" he said in an aggrieved voice. "Nothing dirty done, just good business practice."

"You call it good business practice when you and J.C. Fallon lean on those elevator owners and force them to do what you want?"

Seymour didn't blink. "Yup, that's what I call it. What do you call it, sugar?"

"Why, I . . ." She broke off, seemingly at a loss for words.

"I'll tell you what I call it," Dudley said harshly. "I call it dirty pool, scaring all those wheat farmers into turning their backs on Amanda."

"Shit! What do you know about pool, peckerwood?" Seymour eyed him balefully. "Only a real man goes into a pool hall. They wouldn't let a prissy-pants pissant like you in the place."

Dudley went red, but before he could speak Seymour switched his attention back to Amanda. "You know who's going to be hurt by all this? Thaddeus, that's who. It's going to cost him dear to hire all those trucks. The other wheat farmers, they won't suffer any."

"I thought it was a fine gesture on his part," she said stiffly.

"A fine gesture, huh? If you admire old Thaddeus as a Good Samaritan, whyn't you follow his example and call it quits, Amanda? Then Thaddeus wouldn't be hurt, only you, and you're going to give up the ghost sooner or later, anyway."

Her head went back. "You'd like to see me do that, wouldn't you?"

"Hell, yes. It'd make things simpler all around."

"Well, I have a flash for you, Seymour. I'm not going to. In fact . . . " She crossed an arm under her breasts, propping her chin. "I got a phone call from Thaddeus just awhile ago. He made me promise not to quit."

"Well . . . I reckon that covers it then." He shrugged, grinning. "Now that that's settled, whyn't I take you out to supper, sugar?"

She stared at him, then burst out laughing. "I declare, Seymour, you are a caution, do you know that?"

"Wouldn't have it any other way. But you didn't answer my question. You going to have supper with me or not?"

Still laughing, she gasped out, "Okay, I suppose I might as well. What do I have to lose?"

A strangled sound came from Dudley Graham. "You're going on a date with him, after what he's done?"

"I don't know about a date," Amanda said, "but I'm hungry, and I'm sick and tired of cook-wagon food."

"Jesus, I can't believe this, I really can't! What does he have to do, Amanda, before you stop going out with him? Kill somebody?"

"Now you watch it, Buster Brown." Her eyes blazed. "My personal life is not your concern."

Seymour grinned. "You heard the lady, peckerwood. So why don't you buzz off?"

He doubted that the man even heard him. Dudley was glaring at Amanda, so steamed that Seymour expected to see smoke coming out of his ears any second. "You make me sick, this bastard here makes me sick, and I've had it with both of you!" He spun on his heel and stomped off.

He was only a few yards away when a loaded grain truck started away at a crawl from one of the threshers. Dudley shouted and broke into a run. They watched as he ran alongside the truck, opened the door, swung up onto the running board and inside.

"Oh, shit!" Amanda said in a low voice. "Looks like I've lost him for sure this time, and I'll never find another man as good around machinery as he is."

Seymour was laughing. "Don't fret it, sugar. If he up and quit on you, I'll send one of my guys over. He's good with motors."

Her head swung around. "Good at what? Putting gravel in gears, maybe?"

"Naw. I swear to you, Amanda, I wasn't behind that." He held up both hands, palms out. "Scout's honor!"

"Honor!" she scoffed. "I'll bet you can't even spell the word." But amusement tugged at her lips.

"How soon can you be ready to go to supper?"

"Just as soon as I wash up and change into something decent. Okay?"

"Fine! Since I ain't far away, I'll run over and make a quick change as well." His grin was lopsided. "Can't take my best girl out to supper looking like a tramp, now can I?"

Dudley was, in truth, as angry as he'd ever been in his life—as mad at himself as he was at Amanda and Hooker. He must really be a glutton for punishment, he thought, taking all that guff Amanda gave him and hanging around for more. But what really galled him was the fact that Seymour Hooker was an unabashed reprobate, would always be one, and Amanda knew it by this time. What with the things he'd done lately, she *had* to know it!

Yet, what did she do? Hooker came strutting around, she scolded him, then ended up not only laughing at his dirty tricks, but going out with him!

Well, this time he was through! He'd be better off on the road, scrounging a meal when and where he could get it, instead of sticking with her, panting around her like a puppy, wading in crap up to his knees.

So he was in love with her. For the first time in his life he was in love with a woman, but it didn't seem worth it. Besides, even if he stuck it out, it would come to nothing. At the end of the season she'd kiss him off anyway: "So long, Buster Brown, see you next year." He probably wouldn't even be able to come back next year, because the way things were going there'd be no next season, not for the Cayne threshing crew . . .

He gave a start, turning his head toward the truck driver. "I beg your pardon? I wasn't listening. What did you just say?"

The driver grinned slyly. "From what I hear, I'd say I won't be hauling any more grain for you people."

"Now what makes you say that?"

"Well, the way I get it, the elevators have stopped taking threshed wheat. I'm told they're only taking this farmer's crop 'cause he'd already started threshing, and they didn't want to see him lose his ass."

"Big-hearted, aren't they?"

"Huh?" The man's mouth gaped. "Don't jump on me, Mac, I'm only repeating what I heard."

"Gossip, you mean? Your business is driving this truck. Why don't you stick to it, and leave the gossip to women over their backyard clotheslines?" Dudley said nastily. But he was feeling nasty, and the guy across the seat from him was the only one handy.

The driver touched his brakes and the truck slowed jerkily. "I don't have to take that kind of talk from you!"

"That's right, you don't." Out of the corner of his eye, Dudley noticed that they were on the outskirts of town. He also noticed something else in passing—a canvas banner strung across the front of a long, low, wooden building with the words, *Annie's Place*, in a big, gaudy splash of letters. "So why don't you just let me out here?"

"That's just what I'm going to do. And don't

think I won't have a word with Amanda Cayne about you mouthing off like this when I get back."

"You do that, buddy. I'm sure she'll be delighted to hear it," Dudley said, and hopped down out of the truck before it came to a full stop.

It was dusk now, and the lights came on outside the honky-tonk as he approached it. But it was still dim inside as he poked his head in. He went on in, blinking, trying to adjust to the dimness. It was steamy, the heat of the day still trapped inside, and the stench of spilled whiskey and beer was powerful.

"Hey, you sweet thing!" a voice bellowed, and Annie swooped down on him, folding him in a tight embrace.

Grinning, all his troubles shoved aside for the moment, Dudley rested on the yielding cushion of her ample breasts. Annie Mae Delong smelled of talcum powder, gin, and a musky perfume evocative of sex.

Now she stood back from him, beaming. "Am I glad to set eyes on you, sweetness," the big woman said. "Whooee, am I ever! I was hoping I'd see you while I was in this tank town. We got us some reacquainting to do, Dudley." She leaned in to kiss him, lips open and wet. "How you been, hon?"

Dudley felt a foolish grin stretch his face. "Fine, Annie. And you?"

"I'm fine, now that I see you. I've missed you, Dudley. Most of the men I see through these parts are as crude as a cow barn. Hey!"

She looked alarmed. "I hope you've got the rest of the night free?"

His foolish grin broadened. "I'm all yours, Annie."

She whooped with laughter. "Now that's what I like to hear!" Her voice dropped to a conspiratorial rumble. "There's no sleeping quarters in this dump, but I've got a comfortable tourist cabin on the edge of town."

Dudley felt his face burn and he thought, *Damnit, I'm blushing!*

Annie laughed, giving him a bawdy wink. "That okay with you, hon?"

"Sure," he mumbled. "Sounds great."

"I don't have to be on here till eight. I'm only here now to see that my piano is placed in the right spot. I'll just be a sec. Whyn't you have a beer, and we'll be on our way in a jiffy. I have some good gin in my cabin." She faced around, and bellowed at the two men pushing a piano onto the small platform at the end of the room. "Hey, you two birds! Careful with that. It's a musical instrument, for God's sake, not a boxcar you're shoving around!"

While Annie dealt with the piano movers, Dudley crossed to the empty bar and ordered a bottle of 3.2 beer. He built a cigarette and smoked it between sips to kill the awful taste of the beer. Someone had once said, he couldn't recall who, that 3.2 beer tasted like cold cow piss, which made it even worse than *warm* cow piss.

In her bouncy stride, breasts in full motion, Annie came toward him. "We can hightail it now. Hey, Joe," she said to the lone bartender, "how about a block of ice? That place I'm stay-ing in never heard of ice. Throw in an ice pick, too. That's a good guy."

With Dudley toting a block of ice in a tow sack, they left the honky-tonk and went outside to the parking lot, where a two-year-old Buick, hearse-black and square as a box, was parked.

His face must have mirrored his surprise, for Annie laughed and bounced her knuckles lightly off his shoulder. "I do pretty good for an old, knockabout broad, Dudley. Paid cash for it, too."

She didn't offer to let him drive. She got be-hind the wheel and drove with complete disre-gard for other vehicles or pedestrians, talking constantly. By the time they had reached the tourist court on the other side of town, the soles of Dudley's feet were numb from trying to push his feet through the floorboards. She turned the Buick into a parking stall between two cabins, crunched into the back of the wooden stall, and was out of the car before it had stopped vibrating.

Dudley, sack of ice over his shoulder, fol-lowed her into the cabin. It was a typical tour-ist cabin—a single room, with a high chest of drawers, a bed, a washbasin, and a toilet bowl and tin-lined shower stall behind an oilcloth curtain. Suitcases stood open and clothes were strewn on the floor, the two chairs, the bed, and hanging on every available protuberance.

The one small window was open as far as it would go, but the heat inside the room was un-pleasant, even with the sun down.

Annie said, "Whew! It's hot in here! Dump the ice into the washbasin, chip us enough off for drinks, then hang the sack and the rest of the ice over the window. That might cool it off a little." She grinned. "At least until we get enough gin in us so we won't notice the heat."

Dudley did as instructed, using the ice pick to break up the twenty-five-pound block of ice. The larger chunks he crammed back into the tow sack, then hung the sack across the curtain rod of the window. What little breeze could be felt was hot, but he noticed that it was cooled slightly by the time it had filtered through the sack.

Before he was finished, Annie had made two drinks for them and was on the bed, pillows behind her back. She had rolled her stockings down below the knees and had her legs drawn up. Her skirt was bunched up in her lap and Dudley blinked at the display of splendid thigh.

Annie gave her bawdy laugh and raised the water glass. "Yours is on the bureau, Dudley."

Dudley, his back to her, grimaced when he saw the drink she'd made. It was orange gin, a drink he hated. But at least it was cold, the glass already beaded. He sat down in one of the room's two chairs, gaze carefully averted from Annie's exposed thighs.

She hoisted her glass again. "Here's to all the good things in life, Dudley. Good booze, good sack-time, whatever."

"I'll drink to that," he mumbled, and drank, gamely swallowing the vile-tasting gin. He knew from experience that, if he got past the first few sips without throwing up, he wouldn't be bothered much by the taste after that.

"I haven't seen anything of the stud lately," Annie said.

"The stud?"

"Seymour Hooker. Haven't seen hide nor hair of him since the night he whomped on you."

Dudley grunted. "He's been busy as a little beaver, maybe that's the reason."

"How's that?" Annie asked interestedly.

Dudley gulped at the gin and gave her an abbreviated, but highly colorful, account of Seymour Hooker's activities.

Annie chuckled. "He *has* been a busy little feller, ain't he?"

"It's not funny!" Dudley said explosively. "He's a son-of-a-bitch, capable of just about every dirty trick in the book."

"Oh, he's not a bad guy, old Seymour. I know, I know. You have reason to dislike him, not the least of which was his beating on you. Here, fix me another snort, will you?"

Dudley took her glass and made them two more orange gins. The taste wasn't so bad now, and the heat of the alcohol in his bloodstream was making him break out in a sweat, yet it wasn't an unpleasant feeling.

Accepting her drink, Annie said, "You have to understand about Seymour. I've known him . . . what? A long time, back before he got into this wheat business, back when he was still working in the oil fields. Seymour has to win,

295

you see, at everything he does. But in that he's not much different from most men. Come on, Dudley, fess up now." She grinned. "Wouldn't you feel better about it if you had licked him that night?"

In lieu of a direct answer, Dudley made a growling sound.

Annie laughed. "Course you would have, it's the nature of the male beast. To show you got balls, you have to win, right? At whatever you do?"

"You're the one talking."

"That's right, I am." She took a pull of her drink. "First time I saw Seymour was in a roadhouse outside of Odessa, down in West Texas. He came stomping in, stinking of oil, proceeded to get roaring drunk, and took on not one but two cowpokes. He whapped their butts, then took me home and proved what a stud he was . . ."

It suddenly occurred to Dudley that Annie was Hooker's woman. What was he doing taking that bastard's leavings?

Reading him as easily as a newspaper, Annie leaned forward. "Don't go getting your dander up, sweetness. I'm not Seymour's woman anyute. Seymour hadn't been in bed with me since I like ballsy men, but not one who has to go around proving he's king of the hill every minute. Seymour hadn't been in bed with me since weeks before I met you. That's his trouble, you see. He's so busy winning, by hook or crook, proving he's best at everything, that he's got little time or patience for anything else." She chuckled. "The hell of it is, he *is* just about the best at anything he takes on . . . except being human. There, he falls down. A woman likes a little consideration in her man." She looked at him, her features softening. "That's where you've got it over Seymour, Dudley, four ways from Sunday."

Dudley was warmed by her words, and at the same time inexplicably embarrassed.

She finished her drink, set the glass on the floor and beckoned. "Come here, sweet thing. I'm ready for some of your special brand of consideration."

He went to her, speechless, tongue thick in his mouth. She reached up and looped her arms around his neck. They kissed that way, Dudley still on his feet, weight supported by his hands flat on the bed. Annie worked her tongue into his mouth. She unbuttoned his trousers and took out his stiffening cock. She ran her thumb back and forth across the head. Dudley groaned with pleasure.

She tore her mouth away from his. "Yes, oh yes! In me! Do, do!"

She flipped her skirt up above her waist, and drew up her knees. She wasn't wearing panties. The thicket of pale blonde pubic hair was the most luxuriant he had ever seen.

She tugged at him, and he was inside her easily, already pumping, without any thought of getting out of his trousers. Annie lay with her head turned aside, eyes clenched shut, only her hips moving, rising and falling in counterpoint to his quickening rhythm. The slapping noise their flesh made as they clashed together was the most exciting sound Dudley had ever heard.

"Now?" she said hoarsely. "I'm about there."

"Yes!"

Her body convulsed and she shouted out her pleasure.

They held onto each other tightly, until the spasms had subsided. Then Annie raised her head and laughed. Dudley drew back from her and winced, when his now-limp organ was pinched in his unbuttoned fly.

"Why don't you shuck your clothes and get comfortable, Dudley? We may be here awhile. I don't have to show up at the place for a spell yet."

Dudley leaned on the bar, smoking a hand-rolled cigarette, as the clapping from the sparse crowd died. At the piano Annie was giving her last performance of the night.

Dudley was pleasantly tired from the matinee duet they had performed in Annie's cabin, and he was still lightheaded from sex and all the orange gin he had consumed.

At the piano Annie said, "This next little number is my last song for the night, gents." She winked at Dudley over the heads of the crowd. "It's a special song, for a very special guy."

The number was "Honky-Tonk Woman," which was becoming Annie's theme song, but Dudley, who ordinarily didn't care all that much for country songs, listened with a smile.

Yes, I can hear them whisper.
I see their secret eyes.
They hold their husband's arm
when I walk by.
It hurts me so to see them,
Why can't they realize,
The past is gone, why can't they
let it die?

I was a honky-tonk woman,
No better than I should be.
I layed around, and played around,
My life was wild and free.
I was a honky-tonk woman,
Yes, I led me a real wild life.
But that was before you asked me
to be your wife.

Someday they may be sorry,
They treated me this way,
For who can say just what their life
will be?
And if they ever falter,
Or ever go astray,
They might be treated like they're
treating me.

I was a honky-tonk woman,
No better than I should be.
I layed around, and played around,
My life was wild and free.
I was a honky-tonk woman,
Yes, I led me a real wild life.

But that was before you asked
me to be your wife.

The applause was more generous this time.
Dudley clapped his own hands vigorously, and
there were calls for an encore.

Smiling, Annie batted her hands at the
crowd. "It's late, near closing time. I know you
all have to work tomorrow, and me, I've been
working the night away. Now it's time for me
to have some fun with my guy." That familiar
bawdy grin flashed. "You wouldn't deny a gal
some fun of her own, now would you?"

Ribald remarks bombarded her:

"Let me give you some fun, Annie!"

"Let me give you some of *this*!"

"Whoo, such a time I could give you, doll
baby!"

"You ain't seen nothing yet, Annie, till you've
seen me in action!"

Annie's smile was good-natured. "Now ain't
that nice of you gents, offering like that. But
I'm spoken for tonight. Tell you what, whyn't
you all offer tomorrow night? Never can tell, I
just might take you up on it."

With a wave and a swish of hip, Annie
crossed the room to Dudley. Hooking her arm
in his, she whispered in his ear, "And if I did
offer to take 'em up on it, most would run like
scalded rabbits!"

Outside, she hugged his arm to her breast.
"Tonight, you're my guy, sweetness, and we're
going to have ourselves a high old time. But
come morning . . ." Her voice hardened. "In

the morning you're going back to your threshing crew. Despite what you told me, I know it's
what you want to do."

Laughing, he said, "That's not what you told
me once. You told me you'd be happy to have
me stick around."

"That was before."

"Before what, Annie?"

"Before I knew you very well. Then you were
just another guy to warm my bed. Now you're
a guy I like, and it's not my way to try to
change a man from what he is to what he
ain't."

19

The tempo of the work stepped up now. They had three more small farms to harvest before the Martin place, where they were due in five days. Amanda was determined to make up as much of the lost time as possible.

She drove the crew hard, getting as much work out of them as she could, but drove herself even harder. When grumbling began to surface, she faced it during a noon hour, hands on hips, ready to blast the men. But she changed her mind before the first words were uttered, and said instead, "I know I'm pushing you hard. But I'm also pushing myself . . ." She ran the fingers of one hand through sweat-matted hair. How long had it been since she'd washed it?

She pushed the distracting thought out of her mind and swept on, "All I ask is that we try to make up as much of the lost time as we can. If we get to Thaddeus's place only two days behind schedule and thresh his wheat okay, I'll cough up a bonus for each and every one of you."

She was amazed at the words spilling out of

her mouth. A *bonus*? She'd be lucky to have enough money to pay their wages from week to week, never mind any bonus!

A voice jeered, "How much bonus, Miss Amanda? Six bits? That's about all you can afford!"

Amanda focused on them, gaze jumping from face to face. "What smart Skeezix said that?" No one answered or altered his expression under her searching glance. Her resolve firmed up. "What ever else I may do, I don't make empty promises!" I'll come up with it some way, she vowed to herself. "But first you have to earn it, so get back to work."

Slowly, they got to their feet and returned to their various duties. It wasn't until then that Amanda noticed that Dudley wasn't there. Looking around, she saw a pair of feet sticking out from under one of the tractors; the feet weren't moving. For the past couple of nights he had been going into town after supper, and coming back at all hours.

She walked over to the tractor. "What are you doing, Buster Brown, taking a snooze under there?"

The feet jerked, then Dudley came sliding out on his back, feet first. His face was splotched with grease, his hands black with it. In one hand he held a wrench.

"No, I was trying to make this thing run."

Mollified, she muttered, "Oh . . ."

"Oh?" he said sarcastically. "Is that all? I heard your little pep talk to the team, Coach. No do-or-die speech for me?"

"I figured you didn't need one."

"The way things are going, I may need more than a pep talk to keep these tractors running, not to mention the other machinery."

"What's wrong with this one?"

"The gear teeth are ground down so badly they won't mesh right. They keep slipping."

She went tense. "Gravel? Sabotage again?"

Dudley shook his head, almost regretfully. "Nope. They're just worn down. Damnit, Amanda, do you know how old this pile of junk is? It was made so long ago, I may not be able to get replacement gears for it."

"I know how old it is!" she snapped. "It was bought by my daddy!"

"Before you were born, I'll bet." Grinning, he climbed to his feet.

"Never mind that," she said, arms akimbo. "Can you get it running again?"

Wiping his hands on a rag, he nodded. "I imagine so. There're still some of these old jobs around. Probably find one in a junkyard in town."

"You were just saying gears might be hard to get."

"Hell, yes, it'll be hard. I can't just walk into a shop and buy them new. I have to find used ones." He grinned again. "I was just ragging you a little, for that pep talk you gave. God, what corn! And a bonus yet!"

"There certainly won't be any bonus if you don't get this tractor back to work, and soon. It strikes me, freight rider, that you're pretty fresh-mouthed the last couple of days. It come about from the time you spend in town at night? Got a girl, Dudley?" Her voice became taunting. "Is that what's got you jazzed up?"

He flushed a beet red, and Amanda knew that she was on target.

He said in a low voice, "As I recall you telling *me*, Amanda, what I do on my own time is none of your business. God knows you've made that clear enough!"

"What do you mean?"

"You're too busy with Seymour Hooker and Thaddeus Martin to notice that I'm even alive."

She was suddenly furious with him. Yet, at the same time, a question nudged at her mind— why? Was she angry because he was seeing some woman in town, or because he dared to comment about her personal life?

"I know you're alive," she said tightly. "You work for me."

"You've made that clear enough, too."

They stood glaring at one another. Amanda, aware that this whole exchange was ridiculous, couldn't seem to help herself.

Then, at the sound of a truck door slamming, Dudley's gaze went past her, and his anger switched focus. "Now what in the holy hell is *he* doing here?"

He plunged past her. Amanda whipped around, and saw Bud Dalmas leaning against the fender of a grain truck backed up to the stack of grain sacks, waiting for the truck to be loaded.

Amanda hastened after Dudley, who had skidded to a stop before Dalmas. Hands on hips, Dudley demanded, "Didn't I tell you to never come around these threshers again?"

Dalmas spat a stream of tobacco juice and laughed his silent laugh. "I ain't working for Miss Amanda now, not rightly. I got me a job driving this grain truck. Feller who owns it took sick and needed a driver. I reckon you could say I'm working for Thaddeus Martin, since he's footing the bill to haul this grain all the way up north to an elevator."

Dudley's fists were doubled. "I can't afford to have you hanging around. I'll have to spend all my time watching to see that you don't do something to the machinery."

"Naw now, why'd I do that, Dud? I ain't being paid to do that now. I'm paid to drive this truck."

"Then Hooker *did* hire you to sabotage the tractors and threshers?"

"Yup. That he did. Who else would be interested? Except . . ." His looked darkened. "Except he still owes me."

Dudley swung on Amanda. "You see? I told you Hooker was behind it!"

She made a weary gesture. "What does it matter, Dudley? It's over and done with."

"What does it matter?" he said hotly. "We can send him to jail for it, that's what matters!"

"What proof do we have?"

"You don't want to see him in jail! That's it, isn't it?" His face twisted. "As for proof, Dalmas here can testify to it!"

"Naw." Bud Dalmas spat. "Naw, I ain't testifying to nothing. You think I'm crazy, getting Seymour Hooker down on me like that?"

"But you said he owed you money." Dudley's look was deceitfully innocent. "This is one way you can get even, seeing that his ass lands in jail."

"Don't hold much with courts, all that lawing." Dalmas turned a dark look inward. "I got my ways of getting even with Mr. Hooker."

"Well, Buster Brown?" Amanda said. "Now what?"

"I give up!" Dudley threw up his hands. "Hooker makes me think of a Western movie I saw once. There was this bad gunslinger took over a Western town for his own, ran it just like he wanted. The men were all afraid of him, and most of the women were in love with him. He could do anything he damn well pleased and get away with it. That's Seymour Hooker!" He started off, then swung back. "Now you listen to me, Dalmas. If I see you with your cotton-pickers even *near* a piece of machinery around here, I'll break your fingers one at a time! You hear?"

"Oh yes, Dud. I hear." Dalmas laughed soundlessly. "I'll be good. I got other taters to fry."

Dudley glowered at him, then started off again. Amanda hurried after him. "Dudley, wait up!"

"What do you want now?"

"That movie . . . I'm curious. How'd it end? Did the gunslinger get his just desserts?

He slowed his step. "How do you *think* it ended?"

"If I knew, I wouldn't be asking you, now would I?"

"He fell for a preacher's daughter, threw away his guns, and reformed," he said disgustedly.

"All for the love of a good woman, huh?" She began to laugh. "But then I'm not a preacher's daughter, am I?"

Dudley kept going, his step quickening. Amanda stopped, laughing helplessly.

Bud Dalmas put the truck into low gear and ground off the wheat field. The truck badly needed a ring job; it farted black smoke, and gasoline fumes leaked up through the floorboard cracks.

But it was a job, a better job than driving a bundle wagon, come to think of it. Best of all, it gave him a legitimate excuse to be around Dudley Graham. Dalmas hadn't yet figured out how he'd fix Dudley's wagon, but he was sure he'd think of something fitting.

He'd been really boiled when he learned that Seymour Hooker had survived the accident with only a few scratches. Damn Hooker, he had more lives than a cat! Dalmas knew that the Cayne crew and Hooker's combines would be working almost side by side, starting next week when Amanda Cayne moved her outfit onto the Martin place and Hooker's combines moved onto the adjoining farm.

That would be the time. Maybe he could get

both of 'em at once. Wouldn't that be something!

Once on the highway, he settled down to the monotony of the long, grinding haul up to South Dakota.

Dalmas entertained himself with daydreams of possible dire fates in store for Dudley Graham and Seymour Hooker: flattened to cardboard beneath a steamroller; disemboweled like a shoat at hog-killing time; chewed up by the combines . . .

He suddenly remembered an incident down in West Texas a couple of years back. He'd been working with a hay-baling crew. One of the hands had staggered back to the field drunk one night and passed out in the wrong place. The next morning, before anyone realized what had happened, the drunken idiot had been caught up in the baler and ground up like chopped liver, the dismembered parts pressed into a bale of hay.

Dalmas grinned faintly as he recalled what had happened when the discovery was made, and the hay baler halted. The bale of hay had been streaked with red, like cake icing, and one eyeball had rolled across the ground like a kid's marble when the baler belt finally stopped. Most of the crew had turned white as bedsheets and puked their guts out.

Now if something like that could be worked out for old Dud and Mr. Hooker!

Dalmas cursed as his attention was jerked back to the truck. All the roads up here were blacktopped; concrete cracked like an ice pond in the severe winters. Now, under the broiling sun, the asphalt had softened to the consistency of chocolate candy, and the truck crept along, laboring mightily.

Dalmas cursed again and geared down. It was going to be a long, deary haul. He glanced at the sun, a fireball in the west. A wheat field stretched endlessly on his left, and the sun's rays turned it into a field of rippling fire.

Dalmas blinked, began to grin. He sent a brown stream out the window, not bothering to wipe the dribble from his chin.

What did wheat farmers and harvesters fear more than anything? A wheat fire!

And there it was, what he'd been wracking his brain for—a sureshot way to get back at Dudley Graham and Mr. Seymour Hooker in one swoop!

20

Although summer's zenith, reckoned by seasonal time, had passed, it seemed to Dudley that the days were longer and hotter. Certainly they were drier. Not a drop of rain had fallen in weeks, which seemed to make everybody else quite happy, but he would have been delighted to stand under a brief downpour, head turned up and mouth open like a chicken.

The afternoon they finished up a small farm and headed for the Martin place was as dry and hot as the ones before. The sky was like an inverted brass bowl. There was a carnival atmosphere about the crew as they crawled up the road. Dudley viewed this attitude with sour skepticism. He could see why Amanda might be happy, it represented not only a seasonal landmark for her, but a triumph as well—a triumph over adversity, Seymour Hooker, J.C. Fallon, and "the whole damned state of Kansas," as she had declaimed somewhat ambiguously.

But Dudley failed to see why the others should be in such a holiday mood. There were still several weeks of hard labor ahead, even after the Martin farm, and surely no one believed that bonus bullshit. It wasn't as if they *liked* Amanda . . .

His thoughts stopped short. Damnit, they did like her! Why hadn't he been able to see that before this?

Sure, they'd all hated her when Dudley joined the crew, as had he, and some still liked to rawhide her, when they could get away with it. Yet a change had taken place, so slowly and subtly that he hadn't noticed it. His own attitude had changed, so why was it so hard to believe the other crew members had come to like her? Of course, his own feelings toward Amanda weren't liking as much as a love-hate relationship, but he should have realized how the men felt the night Rooster Cockrun led the sneak attack. They had agreed to fight, to a man. Certainly it hadn't been the money, not at the wages they were being paid, and it hadn't been because he, Dudley Graham, was held in such high esteem. No, it had been out of loyalty and liking for Amanda, a woman they'd all held in contempt in the beginning.

Dudley shook his head in wonder. How the hell did she do it? What was it about her that caused men to fall all over themselves?

The pickup he was riding in slowed, making a turn. From the back, Dudley peeked around the cab. Ahead stretched a dirt lane, lined with stately elms. He saw Amanda's pickup parked off to one side. He hopped out of the slow-moving pickup and walked over.

He propped his foot on the running board. "Well, you made it, Amanda."

"I thought I never would. I've always wondered why Texans are so nutty about football. Now I think I know. I feel like I've been struggling down a football field, fighting for every yard, and suddenly there's the goal line, close enough to touch! Sound crazy to you, Buster Brown?"

"Not crazy at all," he said gravely. "I think you're entitled to feel that way."

She gave him a flashing smile. "You see, you can be nice, if you try." She touched his cheek with just the tips of her fingers, lightly as a feather, then said briskly, "Hop in, I'll give you a ride up to the house."

He went around to the other side of the pickup and got in beside her. Motor idling, she sat for a moment looking back at the main road. Dudley took out the Bull Durham sack and built a cigarette.

Without looking around, Amanda said, "Roll me one, will you, Dudley? I'm all out of tailor-mades."

As he finished the second cigarette, she withdrew her head from the window. "There, that's the last tractor. Looks like we made it all in one piece yet another time."

He gave her the cigarette, held a match for her, then lit his own.

Amanda put the pickup in gear, gave a toot on the horn, and pulled far over on the lefthand side of the lane to pass the caravan. She swerved back over after passing, took a drag of the cigarette, coughed, and threw the cigarette onto the floorboard, mashing it out with her toe. "My God, what's that you smoke, Buster Brown? Cowshit?"

"For your information, it's Bull Durham, the freight rider's delight," he said. "You asked, I didn't offer it to you. And you, *you* can't be nice for very long, can you, Amanda?"

She slanted a mocking look over at him. "Aww, did Mommie hurt'ums feelings?"

"Goddamnit, Amanda, don't patronize me!" He slammed his fist against the dashboard, pain shooting up his arm at the force of it. "By God, I don't know why I put up with it. Just when I begin to think you're human, you become as prickly as a porcupine!"

"Speaking of prickly . . ."

"I know, I know, you bring out my worst side. I've left several times, but I always come back. And for what? More abuse."

"Nobody said you had to stay."

"And foul-mouthed at that. I've never heard a woman, not even a honky-tonk slut, use language like you've been using lately."

"And you should know about honky-tonk sluts, from a few things I've heard about you," she said icily.

He gave her a flinty look. "From Seymour Hooker, probably, since Annie was once his girl. That probably boils his ass!"

"Now who's talking dirty?" Then she said musingly, "Annie, huh? I met her a few weeks back. I can't say a great deal for Seymour's taste, or yours."

"At least Annie doesn't pretend to be anything but what she is."

"And I do?"

He considered that for a moment, then admitted reluctantly, "No, you don't. You don't play that game. You're what you are, I have to respect you for that."

"Respect, no less! My God!" She threw her arms wide, letting the pickup go down the lane unguided. "I never thought I'd hear that word from you!"

Dudley wasn't paying attention. A house had come into view up ahead some time back, but he had noticed it only peripherally. Now his gaze was riveted on it.

The unpainted, two-story structure, without a single tree, shrub or flower around it, struck him as eerie, like some obscene growth sprouting out of the earth—something dreamed up for a story by a writer for *Weird Tales* magazine.

"That's," he pointed, "that's Thaddeus Martin's house?"

"It must be," she said, staring at it. "It's been some years since I've seen it, when I used to come along with Daddy. But I see what you mean, Dudley. I remember now. The first time I saw it I thought it was a witch's castle out of a fairy tale."

They were driving up before the house now, and Dudley saw Thaddeus Martin standing on the stoop, black pipe going. As Amanda braked the pickup to a stop, he came down the steps and crossed toward them. In overalls and faded-blue work shirt, he looked far more at home to Dudley than he had in the shiny suit he'd worn downstate.

Thaddeus opened the door for Amanda to get out, and Dudley slid out on his side and came around the pickup, as Thaddeus said gravely, "You made it, I see, Amanda."

She grinned at him. "I made it, Thaddeus. Were you afraid I wouldn't?"

"I had some doubts, at first," he admitted, with his usual honesty. "But those went away after I watched you and your crew in operation." He nodded to Dudley, then moved his gaze back to Amanda. "When you get your camp set up for the night, I'd like you to come up to the house and have supper with me."

Dudley felt an angry flush heat his face. Although there was no earthly reason why he should be included in the invitation, the way Thaddeus had couched it struck him as a deliberate snub. Catching Amanda's amused gaze upon him, he looked away.

She said, "I would be pleased, Thaddeus. Thank you." She became brisk. "Now, we have a lot to do. Come on, Dudley, let's get at it."

The sky was stained a dying pink when Amanda left her tent that evening. They had set up camp in a cow pasture behind the Martin house, right at the edge of the vast wheat field. The threshers were in place, ready for an early start in the morning. Amanda stood for a moment, gazing across the Martin acreage. It was like looking over an immense, golden lake, the wheat stubble dotted at regular intervals with the shocks of mowed wheat. Unlike most of the farms they had harvested, the acreage here was so huge they would have to move the threshers many times before they were finished.

She breathed a sigh of satisfaction and started across the pasture toward the house, which was bulking forbiddingly in the gathering darkness. She had put on a dress for the occasion and the hot breeze whipped the skirt about her long legs. She even had on silk stockings and high heels, which made walking difficult on the uneven ground of the pasture. She stopped to light a final cigarette, from a pack she had cadged off Jack Rollins. She ground it out under her toe before going up the steps to the house.

The front door stood open, but there was no answer to her knock. Assuming Thaddeus had left the door open for her, Amanda tentatively ventured inside. She had never been inside the house; the times she had been there with her father, Thaddeus had never, at least to her knowledge, invited any of the threshing crew into the house, not even Amos.

Curious about this legendary house of Thaddeus Martin, Amanda looked around as she went down the long hall. There was actually little to see, since all the hall doors were closed except the one opening into what was clearly a parlor—crowded with old-fashioned, uncomfortable furniture.

She paused for a moment, listening. She heard the banging of pots and pans in the back.

She gave in to an impulse and carefully opened one door to peer in. Heavy curtains were drawn across the windows, making the interior very dim. The pieces of furniture in the room wore dust covers. The room had apparently been intended for use as a sitting room, or perhaps a music room, since she recognized one bulky piece as a piano. Had Thaddeus's wife played? For the first time she sensed the melancholy scope of Thaddeus's loss, and realized that this house was something of a shrine to his dead Martha.

Feeling vaguely guilty, she softly closed the door and called, "Thaddeus?"

The noises stopped and Thaddeus appeared at the back of the hallway. "I'm working in the kitchen, Amanda." As she started toward him, he held up a hand. "No, don't come back here. The kitchen's hot as Hades."

"Then you shouldn't be going to all that trouble just for me."

"I'm used to it," he said with a shrug. "I don't care for cold food, and I make a hot meal three times a day, no matter if it's just for me. I have some ice tea, if you'd care for a glass. I know you'd like something stronger, but I don't hold with liquor in the house." He smiled at her expression. "Oh, I know you'd liked to have had a liquor drink that night I took you to supper."

She laughed. "Ice tea sounds fine, Thaddeus."

He nodded. "You sit out on the front porch, where it's some cooler. I'll bring your tea out in a jiffy, and I'll join you from time to time while supper's cooking. We'll eat in about a half-hour."

"You sure I can't help you, Thaddeus?"

"Seems to me I remember you making a sharp remark once about how men think a woman's place is in the kitchen. This time you stay out of the kitchen. Fact is, I don't care for somebody else puttering around in my kitchen. I guess a man gets to be something of an old maid, if he does for himself long enough."

Amanda laughed again and went back out onto the veranda. The only two chairs were straightbacks. Most front porches had at least one rocker. Typical of Thaddeus, she thought, smiling; anything that smacked of comfort and luxury also smacked of sin.

Sitting down, she found herself wondering what it would be like to be married to Thaddeus Martin. He seemed to be well-to-do, and she had a feeling that his frugality and spartan lifestyle would not extend to the woman in his life, that he would tend to spoil her . . .

She pulled herself up short, appalled. For God's sake, what on earth was she doing thinking of marriage to Thaddeus Martin?

She dug into her purse for the pack of cigarettes. About to light one, she heard his footsteps in the hall and paused. She started to return the cigarette to her purse, then changed her mind. What did she care if Thaddeus disapproved of her smoking?

The cigarette, unlit, was dangling from her lips as Thaddeus emerged from the hall. In one hand he had a tall, frosted glass of tea, and in the other . . .

She stared as he handed her a large glass ashtray. She burst out laughing when she saw the price still marked on the bottom.

Thaddeus looked sheepish, shuffling his feet. "Like you said, a man has to change with the times. At least he has to *try*."

"You're sweet, Thaddeus. Thank you." She motioned to the other chair. "Can you sit for a minute?"

"Just for a little." He perched gingerly on the other chair, stiff as a cigar-store Indian.

Amanda lit her cigarette, blew smoke. "I haven't thanked you properly yet for what you did at the Grange meeting the other night. It was a generous gesture, Thaddeus, and I do appreciate it, as I'm sure the other threshermen do. With the elevators refusing threshed wheat, we'd've all been out of business."

"That's what Hooker and J.C. Fallon had in mind, I'm sure. And although I did do it to help you, Amanda, I must confess that," his smile was wintry, "it gave me great pleasure to throw a roadblock in Hooker's way."

"And that disturbs me a little," she said. "You two seem to have become enemies, Thaddeus, and I feel it's my fault. I know you were friends once."

He was shaking his head. "Not true friends, Amanda, not much more than speaking acquaintances. I have never approved of some of the things Hooker does. This time, he just went too far. And don't go blaming yourself. I think it would have happened anyway." His face became somber. "It does bother me that balking him gave me so much pleasure. Fighting him and beating him gave me even more pleasure. It's against the laws of God for a man to take delight in such things."

"Don't be hard on yourself, Thaddeus." She leaned over to touch his hand. "I don't approve of fighting, God knows, but I must admit that I got a boot out of the news that you'd taken on Seymour and won. It's a human failing, Thaddeus. I doubt that God would frown all that hard. I'm not a Bible scholar, but I do seem to remember a couple of things . . . 'Smite thine enemies with a righteous fist . . . An eye for an eye, a tooth for a tooth.'" She laughed. "I may not have the quotes exact, but I'm sure I have the essence of it."

Her voice died as she realized that she was staring directly into his eyes. A quiver sped along her nerve-ends; it was the first time she had felt the impact of his virility. Had he been chaste since his Martha died? What would happen when a powerful, but long-damned-up, sexuality broke free of all restraint? The thought made her giddy.

She realized that he was speaking, his face so close to hers that his warm breath fanned her cheek. She caught the tag-end of a phrase, ". . . flesh of woman," and she said, somewhat breathlessly, "What did you say, Thaddeus?"

He started and almost bolted to his feet. "I have to tend to my cooking," he muttered, and hastened out of sight down the hall.

Shaken, Amanda drew on the forgotten cigarette and found that it had gone out. She drank thirstily from the glass of tea, toying with the thought of leaving right now. If he had in mind to take her to bed, the evening could end in embarrassment for both of them.

Even though she had felt a strong sexual pull toward Thaddeus a few moments before, Amanda had no intention of getting emotionally involved with him. Not only would it be lousy business practice, it could destroy her emotional well-being.

Amanda laughed shortly, as she remembered Dudley's words: "Sniffing around you like dogs in heat." She had to admit there was some justification for his charge—Seymour, Dudley himself, and now Thaddeus. But she had done nothing to bring it about. Just because she was more liberal with her views, more open and frank in her relationship with men, was that any reason for them to think she was available?

She was spared further self-analysis by Thaddeus's appearance in the doorway. "Supper is on the table, Amanda."

Not only did Thaddeus set a good table, he was an excellent cook. Supper was fried chicken, crisp and golden, with gravy thick enough to eat with a fork, mashed potatoes whipped until they were white as snow, small green peas, baking-powder biscuits flaky and tender, and tall glasses of cold buttermilk.

"This, Thaddeus, is without a doubt the best food I've eaten in ages, and I don't just mean cook-wagon grub. This is better than anything

I had to eat *before* I went out with the threshing crew."

He flushed with pleasure, looking down at his plate. "Martha taught me all I know about cooking, and living alone here, I've had plenty of time to practice. Even without company, a man likes to eat good victuals." He glanced up with a smile. "I have an apple cobbler for dessert, so be sure and save room for it."

That was about it in the conversation department for a time. Amanda knew that eating was a serious business with farm people, verging, she often thought, on the religious. And who would be so crass as to talk in church? Amanda respected this and kept silent.

Even with all doors and windows open, it was stifling hot in the dining room, and all the food she stuffed herself with didn't help. Before long, she felt perspiration beading her face and running down her sides in rivulets.

Finally she leaned back. "My God, I'm so stuffed it's downright sinful! I see now why gluttony is considered one of the deadly sins."

"There's nothing sinful about a healthy appetite." He scraped his chair back to get up. "I'll dish up the cobbler."

"Please, Thaddeus, no!" She held up her hand. "I have no place to put it. Maybe later, okay? Let's go out on the front porch and cool off a bit. If that's possible in this weather."

"This is fine threshing weather," he said sententiously.

The remark was so typical of a farmer that Amanda hid a smile. He came around to pull her chair back, and Amanda went ahead of him down the hall. Sheathed in perspiration, she felt almost chilly for a delicious moment when what breeze there was struck her.

She sat down with a sigh and Thaddeus took the other chair, brogans planted solidly on the porch planks, his big hands, fingers spread, resting on his thighs. Amanda thought what a luxury it would be to prop her feet upon the porch railing and let the breeze blow up under her dress.

She didn't, of course, knowing that it would shock him to the depths. She took out a cigarette, picked up the glass ashtray from the porch where she'd left it, and fired the cigarette. Thaddeus filled his pipe and held a kitchen match to the bowl, face wreathed in fragrant smoke.

It was full dark now, and a few late-season fireflies blinked on and off. A horse neighed from somewhere nearby, and cows mooed in the barn.

Amanda turned to Thaddeus. "Going back to what we were talking about before supper . . . I know you're going to have to dig deep in your pocket, Thaddeus, to pay those trucks. I just wish I could do something in kind, like charge you less per bushel, but I simply can't. I wouldn't be able to pay the crew's wages if I did. I'm sure you know how close to the bone I'm operating."

"I do know, Amanda, and I appreciate the thought, but don't trouble yourself. If I hadn't wanted to do it, I wouldn't have made the offer. Since Martha died, I have little to spend money on, and I am comfortably well-off. I have no kin and I won't live forever, so who would the money go to? Unless . . ." He cleared his throat. "Unless I get married again."

"Are you thinking of getting married again, Thaddeus? How nice!"

"I have been thinking about it of late, yes."

Amanda silently berated herself for being so slow to catch on. All that food must have addled her wits.

Thaddeus was going on, ". . . well-off, like I said. It's not a bad life, that of a farm woman. And I can afford hired household help. A city girl might find it a little dull at first, but with a baby to raise . . ." His voice was shaded with sadness. "Martha couldn't have children, you know."

"Thaddeus," Amanda interrupted in a soft voice, "what are you getting at?"

"Why, I'm asking you to be my wife," he said, voice rising on a note of surprise.

"Thaddeus . . ." She sighed. "I wish you hadn't. Dear God, I wish you hadn't!"

"Why? Am I that repulsive to you?"

"Oh, no! I didn't mean that at all. You're a dear man, Thaddeus Martin, and any woman should be proud to be your wife, the mother of your children." She leaned across to touch his hand. "But there is a problem, you see. I don't love you, Thaddeus. I like you, I like you very much. I respect you, and think you're a hell of a man, if you will forgive the profanity, but I do *not* love you."

He was still for a moment. Then, in the silence she heard his knuckles crack. "I thought that, after Martha, I would never love another woman. I thought I was content with my life. Then you came along, and I knew differently. I realized that I would grow old here, grow old all alone, and die, and everything I have will go to the state."

Amanda stirred, making an exasperated sound. "Self-pity doesn't become you, Thaddeus. You would have no trouble finding a woman happy to marry you."

"Self-pity?" His voice held astonishment. "Is that how I sound to you?"

"It is, yes, and I can think of no man less needful of feeling sorry for himself."

His bulk shifted in the chair, and he gave a short laugh. "You're right, and I apologize for that. You said I'd have no trouble finding a woman to be my wife. Perhaps so. But how would I know she wasn't just marrying me for what I have, for what I could give her?"

"And how would you know that isn't why I'd be marrying you?"

"Because I know you, Amanda," he said stoutly.

"You don't know me that well, Thaddeus. You know what I was thinking while I waited out here for supper? How nice it would be here, how easy things would be."

"And that's why you said no?" There was a

note of eagerness in his voice. "Afraid I'd think just that?"

"No, Thaddeus. I told you. I'm not in love with you."

"But you could come to love me, if you gave yourself half a chance. I'm sure of it!"

"You told me once you don't go to movies," she said with a wry laugh, "but you must have seen a few. How many times have I heard that line in a movie!"

He said stiffly, "Now you're making fun of me."

"No, I'm not. Honest, I'm not. But it doesn't work the way you have it, Thaddeus. Believe me, you either love someone or you don't."

"All I ask is that you don't make up your mind definitely until you and your crew are finished here. Give me that much time at least."

"What can I say to that?" She blew out her breath. "Okay, but I won't change my mind."

"You might. People do change their minds. Even if you don't come to love me . . ." He hesitated, then plunged ahead. "I'll still marry you, on any terms."

"Thaddeus, please! This is becoming embarrassing!"

"I'm sorry, not another word tonight." He got to his feet. "I'll fetch the cobbler."

"No, I've already eaten too much." She also got up. "I want to walk for a bit, walk off some of that food. And think a little." She knew the last words were a mistake even before they were out.

Thaddeus pounced. "Yes, you do that. You have a nice walk and think it out."

"Damnit, Thaddeus!" She checked herself, then said resignedly, "Yes, Thaddeus, I'll think it out."

She hurried down the steps, feeling his gaze on her every step of the way until she turned the corner of the house. Then she slowed to a walk. She scolded herself for being so damned stupid as to not know what he was leading up to. She should have stopped him before things had advanced as far as they had.

She laughed to herself. Within the space of three weeks she'd had not one, but two proposals of marriage, both from men she would never have dreamed had matrimony in mind. Most women would consider themselves lucky, and she only felt depression! Beyond that, she couldn't account for it. Without undue vanity, Amanda knew that she was a good-looking woman, and she also knew that her personality was somewhat abrasive. Where did the idea come from that a woman trying to take a man's place was unattractive to the very men she tried to compete with? If nothing else, she had proven that old saw to be false.

Lighting a cigarette, she walked on. As she neared the camp, she saw a light hooked over the motor of one of the tractors. Coming closer, she saw that Dudley was buried up to his hips in the innards of the motor.

She said, "You're an industrious bugger, I'll say that for you, Dudley."

He drew back, straightening up. He said grumpily, "I figured this tractor had to be in the best shape possible, since we're going to be threshing at top speed starting tomorrow."

"You're a good man, Buster Brown," she said sincerely. "And I want you to know that I truly appreciate it. Not many men would work their tails off for the money you're being paid."

He peered at her suspiciously. "Compliments yet? From Amanda Cayne?"

"You're a hard man to compliment," she said tartly, and just like that she was weeping, silent tears running down her cheeks.

"Hey, now!" he said in alarm. "What's wrong, Amanda? If it's me and my big mouth, I'm sorry."

"I don't know. That's the hell of it, Dudley," she wailed. "I don't *know*!"

He took her in his arms, cradling her head on his shoulder. "There now, whatever it is, it'll be all right." He stroked her hair tenderly.

It was the first time she'd been in his arms, and Amanda realized that they were almost the same height, Dudley perhaps an inch or so taller.

God, what a thing to think of at a time like this! She made a sound halfway between laughter and a sob, and fresh tears poured from her eyes.

"For God's sake, Amanda, what *is* it?" He went rigid. "Did Thaddeus Martin say something, do something? If he did, I'll bust his head for him!"

"Thaddeus? Don't be ridiculous! Of all the men I know, Thaddeus comes closest to being the perfect gentleman."

"Then what is it?" He sounded cross and baffled. "I never thought I'd see tears from you."

"Why not? I'm human, despite all rumors to the contrary. I cry." She swallowed, gulping air, and stepped back, knuckling the tears from her eyes. "I guess it's just been building up in me. Daddy having a stroke, the strain of taking over the threshing crew . . . it all finally got to me."

"Amanda . . ." He cupped her face between his hands. "If there's anything I can do to help, just ask. You must know how I feel about you. I love you. Why else do you think I've stuck around?"

A thought skipped through Amanda's mind —is he going to ask me to marry him? She had an impulse to giggle. Then his face was close to hers. His lips had just touched hers when a voice drawled behind her, "Well now, if this ain't a touching sight!"

Dudley gave a leap and stepped back quickly. He sent a furious look past her and spun away without a word. In a moment he was buried to the waist in the tractor again.

Amanda took a moment to compose herself before turning. "Do you make it a habit sneaking up on people like that, Seymour?"

"Aww, sugar, nothing like that." Seymour Hooker gestured with the smouldering cigar in his hands. "I'm starting to work over on the adjoining farm in the morning, and I thought I'd drop over to see how things were with you all here. Didn't dream I'd be dropping in at what might be called an inconvenient time." He was grinning, but it looked forced, as though he was in the grip of tightly controlled anger. "And I didn't know you and the peckerwood were on kissing terms. When did that come about?"

"That, Seymour Hooker, is none of your damned business. Now, if you will excuse me, I'm going to bed. I have a hard day coming up tomorrow."

She strode toward her tent set up a few yards away, ignoring Seymour as he called after her.

21

Bud Dalmas was growing frustrated. The threshers had been working the Martin farm for two days, and Hooker's men were combining the small Moore farm, but the two crews were more than a mile apart. It was unlikely that one fire, even with the wind from the right direction, would trap both crews, so that the fiery deaths of Graham and Hooker would be assured. It didn't bother Dalmas that others, many others, would likely perish in a raging wheat fire. Anyone working for or with either man deserved a like fate.

The thought that Amanda Cayne might be caught in the fire did give him pause briefly, but only because she was a juicy dame, and he would dearly love to have him a piece of that. Maybe it could be managed so that he could get at her before the fire roared out of hand.

There was one thing in his favor—the Martin place was only a relatively short haul to the elevators across the state line. Loaded early in the morning, Dalmas could make the round trip and be back before dark. But even that was too long to be away, in case his chance came.

Then, on the morning of the third day, he received news that set his pulse to racing. The threshers were moving to another section of land; they would be setting up only a hundred yards or so from the property line between the Martin acreage and the Moore place. Hooker's combines would be nearby, as close as they were ever likely to be!

Dalmas knew that this would be the best chance he would ever have. He had to start the fire this very night. Naturally he couldn't do it in daylight, since he might be seen. Starting it late at night, an hour or so before dawn when everybody was dead asleep, would be best, giving the fire a good start before it could be spotted.

There was one problem, he found. The threshers were moved early in the morning and didn't start threshing again until past noon. Dalmas's grain truck was last in line to be loaded, and he knew that by the time he was ready to leave for the elevators, it would be late afternoon. He wouldn't be able to reach the elevators before they shut down for the night, which meant that he'd be expected to wait there until morning. Something would have to be done about that.

The first thought that came to him was to start out with the truck, then park somewhere and sneak back under cover of darkness. He discarded that plan almost immediately. If he wasn't parked at the elevators in the morning, there might be some question raised later as to why he was delayed.

The idea he finally acted upon came to him as they were loading the grain sacks onto his truck. Thaddeus Martin had come out to the threshers, and Amanda left with him in his pickup. Dalmas waited until he was unobserved and raised the hood of the truck, pretending to be tinkering with it. With his knife he sawed partway through a wire leading to one of the spark plugs. Then closed the hood and got back into the cab.

He'd hardly had time to bite off a chaw of tobacco and work it into a juicy cud when a hand slapped the truck window by his elbow. "You're loaded, Dalmas. You can pull out now."

Dalmas started the truck, laughing silently when he heard the motor miss. He jammed the gearshift into low and eased the truck forward, feeding it just enough gas to inch along. Under the pull of the heavy load, the motor missed again, backfired, then died.

He started it up once more and went through a repeat performance.

In the silence generated by the stalled motor, he heard a shout, "Now what the hell!"

He kept a sober face turned toward the window as Dudley Graham charged up.

"Oh . . . it's you, Dalmas. What's wrong here?"

"I don't know, Dud." He gave a helpless shrug. He started the motor and raced it. "Hear that? She's missing pretty bad, and when I feed her the gas, she dies."

"Oh, shit," Dudley said.

He took a step toward the front of the truck,

then froze as Dalmas said, "But I reckon you can fix whatever it is, huh, Dud?"

Dudley glared. "Why should I?"

Gleeful at the reaction he'd hoped for, Dalmas said guilelessly, "Why, you're the mechanic, ain't you? I recollect hearing Miss Amanda say how you can fix anything. Reckon a little thing like a miss won't faze you."

"I work for Amanda Cayne, not Thaddeus Martin, and not you," Dudley said furiously. "I'm not paid to work on your truck, so if it needs fixing, fix it yourself. I'm busy. You know how to foul up a piece of machinery, now see if you can fix it." He started to turn away, then looked back. "But get it the hell out of the way first, you're blocking off the other grain trucks."

Chortling with secret glee, Dalmas started the truck, and drove it, bucking and backfiring, off to one side. He got out and raised the hood, spending some time pretending to be working on the motor. Finally, he stood back, spat a stream of brown juice, and stood scratching his head. Clearly, to anyone who might be watching him, he was baffled by the mysteries under the hood.

With a shrug he got into the cab and slouched back. Through slitted eyes he saw that the sun was low in the west.

He shook with silent laughter. It had worked out fine! He was stuck here for the night.

Thaddeus had been solemn when he came to fetch Amanda. "There was a phone call for you.

From Wichita Falls, a Doctor Anderson. He's waiting for you to call him back."

She went cold with apprehension. "Is it about Daddy?"

"I expect so, Amanda. He wouldn't say, just that it was urgent he talk to you."

She sent a despairing glance at the threshers. Just when everything was going so well! She dreaded to go to the phone, sure that it would be bad news. Yet she had little choice.

With a sigh she said, "Okay, let's get it over with."

At the house Thaddeus got the local operator on the wall phone in the hall and asked her to ring the hospital in Wichita Falls.

He handed the earpiece to Amanda. "I expect you could use a glass of ice tea," he said, and discreetly disappeared in the direction of the kitchen.

Amanda held the earpiece to her ear, trying to keep her mind as empty as possible, endeavoring not to speculate as to the reason for Dr. Anderson's call. She heard the tinny-sounding voices of one operator after another until finally the local operator chirped, "Your party at Wichita Falls is on the line, Miss Cayne."

Gripping the slippery phone tightly, Amanda said, "Dr. Anderson?"

"Yes, speaking." The distant voice had an eerie, echoing quality. "Miss Cayne?"

"Yes, Doctor. Is it bad news about Daddy?"

"I'm afraid so." There was the sound of a windy sigh. "Your father had another stroke early this morning. The extent of it I don't know as yet. At least his condition at present is stable, but he is comatose. I won't know how severe the damage is until he regains consciousness, if he does. Forgive me for being so blunt, but you struck me as a young woman who would prefer the truth instead of my hedging."

"I appreciate that, Doctor." She drew a breath. "Should I come down there?"

"That, of course, is a decision only you can make. If you're thinking that is the reason I called you, it is not. I promised I would keep you informed, and that is what I'm doing."

"There is nothing I can do there," she said, almost to herself.

"In that you are correct. Your father would not be aware of your presence, and you naturally wouldn't be able to talk to him. I gathered from what you told me when you were down here that your presence is needed there."

"That's true."

"Then I would advise you not to make the trip down at this time. Your father will have as good care as I am capable of giving him." There was a pause. "But there might be one problem . . ."

"What is that, Doctor?"

"The problem would be with you, if there is one. Your father might die at any moment, I must warn you of that. Some children take on a huge load of guilt if a parent dies in their absence, if they don't see him one last time. Would *you* feel such guilt? From my experience, it can be quite traumatic, at least for many. So it is a question only you can answer."

Amanda was silent for a moment, thinking. She would feel some guilt, she realized that. But she would also feel guilt if something went wrong with the threshing operation in her absence, especially if Amos Cayne survived this last stroke and regained his faculties.

"Okay, Dr. Anderson, I'll remain here," she said in a sudden decision. "If there is any change, you'll let me know?"

"I'll let you know, Miss Cayne, you may be sure. And may I say that it took courage to reach that decision? Goodbye, Amanda Cayne."

Amanda hung up, her thoughts in a turmoil. Courage? Or simple cowardice? She well knew how much of a drain on her emotions it would be to see the once-vital, once-vigorous Amos Cayne even more helpless than he had been after the first stroke.

At the sound of footsteps she turned. Silently Thaddeus held out a glass of ice tea. She seized it, welcoming the bite of the cold liquid on her parched throat. She squinted her eyes to squeeze back tears.

"It *was* about your father?"

She nodded her head.

"I'm sorry, Amanda. He's worse?"

"Much worse. He had another stroke, a bad one."

"Then you'll be going down to visit with him. Why don't you let me drive you? It'll be too much of a strain on you . . ."

"No, Thaddeus, I'm not going."

His face mirrored surprise, and for just an instant, disapproval. "You're not going?"

"I'm needed here. Besides, what can I do down there? Sit and stew?" she cried. "The doctor said Daddy wouldn't even know I was there! What good would I do him? But you don't approve, do you?"

His face closed up. "It's not for me to approve or disapprove, Amanda. He's your father."

"That's right, he is!" She was angry now, but not sure whether the anger was directed at herself or at Thaddeus. "Would you drive me back to the threshers, please?"

"Of course, Amanda."

They were silent for most of the way. Then, as they drew near the threshers, Thaddeus said, "I'm sorry, Amanda. For a little while there, I did disapprove. It goes back to my own childhood, I suppose, guilt over what happened between my father and myself. We never did get along. He was a drunkard and a no-account. He drove my poor mother to her death. Then, when I prepared to leave home, I struck him in anger. I have never seen him since. He must be dead now, but I've never heard a word about him since I left home. But no matter what else he was, he was my father, and I suppose I have felt guilty ever since. Still, that gives me no right to try and transfer that guilt to you."

"No, it doesn't," she said tightly. She was fighting back an onrush of tears. "I love Daddy, whatever his faults, and he has many. Yet he was always good to me, and I love him dearly. The truth is, it tears my heart out seeing him the way he is. That's the reason I shy away from going. You think that doesn't rip me up with guilt?" Now she was crying.

"I should be shot at sunrise, Amanda," he said wretchedly, "for bringing this up. I understand, believe me, I do. Don't cry, please . . ." Stopping the pickup, he groped for her hand.

Amanda eluded his grasp and was out of the pickup, striding toward the threshers. She dashed the tears from her eyes, and walked with her head high, refusing to look back at Thaddeus's pickup.

She was pleased to see that everything seemed to be proceeding smoothly. Although it was close to sundown, both threshers were going full blast and the bundle wagons were bustling back and forth.

Then she noticed something that gave her pause. Pulled off to one side was a fully-loaded grain truck, just setting there.

Again, her gaze swept the area until she located Dudley, standing by one of the tractors, hands on hips, watching the threshing.

She strode over to him. "Why is that one truck just setting there?" With a jerk of her head she indicated the truck.

He gave a start. "What? Oh . . . that's the truck Bud Dalmas is driving."

"I don't care who's driving it. Why is it simply setting there?"

"It's broke down. Something wrong with the motor."

"Then why haven't you fixed it? How long has it been there like that?"

"Since around the time you went kiting off

with Thaddeus Martin." He shrugged. "And I didn't fix it because Dalmas is a bastard, and he doesn't work for you."

"I don't care if he's the devil himself, and he works for me to the extent that his truck is loaded with sacks of wheat that should be on the way to the elevators! What did you have in mind, letting it stay there until the grain rots?"

"If he can't fix it, let him hire his own mechanic."

"Now you listen to me, Buster Brown!" she said harshly. "You get your tail over there and get that truck running, okay?"

He gave her a dark look, started to speak, then clamped his lips shut and started toward Dalmas's truck.

After another look around, Amanda followed him, already sorry she had spoken so harshly. But she had to take her anger out on somebody. Besides, he should have got the truck running again; it was his job.

As she neared the truck, Bud Dalmas hopped down out of the cab. "Sorry about the breakdown, Miss Amanda. I would have fixed it myself, but I ain't much good around motors."

Dudley had his head and shoulders under the hood; a growl came from him at Dalmas's words.

Dalmas said blandly, "What was that, Dud?"

Dudley back out and turned a scowling face on the man. "I said, you know enough to foul a motor up, you should know enough to fix one. Nothing wrong here anyway but a broken wire, which you probably did yourself. And I've told you for the last time to stop calling me Dud!"

"Yessir, *Mister* Graham. But! Why would I be breaking a wire on my own truck, Mister Graham?"

"How do I know what's in that head of yours? Just plain orneriness would be enough reason for you."

Amanda sighed. "Dudley, will you please fix the damned thing, so we can get this truck on its way?"

Dudley shrugged and ducked back under the hood.

Bud Dalmas said, "Oh, I can't do that, Miss Amanda."

She transferred her gaze back to him. "Can't do what?"

"There'd be no point in my heading out tonight, not this late. Late as it is, I'd be driving all night, no sleep, not good for nothing."

She tapped a thumbnail against her teeth. "You've lost a half-day already."

"Not my fault," he said aggrievedly. "The other trucks, they been gone a spell, long enough for them to get there, unload, and head back."

Dudley backed out from under the hood, climbed into the cab, and started the truck. He raced the motor; it ran smoothly, no sign of a miss. He got out and came over to them. "It runs fine now. Hell, a child of ten could have fixed it in half a minute."

Bud Dalmas grinned in mock admiration. "They ain't lying when they say you're good

345

with motors, Mister Graham. Me, I'm just lost under a hood."

Wiping his hands on a rag, Dudley growled, "If I had my way, you'd get lost, period."

"Okay, okay!" Amanda snapped. "I'm tired of listening to you two snipe at each other." To Dalmas, she said, "You're right, there's not much point in your starting out this late. But I want to see this truck gone when I get up in the morning, okay?"

Dalmas smirked. "It'll be gone in the morning, depend on it, Miss Amanda."

Amanda started off. Dudley hurried to catch up to her. "What was so urgent that Thaddeus Martin had to come after you?"

"Daddy had another attack. The doctor was calling from Wichita Falls."

"Ah, I'm sorry, Amanda. Bad?"

"Bad enough," she said shortly. "I'd rather not talk about it just now, Dudley. Okay?"

It was after sundown now, and the crew was winding up for the day. Most of them were already gathered around the wash bench alongside the cook wagon. Jack Rollins and another man were closing down the threshers for the night. Dudley hastened over to help them. Amanda went on to the cook wagon, got a pan of hot water, and carried it to her tent, where she washed as best she could and changed into a fresh shirt and pants.

She rummaged in her trunk and found an unopened pint of whiskey she'd remembered putting in there. In defiance of anyone who might be watching, she placed it in plain sight on the

346

card table just outside the tent. Carrying the water pitcher, she made another trip to the cook wagon. Men were lined up at the back with their tin plates and cups. The cook's helper was serving stew off the counter hinged to the back of the wagon.

Amanda mounted the three side steps and rapped on the door.

She had to rap again before it was opened and a voice snarled, "Goddamnit to hell, ain't I told and told you men to line up in back for your . . . oh, it's you, Miss Amanda. I thought . . ."

"I know what you thought, John. Forgive me for bothering you at your busiest time . . ." She managed a weary smile and thrust the pitcher at him. "Could you spare me a few chunks of ice?"

John Sanders—a lean, scrawny individual who looked as if he'd never had a square meal in his life—was shirtless, and had a towel wrapped like a turban around his head to keep the sweat from running down into his eyes. He said, "Sure thing, Miss Amanda. Pardon the language." He took the pitcher.

"Don't bother to apologize, John, for heaven's sake. In your place, and in weather like this, I'd probably use far worse."

He turned back into the cook wagon. Amanda stood on the steps, waiting. She saw Dudley coming from the threshers. Seeing her, he arched an eyebrow and veered toward her. She averted her gaze. With a shrug he went on around to the wash bench.

"Here you are."

John was holding out the pitcher in one hand and a covered sauce pan in the other.

"What's in the pan?"

"Your supper, Miss Amanda."

"Stew?" She made a face.

He laughed. "What else? You have to keep up your strength, like they say, and," he winked, "if you're going to put away some hooch, like I think you are, you'll need something to soak it up."

"You're too smart for your own good, John," she said in a grumbling voice. But she took the pan and walked back across to the tent. She sat down at the table, made herself a whiskey and water, fired a cigarette, and took a sip of the drink.

She leaned back with a sigh, some of the tension draining away. For the first time since the telephone conversation she allowed her thoughts to wing down to Wichita Falls and the man in the hospital bed. Amanda knew herself well enough to realize that her resolve to remain away would gradually erode, and guilt would drive her down there, but hopefully she could hold out until they were done threshing here.

She knew what was in her mind. If she could finish here without a hitch, trek down to Wichita Falls, and relate her triumph to Amos, it would be the high point of her life.

If he was aware, if he had regained consciousness.

She finished the drink and made another. It was dark now, but she made no move to light the kerosene lantern on the table. She sat on, smoking, drinking moodily.

The only light now came from the cook wagon where John and his helper were cleaning up. Amanda saw figures moving back and forth in the light, and voices drifted over to her. She felt lonely, deserted, but had to laugh at herself.

A raucous voice bellowed a verse of "It Makes No Difference Now," a current jukebox favorite telling of a man whose woman had left him, and nothing in his life made any difference now. Amanda recalled that she'd heard Annie Mae Delong sing it that night Seymour had taken her to the honky-tonk.

That's how I feel, she thought, and stirred. For God's sake, *now* who was feeling sorry for herself?

Amanda picked up the pint bottle, held it up between her and the cook-wagon light. She'd drunk half of it! With a muttered obscenity, she hurled the bottle into the night and listened until she heard the faint thunk as it hit the ground.

Lifting the lid from the sauce pan, she peered in. The stew had long since grown cold. Listlessly, she forked out a chunk of meat and put it into her mouth. She chewed and chewed, and finally spat it out in disgust. Covering the pot, she got to her feet and had to catch at the chair to retain her balance. God, she was drunk!

349

Amanda made her way inside the tent. Removing only her shirt and boots, she stretched out on the steel cot. The tent spun wildly around her, and a kaleidoscope of painful colors burst behind her closed eyelids.

She was sober enough to realize that she was going to be sorry in the morning, hungover and with a pounding head, and probably sick to her stomach since there was no food in it.

Almost before the thought was completed, she dropped down into sleep like a stone. Nightmares plagued her. Amos Cayne lay comatose on a narrow bed, set in the stubble of a wheat field. Behind him the two threshers, grotesque shapes against a burning sky, squatted still and rusting. Cobwebs thick as ropes twined about them. Amanda struggled toward her father, but each step she took mired her deeper and deeper in the field. The sky behind the threshers grew redder, brighter . . .

Amanda surfaced, thrashing about on the cot. Strangely, the nightmare still lingered, flames dancing behind her eyelids.

Then she realized what had awakened her. Heavy breathing sounded in the tent like a bellows, and rough hands clawed at the waistband of her trousers, trying to pull them down and off.

Her eyes popped open, a scream of outrage ripping at her throat, and in the reddish light she recognized the red, leering face of Bud Dalmas looming over her. He had her legs forced far apart and was kneeling between them.

His trousers were open, the jut of his erection an obscenity.

"Knock it off with the screaming, you bitch," he said with panting breath. "Let a real man fuck you for once." A fine spray of tobacco juice struck her face.

She shuddered in revulsion. "You're not a man, you're an animal!"

She managed to twist to one side, drawing her legs up. Then she drove one knee into his crotch, against that thrust of engorged cock.

Dalmas yowled like a wounded dog. Doubling up, clutching at his groin, he rolled off the narrow cot, landing with a thud on the ground.

Amanda sat up, reaching for her shirt, noting with alarm that the pinkish glow was coming through the canvas. It hadn't just been a part of her nightmare!

She knew that much even before Dudley pushed aside the tent flap and charged inside, yelling, "Amanda! Wheat fire!" He skidded to a stop, holding the lantern high. "Dalmas! What the holy hell is he doing here?"

"What does it look like? He tried to rape me."

"Did he hurt you?"

"If you mean did he succeed, no, and I don't think he'll be trying it on anyone else for some time to come." She stood up, buttoning the shirt. "But never mind him, he's harmless as a kitten right now. The fire, how far has it spread?"

"I don't know. Not far, I think. Jack Rollins

351

spotted it a few minutes ago and woke me up. Everyone is up now, and Jack is organizing a fire fight."

"Then let's go," she said, and ran from the tent without giving Dalmas another glance.

22

Wheat fire!

Drought, hard rain, hail, locust plague, wheat rust—there were many perils wheat farmers and threshermen dreaded, but always in the back of their minds lurked the special nightmare of a wheat fire.

Amanda had never experienced one, but she'd heard the horror stories. A forest fire, a prairie grass fire—all were frightening and destructive, but a wheat fire held a terror of its own. She recalled words spoken long ago by Amos Cayne: "I guess we all dread a wheat fire because it can, within an hour, completely wipe out a farmer's whole year of sweat and labor. And wheat fires have burned to death many a poor thresherman unlucky enough to be trapped in one."

It was worse, Amanda knew, in a field of unharvested wheat, since the flames had more to feed upon, racing across the beaded heads of ripe wheat, jumping fifty yards at a gulp on a strong puff of wind, yet a fire in a stubbled field of mowed wheat could be just as disastrous, if slower moving.

Running toward the threshers from her tent, Amanda could see the flames dancing across the unmowed wheat of the Moore farm across the way. "How did it start?" she gasped out. "Any idea?"

Dudley, loping along beside her, said, "None. Could have been somebody's cigarette. One of Seymour Hooker's cigars. But it's a little late in the night for that; everybody should have been bedded down for hours. Of course, somebody could have started it."

"I don't think you can blame Seymour for this, since it's his wheat that's burning."

"Not *his* wheat, as such, and you'll notice that it's heading right this way."

They were at the threshers now. Jack Rollins had the cook wagon drawn up beside the threshing machines, and all the other machines around them. It reminded Amanda of a wagon train circled against a band of attacking Indians.

As they came up, Rollins was overseeing the hooking of a plow to one of the tractors; the plow was always carried along for just such an eventuality. The other men were busily engaged soaking wheat sacks and wetting down anything that might burn.

Rollins straightened up as Amanda stopped beside him. "I thought we'd try to save the threshers and everything else we could first."

"Good thinking, Jack," Amanda said.

The tractor started with a roar. Dudley motioned the man down from the driver's seat. He yelled, "I'll drive it, just in case the damned thing breaks down on us!"

He sent the tractor growling forward, the plow gouging a furrow out of the dry ground. Amanda watched for a moment, as Dudley circled the bunched threshers, tractors, trucks and pickups. He made one complete circle, then started a second furrow next to the first. If he was allowed sufficient time, there would be a plowed circle around the area, the turned earth wide enough to, hopefully, halt the fire, which was eating its way toward them, driven by a faint breeze from the east.

Sounds of motors starting up across the way drew her attention. In the eerie light cast by the fire, she saw that Seymour had his combines moving, all lined up abreast. She grasped his purpose almost at once. If there was time enough, the combines would cut a wide swath in the wheat over there, in advance of the flames.

It was a daring maneuver, she realized, but also very risky. The combines would be moving directly across the path of the flames. If they didn't succeed in cutting their swath before the fire reached them, both men and machines could be destroyed.

As a gust of wind caused the fire to flare up, she glimpsed Seymour driving one of the combines himself. He was wearing only his boots and trousers, bare chest gleaming in the firelight, an unlit cigar cocked at a jaunty angle in his mouth. She had to smile. She wasn't close enough to hear, but she would have bet that he was singing at the top of his voice.

She started toward him, then stopped, knowing that she would only be in the way over there. She looked around, feeling utterly helpless. Everyone was busy at something, while she just stood about uselessly. She heard the grinding of gears, and looked around to see Thaddeus braking his pickup to a stop. The bed was filled with water barrels.

Jumping out, he yelled at the men around the threshers, "Here's some more water."

Men quickly gathered around the pickup. Jack Rollins jumped up onto the bed, and dipped wheat sacks into the water as they were handed up to him.

Thaddeus came over to Amanda. "I made some phone calls when I realized there was a fire. Others will be coming along soon, although I doubt they'll be in time to be of much help. It'll be over one way or another before they ever get here." He gazed around, nodding in approval. "It strikes me that you're doing a good job here, Amanda."

"I had little to do with it," she admitted ruefully. "They were already busy before I even realized what was happening."

"And Hooker . . ." He nodded at the whirring combines. "He may be a rascal, but he doesn't hesitate to act, and usually does the right thing when he does. That truck over there, why isn't it into the circle?"

He pointed toward the truck Bud Dalmas had been driving, still parked where it had been the night before. Amanda said, "I don't know, but I'll find out." She hurried to the pickup. "Jack, why is that one truck left out there?"

Rollins leaned down to say, "We tried to start it, Miss Amanda, but it's out of gasoline. The petcock on the gas tank had been opened, all the gasoline drained out."

Amanda felt a chill pass over her. Then the fire had been set! Who could be so low as to endanger the lives of so many? Dalmas! It had to be Bud Dalmas!

She sent a glance toward her tent, had even taken a step in that direction, when a chorus of shouts drew her attention back.

The fire had jumped across the swath the combines had made and was burning its way straight toward them. Amanda saw that the drivers were deserting the combines and racing for their lives out of the path of the flames—all except one man, who was running ahead of the flames, toward where she stood.

It was Seymour Hooker, and for a man his size he was amazingly fast. The men around Amanda were frozen with shock. Only Dudley Graham was still busy. He had plowed a circle several yards wide around the bunched machines now.

Seymour was panting for breath when he reached them. "There's only one way to save around, I think. Hopefully we can send a back-fire. The wind's not too strong, and it's veering around, I think. Hopefully we can send a back-fire against the one back there. You and me, Thaddeus, we'll start it. Over there." He

357

pointed behind them. "Better move your pickup out of the way first. The rest of you men keep wetting sacks and try to keep it from spreading the other way. We don't want it turning back on us. The peckerwood has done good, Amanda, your threshers and other machines should be safe. But your tent, sugar," he gave her a smoke-blackened grin, "may go."

"The tent is the least of my worries," she said grimly. She glanced at the tent, wondering if Dalmas had made good his escape by this time.

For some time after Amanda left the tent, Bud Dalmas remained doubled up on the ground, clutching his genitals, whimpering in his agony. Finally the pain lessened a trifle, and he gingerly sat up. Hate filled his mind like a deadly poison. That bitch! He hoped that she was burned to a crisp!

Reminded of the fire he'd set, Dalmas took note of his surroundings for the first time in a while. He saw with alarm that a pink glow lit the tent brighter than any lamp could have. The fire must be getting close!

Panic brought him lurching to his feet. A fresh onslaught of pain caused him to double over again. After a moment he forced himself upright, and hobbled to the tent flap like an old man.

Once outside, his panic increased. It seemed that the whole world was ablaze from horizon to horizon. No matter where he looked he could see nothing but flames. A line of fire was racing toward the tent. It would be consumed within minutes, and him along with it if he did not get away at once.

He stood for a long moment, wracked by indecision. Which way should he flee? He tried to discern the direction of the wind, but it seemed to be coming from all directions, and it was hot as a furnace breath. He seemed to recall hearing once that a raging fire creates its own wind.

Dalmas had lost all sense of direction. He didn't even know the location of the spot where he'd splashed gasoline across a wide band of wheat and set it afire. Directly before him, outlined by the leaping flames, the two threshers and other machines stood, seemingly untouched by the fire. At a crackling sound behind him, he looked around.

The tent was flaming. With a scream of terror Dalmas ran toward the threshers. In his panic he stumbled over a rock and fell headlong. The fall dazed him for a few moments. It was only when heat began to scorch his back that he roused himself. Springing to his feet, he saw that the line of fire had reached him, and his pants were afire. He beat at the flames, screaming shrilly at the pain searing his hands.

Mad with panic now, he began to run again, a human torch. He couldn't even see the threshers. In his mindless terror he ran right past the bunched machines and sped due east—right into the higher wall of fire.

Now his hair was on fire and his clothes were burned away, leaving his body blackened and charred. He plunged on, straight into the depths of hell.

All feeling had left him, and all thought. Then he felt a final, terrible burst of pain in his chest as he inhaled fire, and he fell forward. In a last action before death took him he curled up into a fetal ball.

For an inordinate time, it seemed to Amanda, the success of Seymour's backfire hung in the balance. The original fire from the east slowed considerably as the wind shifted, but it still advanced. The backfire kept turning on the men trying to contain it. They ran frantically up and down the line, beating at the tongues of flame with wet sacks.

Amanda joined them, slapping a wet sack, ignoring the instant blisters caused by the cinders raining down on her face and hands. Smoke bit into her nostrils, and stung her eyes until tears flooded her cheeks.

Suddenly an apparition loomed up, staggering through a small gap in the line of backfire. It was Dudley. His clothes were blackened and smouldering in several places. She had forgotten about him!

She ran toward him, wrapping her wet sack around him, smothering the few burning places in his clothes.

His eyes glared at her, as red in anger as the flames. "I damned near bought it out there! Why wasn't I told that a backfire was being started?"

Before Amanda could reply, a voice drawled

behind them, "What's the matter, peckerwood? Get your precious tail feathers scorched? That's the way we separate the men from the boys."

"Men from the boys, hell!" Dudley raged. "I was busy trying to save the equipment, and keeping a close eye on the first fire. I didn't know that I should watch for one climbing up my ass! Somebody could have told me about a backfire!"

Seymour shrugged carelessly. "No time, peckerwood. In a situation like this, a man with the smarts watches his own ass, doesn't depend on somebody else to do it for him."

"Dudley . . . I am sorry." Amanda touched his arm. "You're right, we should have warned you. I'll admit, I plain forgot. Things were happening too fast."

Seymour gave her a disbelieving look and shook his head in disgust. He dug down into his pants pocket, extracted the crumpled stub of a cigar, and stuck it between his teeth. "Anybody got a match?"

The bizarre request struck them all at once, and they all doubled up with laughter.

Amanda straightened up first. "Look!" She seized Seymour's arm and pointed.

The two men looked in the direction she indicated. The two lines of fire had met, clashing together like antagonists. For a moment flames leaped high, roaring and crackling, sparks flying.

Even as they watched, the two fires became one and immediately began to die from lack of anything to feed on. The ground was black all around, and everything flammable was burned off. Within the plowed circle, the threshers and other machines stood intact, untouched by the fire.

"Looks like you came out in pretty good shape, sugar," Seymour said, "except for your tent. I warned you that it would probably go."

"If that's all we lost, I won't waste any tears . . ." She broke off as a smoke-blackened Thaddeus Martin came over to them.

Seymour eyed him warily. He said, "You lost a little wheat, Thaddeus, but I reckon you didn't suffer too much."

With a look around, Thaddeus nodded solemnly. "I'd say Don Moore suffered the most. I'd estimate he lost about forty acres of prime wheat." He sighed. "But all in all, I'd say we were lucky. Some thanks are due you, Seymour," he said reluctantly and held out his hand.

With a look of astonishment that quickly changed to embarrassment, Seymour took the extended hand.

"Boss, hey, boss!"

They looked up to see Rooster Cockrun legging it toward them. Stopping, he held up a charred mass of metal. "Look what I found! A gasoline can!"

"It figures," Seymour said. "Some galoot set the fire. The question is, who?" He frowned. "Anybody hurt over there?"

"Our guys came out okay, just a few burns. But," Rooster Cockrun's face assumed a mournful look, "all the combines are gone, burned so bad I don't think they can be fixed."

"Well, hell." Seymour grinned painfully, spreading his hands. "Win one, lose one." He looked off, then raised his voice, "You men with the sacks! Wet them down again and look around for hot spots. We don't want the damned fire blazing up again!"

He went swinging off, bare torso black as tar. He walked with his head down, stopping here and there to point out pockets of flames to the men with the sacks.

Amanda passed a weary hand over her brow; it came away streaked with black. She laughed ruefully. "God, we all look a sight! I think the first thing we need is a good bath . . ." She broke off, startled at how easily she could see everyone. Glancing toward the east, she saw that dawn was breaking.

Dudley canted his head, sniffing. "Hey, is that coffee I smell perking?"

In unison, they looked toward the cook wagon. The counter was down, and Amanda could see John and his helper busy inside.

Smiling, she said, "Trust John to realize that everyone would need coffee and hot food."

"I need a good wash, Amanda, no argument," Dudley said. "But more than anything right now I could stand a strong cup of coffee."

"Then let's go, you guys."

She linked arms with them and they started across the field, Dudley on one side, Thaddeus on the other. As they neared the cook wagon, the pleasant aroma of coffee drifted toward them, more delightful than any perfume.

John said, "Coffee's about ready, Miss Amanda."

"You're making sandwiches? They're going to be starved."

"It's in the works."

"Better make plenty. We'll be feeding Seymour's men, too."

Her glance went to Dudley, expecting a hostile reaction. But he said nothing, busying himself with rolling a cigarette. With some amusement, Amanda reflected that the fire had burned away all hostility, at least for the present. She shook out a cigarette for herself and lit it, just as John handed her a mug of steaming coffee. She blew on it for a moment, while John served Dudley and Thaddeus.

Now others began to drift up, Seymour among them. After a struggle he finally lit the battered stub of a cigar and blew smoke. He said, "I think everything's under control now. We put out the last hot spot."

There was a shout from the east, and one of Seymour's men hurried over. His face was pale and sweating. "I just found a dead man over there, boss." He swallowed convulsively. "It ain't a pretty sight. He's burned to a crisp."

Concerned, Seymour glanced around. "It can't be one of our guys, they're all accounted for. Amanda?"

She shook her head. "Not one of mine, either." Then, in a flash of intuition, she knew. "It's Bud Dalmas, it has to be!"

Seymour stared. "Dalmas? What was that sorry sucker doing around here?"

Quickly, Amanda explained, and after a brief hesitation, she also told him of Dalmas's attempt to rape her.

Seymour swore heartily. "The no-good booger! If that's him dead out there, it serves him right."

"It's your own damned fault he was around in the first place!" Dudley said heatedly.

Seymour showed his most disarming grin. "Now, why do you say that, peckerwood?"

"Because you were paying him to do your dirty work for you, that's why!"

"Aww, hell. You never give up, do you? You remind me of a feisty dog worrying a bone bigger'n he is."

Amanda interposed hastily, "I think he was the one who started the fire."

All eyes swung on her. Dudley let his breath go with an explosive sound. "By God, you're probably right! Now why didn't I think of that?"

Thaddeus said, "Why do you think it was him, Amanda?"

"He was driving that truck." With a nod of her head she indicated the burned-out hulk of the truck Dalmas had been driving. "Jack tried to start it to move in with the others and found that all the gas had been drained out of the tank. And your man, Seymour, found that burned gasoline can. I think Dalmas was off his rocker and for some twisted reason of his own he wanted to get back at all of us."

"Then the son-of-a-bitch *does* deserve what happened to him!" All of a sudden Seymour began to laugh. "All right, peckerwood, I admit it! I did hire Dalmas, but that was back before I got religion. Anyway, I got my just desserts, wouldn't you say? Since I'm the one suffered the most damage. A case of the snake biting his own tail, I'd reckon."

For a moment both Dudley and Thaddeus scowled at the laughing Seymour, but then they relaxed with reluctant smiles. No one could stay mad at Seymour Hooker when he was at his charming best, Amanda concluded. Looking at the three men who had figured so prominently in her life of late, she marveled at the twists of fate. Just yesterday, these three were at each other's throats; now there was an air of camaraderie about them.

As Seymour stepped up to the counter to accept a cup of coffee, she said, "I am sorry about your combines, Seymour. What will you do now?"

"Have to wait for J.C. to ship me another fleet. If I'm still working for him, that is, after he learns what happened here. But what the hell! He can afford it." He tilted the mug of coffee to his mouth.

"I have a suggestion," she said mischievously. "While you're waiting, you can work for me. I could use another man to finish up here."

He exploded with laughter, spewing coffee. He choked out, "By damn, I may just do that! Sugar, you're something, you really are!"

John was setting out plates of sandwiches on the counter now, and the men from both crews were eagerly snatching at them.

Amanda clapped her hands together and said briskly, "Okay, you men working for me! Eat up, we have to get to work." She smiled tightly. "We're getting a late start this morning."

Epilogue

As the man in the wheelchair finished speaking, the writer said, "That was a hell of a story, sir. I gather you're one of those three men? Dudley Graham, Thaddeus Martin, or Seymour Hooker?"

Before the older man could speak, the door to the sun porch opened and a tall, slender woman with pure-white hair stepped through, coming toward them with a swinging stride. Although obviously no longer young, she was still vigorous and strikingly handsome.

"Hi, sugar. You don't know what you've been missing. I've been telling this young feller here the story of my life."

The woman's smile was amused but affectionate. "Considering how many times I've heard it, I'm just as glad I missed it."

The man in the chair bellowed with the laughter of a much younger man. "Damn, but you're a hard woman, sugar." He faced around. "To answer your question, young feller . . . yeah, I'm one of those three men. Seymour Hooker." His face twisted in a bitter grimace. "What's left of him."

"Now, darling." The woman dropped a hand onto Hooker's right shoulder. "Feeling sorry for yourself again?"

"Yes, goddamnit, I am! Who's got a better right, Amanda? Reliving those old days for this young guy brought it all back."

"But it's been a good life, hasn't it?" Crossing one arm under her still-firm breasts, she tapped a thumbnail against her teeth and assumed a look of mock severity. "Unless you're having regrets? About marrying me, say?"

"Now you know better'n that, sugar." He reached up to take her hand. "That's the best thing ever happened to me, marrying you. But the damned doctors!" he grumped. "No booze, no cigars, no nothing!"

Smiling again, she said, "Seymour, you've drunk enough booze and smoked enough cigars to keep two ordinary men. Rest on your laurels, okay?"

The writer said eagerly, "You're Amanda Cayne, I gather?"

"*Was*, young feller," Seymour Hooker said smugly. "She's Amanda Hooker now. Has been since about a month after that fire. See them combines out yonder?" He motioned with his head to the field of wheat outside the sanatarium. "Had two fine sons, Amanda and me. That's their crew and combines harvesting out there."

"The threshers, Miss Amanda . . . uh, Mrs. Hooker. How long did they operate after the fire?"

Again, it was Seymour who answered, "She

370

quit them at the end of that season, and went along with me and my combines the next season, *mine* that year and every year up until I retired." He laughed. "Old J.C. Fallon fired my ass following the wheat fire."

Amanda said, "Yes, Seymour was right about one thing. The day of the threshing machines was drawing to a close. Then, too, Daddy died shortly after the fire, of another stroke . . ." Her glance moved to her husband, then jumped away. "But we were lucky in that there was still some market for threshing machines. I got enough for them and the tractors to invest in a fleet of combines and the rest, as they say, is history."

Seymour grunted. "Wasn't all that easy. Not at first. The Depression was still on. We suffered through some thin times, but things picked up when the war came along."

"Thaddeus Martin?" the writer asked. "What happened to him?"

"Thaddeus died a few years back," Amanda said, face shadowed by sorrow.

"Did he ever get married?"

"No, he lived alone and died alone."

"He never got over Amanda." Seymour was grinning. "Thaddeus told me once, at the christening of our first boy, I think it was, that he could never find another woman like Amanda here, so he finished out his years a bachelor."

"And Dudley Graham?"

"The peckerwood?" Seymour snorted laughter. "He got hitched during the war, has a passel of kids now. He was a hero during the war, out there in the South Pacific somewhere, got a whole chestful of medals. Me, they made 4-F, because of this gimpy leg of mine."

Amanda said, "Dudley opened a garage out in California after the war. The last we heard from him, he now owns a thriving Cadillac agency."

The writer was quiet for a long moment. "Well, I guess that about wraps it up." He punched off the recorder. "To sum up, to satisfy my own curiosity more than anything else . . . would you say that, all in all, you've had a good life, Mr. Hooker? In spite of your . . ." He broke off, flushing.

"Stroke. Don't be afraid to say it, young feller. I've never been a man for mincing his words. A stroke, that's what I had. Just like old Amos. I reckon, in a way, Amanda has had it the worst. The two men in her life felled by strokes."

"Seymour, now you stop that, okay? Have you heard me complaining?"

"Nope. But then you never was much of a complainer, sugar." He grinned up at her. Then he switched his gaze back to the writer. "But you're right. Good times or bad, it's been a good life. A good woman, two fine sons . . . what more can a man ask for? Like I said earlier, life has been a kick in the ass for me." Twilight had fallen now, and Seymour gazed dreamily out at the combines still whirring busily. "Yeah, you could say that. A real kick in the ass . . ."

372

Dear Reader:

The Pinnacle Books editors strive to select and produce books that are exciting, entertaining and readable . . . no matter what the category. From time to time we will attempt to discover what you, the reader, think about a particular book.

Now that you've finished reading *The Harvesters,* we'd like to find out what you liked, or didn't like, about this story. We'll share your opinions with the author and discuss them as we plan future books. This will result in books that you will find more to your liking. As in fine art and good cooking a matter of taste is involved; and for you, of course, it is *your* taste that is most important to you. For Clayton Matthew and the Pinnacle editors, it is not the critics' reviews and awards that have been most rewarding, it is the unending stream of readers' mail. Here is where we discover what readers like, what they *feel* about a story, and what they find memorable. So, do help us in becoming a little better in providing you with the kind of stories you like. Here's how . . .

WIN BOOKS . . . AND $200! Please fill out the following pages and mail them as indicated. Every week, for twelve weeks following publication, the editors will choose, at random, a reader's name from all the questionnaires received. The twelve lucky readers will receive $25 worth of paperbacks *and* become an official entry in our 1979 Pinnacle Books Reader Sweepstakes. The winner of this sweepstakes drawing will receive a Grand Prize of $200, the inclusion of his name in a forthcoming Pinnacle Book (as a special acknowledgment, possibly even as a character!), and several other local prizes to be announced to each initial winner. As a further inducement to send in your questionnaire *now,* we will also send the first 25 replies received a free book by return mail! Here's a chance to talk to the author and editor, voice your opinions, and win some great prizes, too! —The Editors

READER SURVEY

NOTE: Please feel free to expand on any of these questions on a separate page, or to express yourself on any aspect of your thoughts on reading . . . but do be sure to include this entire questionnaire with any such letters.

1. Are you glad you bought this book, and did it live up to your expectations?

2. What was it about this book that induced you to buy it?
   (A. The title_____) (B. The author's name_____)
   (C. A friend's recommendation_____)
   (D. The cover art_____)
   (E. The cover description_____)
   (F. Subject matter_____) (G. Advertisement_____)
   (H. Heard author on TV or radio_____)
   (I. Read a previous book by author_____ . . .
   ` which one? _____)
   (J. Bookstore display_____)
   (K. Other? _____)

3. What is the book you read just before this one?

   And how would you rate it with *The Harvesters?*

4. What is the very next book you plan to read?

   How did you decide on that? _____

5. Where did you buy *The Harvesters?* _____

   (Name and address of store, please):

6. Where do you buy the majority of your paper-backs? _____

7. What seems to be the major factor that persuades you to buy a certain book?

_____

8. How many books do you buy each month?

_____

9. Do you ever write letters to the author or publisher . . . and why? _____

_____

10. About how many hours a week do you spend reading books? _____ How many hours a week watching television? _____

11. What other spare-time activity do you enjoy most? _____ For how many hours a week? _____

12. Which magazines do you read regularly? . . . in order of your preference _____,

_____, _____,

_____

13. Of your favorite magazine, what is it that you like best about it? _____

_____

14. What is your favorite television show of the past year or so? _____

15. What is your favorite motion picture of the past year or so? _____

16. What is the most disappointing television show you've seen lately? _____

17. What is the most disappointing motion picture you've seen lately? _____

18. What is the most disappointing book you've read lately? _____

19. Are there authors that you like so well that you read *all* their books? _____
Who are they? _____

20. And can you explain *why* you like their books so much? _____
_____
_____

21. Which particular books by these authors do you like best? _____
_____

22. Did you read Taylor Caldwell's *Captains and the Kings*?_____ Did you watch it on television? _____ Which did you do first? _____

23. Did you read John Jakes' *The Bastard*? _____
Did you watch it on TV?_____ Which first?_____
Have you read any of the other books in John Jakes' Bicentennial Series? _____
What do you think of them? _____

24. Did you read James Michener's *Centennial*?_____
Did you watch it on TV?_____ Which first?_____

25. Did you read Irwin Shaw's *Rich Man, Poor Man*? _____ Did you watch it on TV? _____
Which first? _____

26. Of all the recent books you've read, or films you've seen, are there any that you would compare in any way to *The Harvesters*? _____

27. In *The Harvester*, which character did you find most fascinating? _____
Most likeable? _____ Most exciting? _____ Least interesting? _____ Which one did you identify with most? _____

28. Do you think any of Clayton Matthews' characters were based on real people? If so, who reminded you of whom? _____
_____
_____
_____
_____

29. Rank the following descriptions of *The Harvesters* as you feel they are best defined:

	Excellent	*Okay*	*Poor*
A. A sense of reality	____	____	____
B. Suspense	____	____	____
C. Intrigue	____	____	____
D. Sexuality	____	____	____
E. Violence	____	____	____
F. Romance	____	____	____
G. History	____	____	____
H. Characterization	____	____	____
I. Scenes, events	____	____	____
J. Pace, readability	____	____	____
K. Dialogue	____	____	____
L. Style	____	____	____

30. Have you read *The Power Seekers*, also by Clayton Matthews? _____

31. Do you have any thoughts regarding the length of this book? ____ Would you have liked it to be longer? ____ Shorter? ____

32. Would you be interested in reading a sequel to *The Harvesters*? _____

33. Would you be interested in reading a similar story, but in a different setting or location? ____ Where, for instance? _____
_____

34. What, in your opinion, is the best or most vivid scene in *The Harvesters*? _____
_____

35. Did you find any errors or other upsetting things in this book? _____
_____

36. What do you do with your paperbacks after you've read them? _____
_____

37. Do you buy paperbacks in any of the following categories, and approximately how many do you buy in a year?

   A. Contemporary fiction _____
   B. Historical romance _____
   C. Family saga _____
   D. Romance (like Harlequin) _____
   E. Romantic suspense _____
   F. Gothic romance _____
   G. Occult novels _____
   H. War novels _____
   I. Action/adventure novels _____
   J. "Bestsellers" _____
   K. Science fiction _____
   L. Mystery _____
   M. Westerns _____
   N. Nonfiction _____
   O. Biography _____
   P. How-To books _____
   Q. Other _____

38. And, lastly, some profile data on *you* the reader . . .

A. Age: 12–16_____ 17–20_____ 21–30_____
   31–40_____ 41–50_____ 51–60_____
   61 or over_____

B. Occupation: _____

C. Education level; check last grade completed:
   10_____ 11_____ 12_____ Freshman_____
   Sophomore_____ Junior_____ Senior_____
   Graduate School_____, plus any specialized
   schooling _____

D. Your average annual gross income: Under
   $10,000_____ $10,000–$15,000_____
   $15,000–$20,000_____ $20,000–
   $30,000_____ $30,000–$50,000_____
   Above $50,000_____

E. Did you read a lot as a child?_____ Do you
   recall your favorite childhood novel? _____
   _____

F. Do you find yourself reading more or less
   than you did five years ago?_____

G. Do you read hardcover books?_____ How
   often?_____ If so, are they books that you
   buy?_____ borrow?_____ or trade?_____ Or
   other?_____

H. Does the imprint (Pinnacle, Avon, Bantam,
   etc.) make any difference to you when considering a paperback purchase? _____

I. Have you ever bought paperbacks by mail
   directly from the publisher?_____ And do you
   like to buy books that way? _____

J. Would you be interested in buying paperbacks via a book club or subscription program?_____ And, in your opinion, what would
   be the best reasons for doing so? _____
   _____ . . . the problems in
   doing so? _____

379

K. Is there something that you'd like to see writers or publishers do for you as a reader of paperbacks? _____

_____

THANK YOU FOR TAKING THE TIME TO REPLY TO THIS, THE FIRST PUBLIC READER SURVEY IN PAPERBACK HISTORY!

NAME _____ PHONE _____

ADDRESS _____

CITY _____ STATE _____ ZIP _____

Please return this questionnaire to:
The Editors; Survey Dept. TH
Pinnacle Books, Inc.
2029 Century Park East
Los Angeles, CA 90067